Loren Teague lives in Nelson, New Zealand.

ULTIMATE BETRAYAL

Katrina Jones is broken-hearted to discover the man she loves is an IRA terrorist on the run from the police. He disappears after a bomb explosion and Katrina sets out to track him down. When she finds Sean McKinlay on a high country station in New Zealand, she confronts him about his past. But what she uncovers plunges them both into danger — and reignites the passion between them. Can their love survive when someone wants them dead?

Books by Loren Teague
Published by The House of Ulverscroft:

TRUE DECEPTION

LOREN TEAGUE

ULTIMATE BETRAYAL

Complete and Unabridged

ULVERSCROFT
Leicester

First published in Great Britain in 2009 by
Robert Hale Limited
London

First Large Print Edition
published 2010
by arrangement with
Robert Hale Limited
London

The moral right of the author has been asserted

British Library CIP Data

Teague, Loren.
  Ultimate betrayal.
  1. Irish Republican Army- -Fiction. 2. New Zealand
  - -Fiction. 3. Romantic suspense novels.
  4. Large type books.
  I. Title
  823.9′2–dc22

  ISBN 978–1–84782–976–4

Published by
F. A. Thorpe (Publishing)
Anstey, Leicestershire

Set by Words & Graphics Ltd.
Anstey, Leicestershire
Printed and bound in Great Britain by
T. J. International Ltd., Padstow, Cornwall

This book is printed on acid-free paper

Prologue

A ten-year-old boy was killed and several people were injured in a bomb explosion yesterday at Covent Garden. This is the third attack in recent months of a new wave of bombing since the peace talks in Northern Ireland have stalled. A spokesman for the Irish Republican Army denied responsibility, citing the bomb was caused by a splinter group. Police are appealing to the public for any information leading to the whereabouts of Sean O'Riley, a member of the Irish Republican Army, who may be connected to this latest incident.

1

Boston — Three years later

Katrina Jones had never broken the law before. She'd never committed fraud, or even had a parking ticket, but what she was about to do could result in arrest and life imprisonment.

Lifting up the newspaper cutting she kept in the back of her diary, she studied the black and white photo of a man she'd convinced herself she hated. Yet, even now, her pulse fluttered as she took in his face and tousled black hair. He had extraordinary dark eyes, lethal in their intensity. He could almost be mistaken for one of the gypsies said to roam the Irish countryside. But he was no gypsy. The man she was looking at was an IRA terrorist.

Sean O'Riley.

He had left her life in tatters and, often, she had wondered if he'd ever regretted what he had done? Well, in one week's time she would find out, she thought resolutely.

Katrina flicked her wrist to look at her watch. It was a quarter to eight. Time to get going.

She backed her vehicle out of her garage attached to her tiny flat, and headed to Newbury Street in the Back Bay area of Boston. Only a few minutes drive away, Parisiana was a combined bookshop and café set amongst elegant boutiques and funky salons.

The traffic lights held her up for a couple of minutes, but Katrina wasn't worried. Never one to waste time, she re-applied her lipstick, and checked her hair in the car mirror. She wore her straight blonde hair long, just past her shoulders, except when she was working at Parisiana. Then she gathered it back primly to the nape of her neck and tied it with a black ribbon.

She drove into an empty car park and jumped out. Several more steps and she stood outside the café. She stopped for a moment to look at the brownstone building, the window frames recently painted a rich burgundy. The place had a Bohemian look about it, reflecting the atmosphere inside. Lace café curtains hung at the windows on a brass pole. Scripted in rolled gold italics high above the windows, as well as on a fancy sign jutting out from the wall, was the name Parisiana.

Climbing the twenty steps, she opened the door and stepped inside. Immediately, she could see it was busier than the night before. Not that she was complaining. She loved to see the place buzzing like this.

A table had been marked reserved especially for her, all set out nicely with a freshly laundered green check tablecloth. A bottle of their best champagne lay nestled in ice in a silver bucket. The head waitress, Jilly, knew her tastes well, she thought, with a smile.

An aroma of freshly baked bread wafted out the kitchen door. With the staff being rushed, perhaps she ought to offer to help? But no sooner had she reached the next table, than a hand was placed gently on her shoulder from behind. It was Jilly.

'Don't you dare, Katrina. It's your night off. We can manage without you for once, you know.'

'But — '

Jilly wagged her finger. 'No buts, OK? If you go into the kitchen, the chef will have a fit. I ought to know. I'm married to him.'

Katrina laughed softly, appreciating Jilly's consideration. 'Hmm . . . maybe you're right. OK then, if the kitchen's off limits, shall I go upstairs? I can help unpack those books that arrived today.'

'Nope. You stay put. Those books have already been unpacked, priced and put on the shelf. We've got thrillers, romances and, if I remember rightly, some poetry. Oh . . . and some cook books as well. Something to suit everyone. Besides . . . ' her voice trailed off as her head shot up. 'I don't think you have time.' Her gaze focused on a dark haired woman who had just entered the café and was now standing in the foyer. 'It looks like your friend from London has just arrived.'

Katrina whirled around, and then gave a smile. 'You're right. She has.' Katrina threaded her way through the tables to greet her. 'Jessie, you made it. How was your flight?'

'Awful.' Jessie rolled her eyes. 'Packed full. But then every flight I've ever taken from London to Boston has been like that.' She shrugged, then gave Katrina a wide smile. 'But now I'm here, I've forgotten about it already.' She pulled out a small parcel from her bag. 'Here, you are. This is for you. A little something I picked up on my travels.'

Surprised, Katrina took the parcel wrapped in silver paper. 'That's so thoughtful of you. But really you didn't have to.'

'I know but I wanted to. Honest I did. Besides, we've been friends for a long time now.'

Katrina pulled off the ribbon around the parcel, eager to see what it was. Her eyes widened. 'Oh . . . it's a novel. *Jane Eyre.*'

'For your book collection,' added Jessie, with another warm smile. 'Seeing as you're a Yorkshire lass, I thought you might like something to remind you of home. It's an old edition.'

Katrina smoothed her fingers over the cover. 'Hmm . . . so I see.' She flicked open the inside page. 'It's in good condition too.' She carefully looked for the publication date and found it. Then raised a brow. 'Over one hundred years old. What a find.'

Jessie nodded. 'I know. I discovered it in an attic of an old farmhouse in Ireland. A lot from a deceased estate up for sale.'

Katrina knew that Jessie's search for antiquarian books took her to all sorts of places. She suspected this particular copy was worth a few hundred dollars. 'Thank you. I'll treasure it always.'

A few minutes later, after taking a seat at the table, Katrina poured them both a glass of champagne. It was so good to see her friend again, thought Katrina. She lifted her glass towards Jessie. 'Here's to life. Wherever it may take us.'

'To life,' repeated Jessie, clinking her glass. She took a sip, then leaned forward in her chair. Her voice lowered. 'So tell me, what's going on? You sounded so mysterious on the phone, I couldn't wait to get here.'

Katrina hesitated. She had tried to plan what she was going to say, but now that Jessie was sitting right in front of her, somehow she couldn't think of the right words. Maybe it would be best to just come right out and say it. Katrina took a deep breath. 'I'm leaving Boston.'

'Leaving?' repeated Jessie, arching a brow. 'That's a big step to take. So where are you going?'

She took another deep breath, knowing that what she was about to say wouldn't go down well. 'To find Sean.'

Jessie's face paled. 'You're what? You can't be serious?'

Katrina nodded. 'I am.'

'But . . . ' Jessie's voice floundered. 'You can't.'

'Can't?'

'You know what I mean.' Her friend's voice sharpened. 'You're getting involved in things that are way out of your depth. Let the police handle it. Sean O'Riley has no scruples. You don't know what he'll do if he is cornered. He might even try to kill you.'

Katrina wouldn't let her friend know that the same terrible thought had crossed her mind too. She shook her head, fear lurking in her heart. 'No . . . no . . . I can't believe he would do that. Not to me.'

'Well, I certainly do. He nearly killed you once, didn't he?' Jessie placed her hands flat on the table.

Yes, he had, thought Katrina painfully. But had he meant to?

She firmed her resolve. 'I'm still going, Jessie. I've made up my mind. And I'm not telling the police either.' She amended quickly, 'At least, not until after I see him.' Seeing Jessie's look of dismay, she rushed on, 'Don't you see? If I let the authorities know where he is, they'll arrest him immediately. I just need to talk to him first.'

Jessie continued to stare at her. 'But what about Parisiana? I thought you loved owning this place.'

'I do. And Jilly said she would run it for me. She's more than capable.'

'And Scott? Don't you love him? He's not going to like you going away suddenly like this. What on earth are you going to tell him?'

Katrina shrugged again. Scott was the least of her worries. 'I'll just say I need some time on my own. Things haven't been right between us for a while anyway.' If only she could unburden herself to Jessie, but she felt this wasn't the time. Telling Jessie about Sean was enough for now.

Jessie gave a sigh. 'I see. That's a shame.

You and Scott seemed to get on so well. Ever since you left London you've been much happier. You've rarely talked about Sean, never even mentioned him, so naturally I thought you'd put all this unpleasant business behind you.'

Katrina couldn't help the unsteadiness of her breathing. 'I'm completely over Sean if that's what you mean.' But even as she said the words, Katrina knew they weren't strictly true. How could she ever forget the man she had fallen desperately in love with? The man who had deserted her after he'd committed a crime against humanity.

'If you were over him, you wouldn't be doing this,' accused Jessie, her eyes narrowing slightly. 'Or is it revenge you're after?'

Katrina shifted uneasily. 'Revenge? No, no . . . it's not that. I just want to understand what happened. You might have been able to forget it. But I haven't, no matter how hard I've tried.'

She had told her friend about the nightmares she'd been having on and off and how they had left her shaken and tearful for days afterwards. Eventually, she had sought help from a psychotherapist. He had told her that some issues in her life hadn't been resolved and, unless she could face Sean once and for all over what he had done to her, she would never be free of him.

Looking back, Katrina realized the first step to making a fresh start had been leaving London for America. Setting up her café and bookshop in Boston had been the second. The café had been open for two years now. She'd always wanted to own her own business, combining her love of cooking with her passion for books. With her knowledge of the book trade, her reputation for tasty food and friendly service, the place attracted every writer and publisher imaginable from the literary set to hard core newspaper journalists. She worked hard, six days a week, and she had to admit Parisiana was now making a fortune. Katrina made sure her staff were well paid, with an added bonus every month in return for their loyalty. Leaving all of this behind, even temporarily, wouldn't be easy, she thought regretfully, especially since she'd put her heart and soul into it, but, she reasoned, the staff would cope fine without her for a while. Jilly and her husband, Jeff, got on well with the staff and would relish the opportunity to be in charge.

'I still can't believe you'd leave Scott,' said Jessie, interrupting her thoughts.

Katrina's voice firmed, though she could understand her friend's worry. 'It's something I have to do. Whether Scott likes it or not.'

Jessie gave an exasperated sigh, then leaned back in her chair. 'Well, I can see there's no talking you out of it. All I ask is that you just be very, very careful.'

Katrina gave a smile. 'I will. I promise. I won't take any chances. Will that satisfy you?'

'Nope, but I suppose I haven't a choice. You've always had a determined streak. That must be the Yorkshire grit in you.' Jessie turned thoughtful. 'So tell me more. I'm interested to know. How are you going to find Sean?'

'I already have.'

'What?'

'I hired a private investigator.'

'I don't believe it,' exclaimed Jessie, amazed. 'You mean a private investigator managed to track Sean down after all this time? Even after the security intelligence services failed. That seems a bit odd, don't you think?'

'Perhaps Sean got careless. I don't know. After all it's been three years since he disappeared. But I hired the best private investigator I could find. It cost me a lot of money and it's taken a while, but at least I know Sean's whereabouts. The detailed report I received also gives information about the people he's staying and working with.'

Jessie pursed her lips. 'A detailed report; I

am impressed. Can I read it?'

'Why not?' Katrina handed over the documents willingly. She wanted to convince Jessie that she wasn't rushing into this blindly, but had thought it all out very carefully. Katrina went on to explain, 'Sean's been living at a high country station in New Zealand. I never thought he'd end up in a place like that.'

Jessie let the information sink in. 'Hmm. Very clever. New Zealand's high country would be an ideal place to hide, I suppose. It's very isolated.' Jessie skimmed the report quickly, then looked at Katrina with surprise. 'It says here he's related to the owner of the station.' She paused briefly. 'You never mentioned he had an uncle in New Zealand.'

Katrina shook her head. 'I never knew. Sean never spoke much about his family though he told me his parents in Ireland were dead. According to Rick Caruso, the private investigator I hired, Sean's been living at Glenroy Station for about three years now, working as a farm hand. He's now known as Sean McKinlay.' Katrina paused reflectively.

'Do you remember the police told me they suspected Sean had left the country? It looks like they were right after all.'

Katrina recalled the London Metropolitan Police had questioned her afterwards. She told them she'd known Sean for several months and had no inkling of his terrorist connections. She could have sworn he was an art dealer as he had talked so enthusiastically about painting and his own work. Talking about Sean like this to Jessie made it all seem like yesterday somehow. Katrina's heart started to pound as the images flowed back in her mind. The last time she had seen Sean was in the London bookshop where she had worked with Jessie. It had been Jessie's day off and Katrina had stayed on longer because they'd been short staffed. Sean had been waiting for her while she finished work, dressed in faded blue jeans, whitened at the knees and sporting a battered black leather jacket with the collar turned up. He leaned against a shelf of books watching her closely as she served her final customer for the day. His roguish smile made him look wild and dangerous. She remembered thinking at the time she could imagine him more at home amongst the bleak moorlands of Ireland than a glitzy London shopping mall.

And now, to think she had finally found him in New Zealand after all this time. What did she feel? It was something she couldn't honestly answer. Not yet, anyway. Her hand shook as she lifted the glass of champagne to her lips, still deep in thought.

'Are you all right?' asked Jessie quietly.

With great effort, Sean's image disappeared and her friend's worried expression came back fully into view. Katrina gave a smile, then rubbed her forehead. 'I'm a bit tired, that's all. Been working long hours and I haven't been sleeping so well lately. I guess I've been a bit worried about how things will turn out.'

Jessie's brows rose, her gaze speculative. 'I'm not surprised. This is a big step to take.' She leaned forward. 'I'm always telling you, you work too hard.'

Katrina gave a laugh but shifted uncomfortably, knowing Jessie was probably right.

'Don't. You're making me feel guilty.'

'Good, I'm glad.'

For a brief moment, Katrina wondered whether to tell Jessie any more of her plans. She had always proved trustworthy in the past and had been a good friend to her.

'There's something else,' added Katrina softly. 'The station does homestays where you can work for your keep. I've been thinking that it might be a good way of getting onto the station initially without alerting Sean.'

Jessie gasped. 'My God, girl, now I know you're completely crazy. You mean you're going to work there as well?'

Katrina tried to explain. 'Sort of. But that

all depends on what happens when I arrive. I've already spoken over the phone to John Forrester, the owner of the station. That's Sean's uncle. He's agreed to take me on for a month on a trial basis.'

Jessie's eyebrows rose again. 'What? Sean's family might know about his past. They might even want to protect him.'

Katrina shook her head. 'The private investigator says they sound very respectable. Typical farmers, and they've owned the station for years. Besides I've given a false surname. Katrina Young. They won't even know who I am.'

'But as soon as Sean sees you, he'll recognize you.'

'That's true. But I'll cross that when I come to it.' Katrina reached into her handbag again. 'Here. This is a copy of the report, so you know where I am. Just in case.'

'What do you mean just in case?' asked Jessie, anxiously.

Katrina hesitated. 'If anything happens to me, I mean.'

Jessie's face paled again. 'Don't talk like that, do you hear me?' With unsteady hands, she took another sip of her champagne, then emptied the glass. 'So what else did you find out about Sean?'

'Not a lot. He's kept a low profile. Never

takes any holidays and rarely goes into town, but when he does it's usually to do with the station, picking up supplies that sort of thing.'

Jessie looked thoughtful. 'Sean has fooled a lot of people. Even you. Possibly even his family. He's a man used to assuming different identities.' Jessie leaned forward. 'He's a professional.'

Bitterness filled Katrina's voice. 'I know all of that. But it makes no difference. I'm still going to New Zealand.'

'Don't you remember what that police officer said to you? Sean is a very dangerous man,' emphasized Jessie.

How could Katrina forget? She hated to say it but even as the police officer's words echoed in her mind, she had to convince Jessie she knew exactly what she was doing, and she knew all the risks involved.

She swallowed hard. 'Yes, I remember. He said Sean is ruthless. He'll kill if anyone gets in his way.'

★　★　★

The next day, Jessie stood at the hotel-room window, overlooking Boston harbour. She hadn't slept very well, tossing and turning until the wee hours. Usually when she visited Boston she stayed with Katrina at her flat but knowing things had gone awry between her friend and Scott, she decided it would be better to stay in a hotel. Katrina had told her Scott had a temper and Jessie had suspected that he might be heavy handed as well, especially after he'd been drinking. The last thing she wanted to do was make things worse for her friend.

Jessie looked at the phone. All night she had thought about what she had to do. Even so, betraying Katrina's confidences didn't sit well.

Dialling the number she knew by heart, she tried to think what to say. And what *not to say*.

A man's voice answered gruffly, 'Maguire.'

'Danny, it's me. Just a quick call.'

'Hi, Sis. Been expecting you to ring. What's happening over there? Did you pass on those messages I gave you to our supporters. We got to keep the flame burning for a united Ireland.'

'I did. Looks like they're donating more money to the cause. But I had a hard time persuading them. Ever since the American Government listed us as a foreign terrorist organization, they're not so keen to dip into their pockets. Still, I did my best.' Jessie hesitated. 'Something else has come up. That's why I'm ringing. I'm worried. Promise me you won't say anything to Carrie. This is between you and me, right?'

'You know I don't like keeping things from Carrie: She's my wife.'

'Promise me?' Jessie reiterated.

She heard him give a sigh. 'OK, I promise.'

'It's Katrina. She's found Sean. Can you believe it?'

Silence. 'Are you sure?'

'Yes. I'm sure.' She hesitated again. 'I didn't know whether to tell you. I don't want any trouble.'

'You're too soft, Sis. Haven't I told you that before?'

'Danny, I'm not like you and Carrie. You know that. I believe in a united Ireland too. I'm more than willing to pass on messages for you, help raise funds for the Real IRA, even spy. But I don't like hurting people . . . ' Her voice trailed off. 'I've always liked Katrina. She's a good friend of mine.'

'Stop worrying, kid. What happens to Sean isn't your problem. And we'll keep Katrina out of it. We've no gripes against her.'

She knew Danny was right. Even so, she felt torn between her friend and her brother. She'd always supported Danny in whatever he did especially his involvement with the Provisional IRA and then, later on when they'd disbanded, he'd joined the Real IRA.

19

Though she was ashamed to admit it, she turned the other way whenever any violence was carried out by those he was involved with. Danny always justified everything to her. He somehow made her see that there was no other way to achieve their goal. She thought the world of Danny, though she'd had a few run ins over the years with his wife, Carrie. Danny had always been her big brother, so strong, so right in everything, even when they were kids. She'd follow him to the moon if she had to. But she'd never do that for Carrie. Personally, she didn't think Carrie was good enough for him. His wife could be such a vindictive bitch sometimes. And one thing she knew for certain was that Carrie hated Sean for betraying them. The rule for betrayal, especially for informers, was death.

Sean was a danger to Danny, she reminded herself. And her brother came first. Always.

Jessie gave a sigh. 'I just don't know. I tried talking Katrina out of going to New Zealand but she won't listen.'

'New Zealand?' exclaimed Danny. 'Is that where Sean is?'

She didn't answer.

'Jessie?' he said sharply.

'I'm here.'

'You know what we *have* to do,' urged

20

Danny. 'We can't sit on this. Sean knows who I am, for Christ's sake. He knows who Carrie is too. If we ever get caught, he's got enough evidence against us to put us away for life. Besides, he ruined months of planning. The bastard. For that alone, he deserves everything he gets.'

Jessie's heart sank. If she gave Danny the full details of Sean's whereabouts there would be no turning back.

★ ★ ★

Katrina glanced out of the window of the plane as it lost height, and thought of Jessie. Her friend would be back in London now working in the bookshop. The same bookshop Katrina had worked in when she'd first met Sean. Jessie often travelled to Ireland, and even America twice a year, to inspect and purchase antiquarian books for sale, then took them back to London for reselling. Every time Jessie came to Boston, she and Katrina got together, and caught up on what was happening in their lives. It had been wonderful to see her again, Katrina thought. Just like old times.

Katrina frowned as she thought of Scott. She had tried to explain to him that she just wanted a break, but when he'd started hurling abuse at her, she'd walked out on him before things had got worse. There had been no mention of Sean O'Riley as Katrina had known that would have made Scott worse. In a moment of vulnerability, just after she and Scott had got together, she had once confessed to him about Sean, then had regretted it ever since.

A light touch on her shoulder reminded Katrina to snap on her seatbelt.

'We're just about to land in Nelson,' said the hostess with a practised smile.

At least, she wouldn't have to go through passport control, thought Katrina, with relief. That had already been done in Auckland earlier on when she'd arrived on an international flight to New Zealand.

Within minutes, Katrina walked across the tarmac to the low, white airport building which lay ahead of her. A sea breeze blew back her hair, cooling her face. She sniffed the salt air, thinking how wonderful it was after the traffic fumes in Boston. Clean, green New Zealand was the slogan she'd seen in an in-flight magazine. Now she could easily understand why this was one of the last unspoiled countries of the world with its wide areas of hilly pine forest, dark green against an azure sky.

For the briefest of moments, Katrina

almost forgot why she was here and imagined herself as a backpacker on holiday. The enormousness of what she was doing almost prompted her to turn right around and head back to Boston straight away. No, she couldn't do that. She'd come too far now.

Once inside the airport building, a voice came over the loudspeaker announcing passengers should go out the main entrance where the luggage could be collected. Perhaps, John Forrester would be waiting for her there. Surely, it wouldn't be too hard to find him since the airport was relatively small.

She didn't even have to try. A tall, elderly man ambled over to her, dressed in typical farmer's cotton shorts and a worn check shirt. 'Katrina Young?'

Katrina started at the unfamiliar surname. She nodded quickly. 'Yes . . . yes . . . that's me. And you?'

'Mr Forrester. But call me John, please,' he added, surveying her for a few seconds. 'I'm pleased to meet you.' He smiled, then lifted off his wide-brimmed hat and held it to his chest. His hair was grey, thinning on top. Katrina thought there was something endearing about the man with his white bushy eyebrows and deep blue eyes. He put out his big hand and Katrina took it, shaking it firmly.

'You'll be tired after your flight, I expect,' he said kindly.

'A little,' she admitted. 'But it's good to be here, at last.'

Within minutes, John had shown her to the four-wheeled drive vehicle parked nearby. Then, out of nowhere, a black and white dog bounded, its pink tongue lolling. The sheep dog obviously belonged to the farmer and had been waiting patiently in the shade. Katrina patted it on the head as it nuzzled her legs. She had always loved animals.

'Seems like you've made a friend,' said John grinning.

Katrina laughed. 'I hope so. I've been brought up with animals. My father was a country vet.'

'Is that so? Makes a change from the usual people we take in. Most of them are from the city and haven't got much of a clue when it comes to animals. That's why they come here, so they can experience something different.'

Katrina gave a rueful smile. 'Don't expect too much from me. I've been living in a city for a long time now — ever since I left home when I was a teenager.'

'Well, at least you can cook from what you've told me. But you might have to go easy on any fancy dishes. You'll have a riot on your hands if you serve up something the

24

farmhands won't recognize. Plain tucker is what they like.'

She couldn't resist saying, 'Perhaps, I can persuade them to try something different.'

John gave a chuckle. 'I'm not so sure. But you're welcome to try.'

Katrina slipped into the front seat of the truck. 'Thanks for letting me stay at short notice. Having a break like this is just what I need.' That part was true, at least, and it made her feel better, though marginally. Then she chided herself. She wasn't going to be playing housekeeper for very long. So why was she so worried?

'Is it far to Glenroy?' she added curiously.

John started the engine. 'A couple of hours' drive. We head inland towards a range of mountains. We'll be there before the sun sets. I just hope you like it. Can be a bit lonely sometimes, especially for the young ones like yourself.'

Katrina was quick to show her interest about the place. 'That won't bother me. Honestly, it won't.' Then, because she was genuinely interested, she added, 'Have you been doing homestays for long?'

'About a couple of years. It's a good way of getting help, especially around the house. We're starting to get more Americans staying with us now. At one time, it was mainly

English tourists who wanted to experience life on a high country station.' He glanced at her. 'And what about you? You like living in Boston?'

'Sometimes,' she admitted. 'I guess being brought up in Yorkshire, you never forget your roots but Boston has been good to me.' Briefly, she told him about her life for the past few years, selectively changing names and places, hoping John would be satisfied with her story and her reasons for coming to New Zealand. 'A working holiday is just what I need,' she said with enthusiasm.

He nodded, informing her, 'We do have tourist buses passing through the station regularly. Occasionally, they stop at the homestead for a chat, and if we've got time, we put on afternoon tea. Sometimes one or two passengers end up staying a few days. I don't mind. It's always extra money for the farm and we've got plenty of room.' John shrugged. 'Mind you, my nephew Sean isn't so keen. He likes his privacy. I can't say I blame him.'

Katrina stiffened at the mention of Sean's name. He was probably afraid someone might recognize him. After all, his photo had been plastered right across the newspaper headlines in Britain.

'Your nephew doesn't like people?' she

enquired, keeping her voice casual.

'I wouldn't say that but he's a loner in a lot of ways. He's Irish. Came out to New Zealand three years ago.'

'And does he plan on staying?'

'Looks like it. He hasn't got any other family left in Ireland. My wife, Jenny, and Sean's mother, Sarah, were sisters. Jenny immigrated here, back in the 1950s to work on the station as a cook. That's how we met. Then later on we married.' He shook his head and sighed. 'She died several years ago.'

Katrina looked at him, her voice softening. 'I'm so sorry. I didn't mean to pry.'

'You didn't. Just thought maybe you'd like to know a bit about us.' He slipped the ute down a gear. 'It's been tough without Jenny, I'll admit it. Sometimes though, I still think she is close by.' He gave her a quick glance. 'Sounds a bit silly coming from an old man like me, I suppose.'

'No,' she said quietly. 'I understand exactly what you mean. When a person has been a special part of your life, they will always be with you.'

While tempted to ask more questions about Sean, Katrina didn't want to arouse John's suspicion. Purposely, she changed the topic. 'Some of the landscape around here reminds me of England. It's so green.'

'You sound homesick.'

'Perhaps, a little,' she admitted. Suddenly, her stomach clenched. Now she was beginning to wonder if she was doing the right thing after all. Coming to New Zealand to find Sean had seemed like a good idea at the time, especially when she was planning it all in the safety of her own home. But who knows what she would find? She tried to steady her breathing.

John's face brightened. 'It might be lush green here, but the scenery changes drastically once we head into the mountains. It's bleaker, more rugged. Glenroy is a special place. I'm sure you'll love it here. My wife did.'

His enthusiasm about his home and family had Katrina shifting uneasily in her seat. Somehow she couldn't believe this man knew about Sean's murky past. She tried to concentrate again on the scenery which had a calming influence. Wild flowers grew everywhere, some shaded purple, others bright pink. The golden tussock stretched forever.

'You're right, the land here is beautiful,' she murmured, impressed with what she'd seen so far.

A thoughtful look crossed John's face. 'Maybe I'd best tell you a bit more about us, so you know what to expect. One of my sons,

Ross, lives on the farm. He's the eldest so he'll take over the place some day. My youngest son, Brent, is a geologist. He lives on the West Coast, a place called Moonlight Valley, several hours' drive from here. Then there's Sean who I mentioned before. He's a deep one. But I think you'll get on grand. There's a few farmhands and they're all a good bunch. Very easy-going. I'm sure you'll like them all.'

'I'm sure I will,' murmured Katrina.

Eventually, they descended into the valley. The winding river shimmered like a living, breathing entity as the sun's rays glided over the surface. Pot holes jolted the vehicle, and John's brow creased in concentration. He gripped the steering wheel harder. Katrina fell silent, not wanting to interrupt him.

Instead she thought about what she would say to Sean when she faced him.

2

Sean McKinlay climbed down from his horse. He leaned against the rickety fence, then took a swig of cool water from his flask. He was due back at the homestead in a couple of hours but there were a few things he wanted to check first.

He gazed at the land in front of him appreciating the harsh beauty of the mountains unfolding dramatically in the evening sun. For a man accustomed to the lush greenness and gentle undulating hills of Connemara in Ireland, he had unexpectedly fallen for a land on the other side of the world, a place he'd once heard described as having a lot of sheep and not much else. He was inclined to disagree. Couldn't they see the tawny gold and browns of the mountains and the darkened streaks of scorched earth which painted a picture so beautiful, you wondered if it was real? He sighed. A man could unshackle the bonds of convention and live exactly as he chose to, right here in the high country.

At thirty-five years old, he'd seen a lot of the world, but it was only here, or in Ireland, that he'd really felt at home. Only now, he knew perfectly well he couldn't live in either country without hankering for the other. New Zealand had been a good choice though — far away from the subterfuge and violence which still left a sore wound if he cared to think too deeply about it. He'd had enough of murder and mayhem to last ten lifetimes. He wanted peace, and on the station he'd found it. Or at least, he'd thought he had.

He raked his hair back from his face, cursing the heat. Maybe he ought to get a number one haircut like his cousin, Ross, and the rest of the farmhands. The men had once made fun of him and his shoulder-length hair when he'd first arrived, calling him a long haired hippy, and saying other things like, 'He looks like a Sheila to me.'

Later, he'd found out 'Sheila' was a slang term for woman. That had got his back up. Ross had tried to stop the men from harassing him and told him every greenhorn went through it. It hadn't even mattered that Sean was the boss's nephew.

'Big woman's blouse doesn't even know one end of the sheep from another,' one farmhand had said with glee. They'd baited and tormented him until finally Sean had lost his temper, throwing the first punch and taking on three of them at once. Sure, he came off worst, but they never called him names again. Instead, the farmhands treated him as one of their own and bought him a beer on the rare occasions he went with them into town.

Sean skimmed the area around him. Where was Ross? He was supposed to be checking some fencing with him. Then, distracted by movement nearby, Sean watched as two red deer bounded out of a gully. He pulled his rifle from his saddle bag and releasing the safety catch, aimed carefully. His finger tightened around the trigger. The shot echoed like the crack of a whip, chasing away the ghosts of the past as if they never existed. He smiled. A crack shot and yet he had missed by inches, simply because he had wanted to. He just hadn't been able to shoot the stag. It was such a magnificent creature, in all its wildness. Ross, his cousin, would have laughed at him, and so would the others if they had known. Now that was something he definitely wasn't going to tell them.

Sean had just slid his rifle back in the saddle-bag when he noticed a dust trail in the distance curling upwards in a spiral. A white ute travelling at a high speed, slowed down to cross the snake-like river in the Acheron valley. Sean shaded his eyes, recognizing the ute immediately. The driver would be his uncle

John on his way back from Nelson with their new housekeeper. An English girl, he'd been told earlier.

Sean scanned the land around him one more time, searching for Ross. Then he saw him. He appeared just over the rise, cantering towards him. When he reached Sean he pulled up his horse, and frowned. 'Christ's sake, Sean. How come you didn't get the stag at that range? Losing your touch or something?'

Sean shrugged, his gaze enigmatic. 'It moved too quick, I guess.'

Ross's tone was sceptical. 'Hmm . . . never known you to miss before.' He flashed Sean an odd sort of look, then turned his horse about, shaking his head.

On the way down, Sean thought about his plans for the future. He'd bought some land and a cottage further up the valley and planned on doing the place up eventually. Ross and his uncle John had tried to put him off saying too much work was needed on the cottage, and there was plenty of room at the Glenroy homestead. But Sean wasn't afraid of hard work. He was patient. He could see its potential. In some ways, he thought, it would be like restoring a piece of artwork, only on a larger scale. The porch might be dilapidated and every window cracked, but he could repair that.

He gave a long sigh, feeling restless. The sooner he started working on it, the better.

* * *

Katrina's first thought when she saw Glenroy Homestead was how quaint it looked. Large baskets of lobelia and alyssum hung on silver chains from the veranda guttering. The roof, made of corrugated iron-sheeting, was long and sloping with a taint of rust but somehow that added to its rustic charm. On the walls of the veranda, a jumbled array of black oilskins and wet weather gear hung on brass hooks.

Behind the homestead, golden light from the setting sun sharpened the contours of the mountains and softened the landscape. Katrina gazed mesmerized. She had never seen anything so beautiful.

'I'll be glad to get my feet up,' said John, interrupting her thoughts. He stretched his back. 'But first, I'd better get these supplies unloaded. We'll need some of them for dinner tonight.'

Katrina watched John at the back of the ute lift out the provisions he'd purchased in town. There were boxes, a few cartons and plastic bags. Katrina grabbed her backpack and whatever else she could carry, and then followed him towards the homestead.

'Where is everyone? It seems awfully quiet around here?' she remarked.

John put the large box down on the veranda, then turned to face her. 'Out working. But they'll be back soon for dinner.' He pointed to a large wooden hut over to the far right of the paddock. 'That's the shearers' quarters,' he told her. 'They won't be arriving until we've got all the sheep mustered . . . maybe in a couple of weeks' time. That's when you'll have your work cut out for you.'

Katrina jumped. Of course, she'd be the housekeeper and cook. How could she have possibly forgotten? 'Yes, I suppose so,' she laughed, but her laugh faltered slightly at the size of what she'd taken on.

The inside of the house was cool, the walls painted a creamy white. Katrina walked along the hallway, behind John. He opened a door. 'This is your room. Make yourself at home. If there's anything you need, just ask.'

She murmured, 'Thanks,' then in one glance took in the furnishings; the white calico cover over the bed and the brass bed ends. Although the room looked fairly basic, the polished wooden floors with a couple of scatter rugs and a built in cupboard along one wall, made it look cosy. Once she had a few items of her own displayed on the dressing-table, it wouldn't be so unfamiliar, she thought. After depositing her backpack on the floor, and deciding to unpack later, she made her way along the hallway to find John. She entered the kitchen. Katrina's gaze swept the room. It looked well laid out, with a log-fired oven and a large pine table standing in the middle of the floor.

She heard a horse whinny outside. Heavy boots thudded on the veranda.

A deep voice called out, 'John, are you about?'

Katrina's heart started to pound. It sounded like Sean, she realized. A sudden urge to run came over her. Get a grip, she told herself firmly. You *have* to face him.

When he walked in, she could hear herself make a small noise in the back of her throat.

He was dressed in stonewashed denim jeans and a cotton shirt. He lifted off his wide-brimmed leather hat and threw it on the bench. 'Phew . . . am I glad to call it a day.' He moved forward to greet her, smiling, holding out his hand. His smile faltered.

Her gaze locked with his. Seconds passed. She couldn't move, or speak. Finally, she said, 'Sean . . . ' But her voice tailed off at the intensity of his gaze.

'Katrina?' he uttered. His arm dropped to his side. He spoke softly, so soft she had to strain to hear what he said. 'Jaysus. Tell me

I'm seeing things.'

He hadn't changed much, she noted. He was leaner with a few more lines around his eyes and slight hollows in his cheeks. She ached to rush into his arms . . . and to tell him how much she had missed him. Instead, with great restraint, she took a deep breath and said in a cool voice, 'Yes, it's me, Sean. Been a long time, hasn't it?'

He took another step forward. 'I can't believe it's you, Katrina. What are you doing here?'

Her chin lifted. She gave a strained laugh. 'Looking for you.'

'But . . . but . . . why now? It's been three years.'

Yes, she thought. Three years, twenty days, and four hours. The longest time of her life.

'You disappeared after the bomb explosion,' she said, her voice a barest whisper. She wasn't sure if she was asking a question or giving a statement. Her mind didn't seem to be functioning properly.

His forehead creased. 'I know . . . but . . . didn't you receive my letters?'

'Letters?' she exclaimed, taken aback. 'What letters?'

'The ones I wrote to you.'

'But I . . . I . . . never received any letters,' she stammered, unable to believe what he was saying.

He looked puzzled. 'Surely you must have. You wrote back to me.'

She gave him a blank look. 'I never wrote to you. How could I? I didn't know where you were. I kept hoping you'd contact me, but there was nothing. Nothing at all.'

'Hold on.' He paused slightly. 'There's been some mistake. You wrote and told me you hated me. That I was never to contact you again.'

Bewildered, she shook her head. 'No . . . no . . . I didn't. I don't know what you are talking about.'

She tried to get her head around what he was saying. She had to be careful. For all she knew, he could be lying, or making excuses, or basically trying to confuse her. Yet, something about the way he spoke convinced her that maybe he had written to her after all but what about the letter supposedly written by her?

His mouth tightened at her silence. 'You don't believe me,' he said flatly.

'No . . . no . . . it's not that.' Yet, even as she said the words, she knew that wasn't totally true. To cover her confusion, she said, 'There's just so many unanswered questions. And now you're telling me you wrote to me. And that I replied.' She shook her head. 'This isn't something I had expected.'

His voice deepened. 'It's the truth. I swear it.'

'Even if it is, you're hiding in the back of beyond because you're on the run from the police.'

He stared at her. 'You've already made up your mind about me. So why come all this way to find out something you already know?'

Her chin tilted upwards again 'but that's just it. I don't know. All that I've ever read in the newspapers or been told by the police never made sense to me. No matter how many times I went over it.'

He said warily, 'If its justice you're after, you'll not find it here, Katrina.'

She shook her head. 'No, not justice. I'll leave that to the authorities.' God, she just wanted some understanding. And some peace within her own mind. As to what there had been between them, she couldn't even afford to think of that. Let alone hope.

She had a thought. 'So why didn't you ring me?'

'I did, a few weeks later. By then your phone had been disconnected. That's when I heard you'd gone to Boston,' he said. 'I tried to follow you. But I couldn't get into the States. They're not too keen on Irish paramilitaries entering the country since the terrorism threat.'

So he had cared enough to try to find her. Her heart leapt a little. 'I had to leave London. The press found out I was your girlfriend and hounded me. It took some convincing the police that I knew nothing about what you'd been up to. That I'd been an innocent party all along.'

Again he stepped forward, reached out for her, and said, 'I'm sorry,' but she stepped back quickly.

'No, Sean. Don't touch me.'

'Katrina . . . I didn't mean for you to get caught up in it all. You have to believe me. Things went terribly wrong.'

A thin chill hung on the edge of his words. Maybe she'd been hoping he'd deny it all but here he was admitting he was guilty. He'd even called himself an Irish paramilitary. She flashed him a look of disdain. 'You're three years late with your apologies, but I'll settle for the truth. That is, if you're capable of it.'

He flinched. 'If I ever lied, it was to protect you. Damn it. Don't you see?'

She stood looking at him, unsure. 'See what?'

'We need to talk this through,' he said firmly 'but not now. Later on, when we're on our own. It would be better that way.'

Katrina felt uneasy. 'Your family don't know about you, do they?'

'John does but he's the only one.' He hesitated. 'Don't say anything yet. Do this for me, Katrina. At least, just until we sort things out. I can't promise to tell you everything, but I'll do my best to make you understand what really happened that day. Maybe then you won't think so badly of me.'

Katrina bit her lip, still filled with uncertainty. 'I've no choice. I need some answers, Sean.' She would just have to be patient and hope he would tell her the truth. Then it occurred to her 'but if I agree, what's to stop you running again?'

He shook his head. 'No, you've got me wrong. I'm not going anywhere. This is my home now. Probably the first one I've had in years.' His eyes fixed on hers in a direct and penetrating gaze that had always brought a flush to her cheeks. 'And now you're here.'

Something intense flared through her. 'Yes, I am but maybe you're wishing I wasn't.'

'That's not what I meant.'

She wanted to believe him, but she still wasn't sure but what had she expected? That he would plead forgiveness, perhaps, even offer to give himself up? He'd said sorry, hadn't he? It just wasn't enough, her conscience told her. Damn him!

A shout from outside interrupted them. Sean gave her a reassuring smile, though she could see the worried light in his eyes. 'That's Ross. My cousin. A bit of a rough diamond. But you'll like him. Come on, let's get the introductions over with. He's been waiting to meet you.'

★ ★ ★

The sun's bright light blinded her for a second after being in the shade of the house. When Katrina's eyes adjusted, she watched Sean greet his cousin before she stepped forward to shake his hand.

Ross was a lot stockier than Sean, but just as muscled. With his blond hair and tanned skin, she couldn't help but compare them.

Ross drawled, 'So you've come all the way from Boston, huh? You don't talk like a Yank.'

'That's because I'm not one. I'm English.'

'Ah, that explains it.'

'And you're a Kiwi?' she shot out, unable to resist his teasing tone.

'Yeah.' He grinned widely. 'You catch on real quick for a Pom.' He swapped looks with Sean. 'Obviously, she's got a sense of humour too. Looks like we've struck it lucky this time.'

Katrina laughed, feeling warmed at his manner. 'That depends.'

Ross leaned forward. 'Best be warned

though: women are in short supply around here. It's mainly fellas that come to stay, keen to experience the outdoors and work on the land.'

'I'm not afraid of hard work, especially on the station. I can toss hay just like anyone else around here.'

'Not with those muscles, you can't,' he mused. 'Maybe you'd be safer in the kitchen pounding dough.' He gave a chuckle. 'Of course, that's not to say we can't give you a chance. That is, if you're really keen?'

Katrina's eyes glinted. 'Of course, I am. Maybe I'll just have to prove to you that women are just as good when it comes to working hard.'

His face turned thoughtful. 'Can you ride a horse?'

She bit her lip. She may have been the daughter of a country vet, but she'd never been interested in riding horses. As a young girl, she'd been too busy reading books and watching romantic movies on the television. 'No, but that doesn't mean I can't learn.'

'OK then. What about riding a farm motor bike?'

She couldn't help but laugh. 'Why don't you ask me about things I can do?'

He gave her a sceptical look. 'Dad mentioned something about you being a good cook, seems to me you'd look more at home in a beauty parlour.' He lifted up her hand and examined her fingertips. 'Thought so. Silver nail polish?' He tutted. 'That won't last long around here.'

'Pretty hands have nothing to do with cooking skills. How about I prove it tonight?' Her chin lifted in challenge.

He nodded, still grinning. 'That's my girl. Just what I've been hoping. How about steak and French fries with plenty of cooked tomato and beans. Meals have been a bit poor around here lately. Usually when we stop work for the day, we're too tired to make an effort.'

Katrina screwed her face up. 'Something tells me you need educating about cuisine. If you think I'm going to fry up steak and chips, you've got another think coming. How about steak in mushroom sauce with potatoes sprinkled with mint?'

Ross swopped glances with Sean. 'Whoa! What do you think? Shall we take a chance on her?'

'I'm willing to,' replied Sean, his gaze settling on her.

He's hoping I won't say anything, she thought, holding his gaze.

The moment was broken by John carrying a trayful of eggs. 'OK, lads, seeing you've all introduced yourselves, how about getting some wood for the fire? We're clean out.'

'I'll do it,' offered Sean. He stepped forward, saying quietly, 'I'll see you later, Katrina.' The way he said her name caught at her. An ache began in her throat. Oh Sean. She took a step forward as if she was going to go after him, but seeing Ross's perceptive gaze she pulled herself up just in time.

John spoke again. 'Here's some fresh eggs. They'll need to go into the fridge.'

'I'll put them away for you,' answered Katrina helpfully. He handed them over without any fuss. She had noticed the tired lines on his face earlier. It was obvious he was feeling the strain of a long day. After all, he must be in his seventies, she thought.

'Right then,' said Ross. 'I'll be on my way too.'

Katrina threw a smile over her shoulder at Ross as if to say, you don't know what you're letting yourself in for. She heard him laugh out loud. Too cocky by half, she thought with a smile. She'd show him.

Later, while she busied herself in the kitchen, her mind touched on what had happened earlier with Sean. This was what she had planned, wasn't it? Meeting Sean again. Finding out the answers to her questions. And yet, why did she get the strangest feeling that things might not go according to plan?

* * *

Katrina rose before seven o'clock the next morning, determined to speak to Sean on his own. She hadn't had a chance the night before since she'd been too busy preparing the meal and clearing up afterwards. The evening had been a great success. Not only had the men eaten the first course, they'd had seconds, then devoured the chocolate cake dessert she'd made before she'd even had time to add the icing. Afterwards, they had all retired early to bed, since they had to be up at dawn. She'd been only too willing to head to her room as well so she could be alone with her thoughts, and to think about what Sean had told her about the letters he'd written to her. If he'd kept them, especially the one he'd received from her, she could, at least, believe it.

Katrina stepped outside onto the veranda. The flowers growing in the hanging baskets were wilted, so spotting an old watering can nearby she looked round for a tap. After finding one jutting out from the outside wall of the house, she filled the watering can quickly.

Footsteps behind her made her whirl around to see who it was. 'Sean,' she said surprised.

He flashed a brief smile. 'Did you sleep well?'

'I did. As soon as my head hit the pillow I was out. I guess I was more tired than I thought.'

At least he was being friendly, she thought. She hadn't been sure what to expect.

'You want to talk?' he asked. 'John and Ross are away for an hour or so.'

She nodded. How was she going to handle this? Yesterday, she wanted answers. Nothing had changed in that respect but more than that, if it was at all possible, she wanted to convince Sean to give himself up to the authorities. She continued to water the plant pots while she formed the words in her mind.

Sean shoved his hands into the pockets of his Levi jeans and leaned against the stone wall waiting for her to reply. Impatience crossed his face. 'Well? Are you going to talk to me or not?'

'I'm just thinking,' she replied defensively. 'It wasn't an easy decision to come here. But now that I am, I want to know your side of things.' Her voice lowered. 'At least, you owe me that.'

He hesitated. 'There's more to all this than

you realize. I'm not sure how to begin. Even how safe it is for you to know.'

'Well, why don't you start with the bomb? That was what changed everything. My life, your life, and a hundred other people we don't even know. The bomb was in your briefcase, wasn't it? You carried it into the bookshop where I worked.'

He swallowed hard. 'The briefcase belonged to me. That's true. But I didn't know anything about a bomb. There were supposed to be only papers inside.'

She said slowly, 'You mean, you didn't make the bomb?'

'No,' he shot out. 'Never. Not in a million years.'

'But you know how to make one?'

He stared at her for a long moment, an odd light in his eyes. Finally, he said, 'Sure. I know how to make a bomb.'

Silence fell. 'Go on . . . '

'I was delivering the briefcase to a contact in MI5,' explained Sean. 'I'd arrived at the bookshop, just before you finished for the day. Do you remember that?'

Katrina jolted. MI5? What connection had Sean with them, she wondered? Could she dare hope . . . ?

Katrina searched her memory, but things were vague. Shadows shifted, merged, then blended into nothing. Part of her memory was lost, perhaps forever. The psychotherapist had called it selective amnesia.

Suddenly, her mind was propelled backwards, trying to make sense of those last few precious moments when she and Sean had been together, and before the world had erupted into mayhem, leaving her life, and so many others, in ruins.

When Sean entered the bookshop, she'd been standing behind the polished wooden counter parcelling up an order of books. 'Hi,' she'd said. She found it impossible not to return his disarming smile.

Sean put down his black briefcase on the wooden counter.

'I'm just finishing up,' she continued. 'Won't be five minutes, OK?'

'I'm not waiting a moment longer,' he'd said softly, his arms slipping around her waist. His lips lightly brushed against hers.

She protested, drawing back. 'Sean, someone might see us. My boss is upstairs. He'll be down any minute to lock up.' Yet even as she had said the words, she'd been unable to resist his touch. She wrapped her arms around his neck, enjoying the feel of his hard lips on hers.

He whispered in her ear, 'I had to see you before I leave.'

Confusion filled her. 'Leave? But you just got here. Where are you going?'

'Ireland.' He spoke casually. 'Got a flight booked tonight. Just some business affairs I have to see to.'

'Let me go with you?' she pleaded. 'I can get a few days' holiday from here. I've always wanted to see Ireland. You did promise you'd take me one day.'

Sean shook his head, his eyes regretful. 'No . . . I can't. Not this time.'

He smiled, an easy smile that almost reassured her, except she still had an uneasy feeling that something wasn't quite right. Sean had been a bit evasive lately whenever she'd questioned him about where he'd been in the evenings. She'd rung him several times and even left a message but he hadn't returned her calls. Then today, he'd sent her a text message saying he'd meet her after work.

'Are you seeing someone else?' she asked suddenly. It was a question which had been playing on her mind, but she had never summoned up the courage to ask him, fearful of what he might say.

'No . . . never,' he said fiercely. 'How could you even think that?'

She hated herself for acting this way but she just couldn't help it. Possessiveness wasn't part of her nature, but it was obvious he was holding something back. For the briefest moment, she saw the desperation in his eyes and with it a darkness she didn't understand.

'Sean, what's wrong?'

He shook his head, and slipped his hand into hers. 'Nothing that I can't handle. Come on, let's go. We haven't got a lot of time. There's something else I need to tell you. Something important. Maybe then you'll understand what all this is about.'

She left him standing there while she walked through to the back of the shop to collect her coat and handbag. It was almost five o'clock and she knew Mr O'Donnell, upstairs in the office, wouldn't mind her going a little early. 'I'm away, Mr O'Donnell,' she shouted at the bottom of the staircase. She heard him answer briefly, 'Right, see you tomorrow.'

When she returned to the front of the shop, a man was standing next to Sean. She hadn't even heard him enter the shop. They were deep in conversation. She noticed Sean handing his briefcase to him. The man took it, glanced up at her briefly, his face taking on a wariness. Then, with a brief farewell nod at Sean, and a quick glance at her, he left, closing the door behind him.

Sean was acting so strange. 'Who was that?'

she asked, noting the man's quick exit.

'Just a business associate. I made arrangements to meet him here.'

'You gave him your briefcase.'

'That's right, I did. But he'll return it to me later on.' Sean slipped his hand into hers. 'Ready then?'

She nodded, still feeling uneasy. Once they stepped out of the bookshop, a warm feeling encased her at Sean's closeness. She had so been looking forward to seeing him again.

The bookshop was situated in a shopping mall and, as they started walking, she saw a young boy hovering outside the toy shop next door. All day long children had been traipsing in and out with their parents taking advantage of the pre-Christmas sale. Next to the fountain, across the way, two men stood, hands in their pockets. It looked like they were searching for someone the way their gazes swept over everyone who passed. As Katrina and Sean neared, the look on the men's faces alarmed her. One of them pointed at Sean.

'Sean,' she began to say. 'Those men — '

'I see them,' he said tightly. 'Just keep on walking.'

'But Sean,' she uttered.

'Don't Katrina. There's no time. Don't even ask me.'

Katrina glanced back, over her shoulder. The men started to follow them. Ahead of her she saw the man who had been in the bookshop earlier. He still carried Sean's briefcase. It looked like he was heading back to the bookshop. When he saw the two men, he started to run.

Sean grabbed her hand and pulled her into the doorway of a jeweller's shop. He rattled the door but it was locked. He turned to face her. 'Damn. Is there another way out of the mall?'

'Yes, but . . . ' Her words faltered as a blinding flash crossed her vision. The sound of shattering glass and screaming echoed in her ears. Then nothing. Only darkness swirled like a never ending gloom.

Sean's face loomed into hers, snapping her back to the present. 'Katrina, are you all right?'

She saw the concern in his eyes and wondered if he had any idea of what the bomb had done to her. Even worse, his betrayal.

I loved him. But he used me.

'I'm not sure,' she murmured, her hands trembling as she fought for control. Her breathing started to shallow. The plastic watering can suddenly slipped from her fingers and landed on the concrete with a thump. Water pooled at her feet like the blood which had run beside her as she had lain injured on the ground. Her heart thudded in her ears.

Don't give in to the fear, she told herself. Remember what the psychotherapist told you. Breathe slowly, in and out. Concentrate on an object you can see.

She focused on a ruby red rose growing from a wooden tub, until she was able to force away the unpleasant images. Her breathing eventually slowed and steadied. Her vision came back into focus again. When she felt calmer, she lifted her gaze and faced Sean accusingly.

'Jaysus,' uttered Sean, his eyes concerned. 'Why didn't you tell me?'

She shook her head, weariness flowing through her. She gave a shrug. 'It happens sometimes. Not very often now.'

He grimaced. 'Post traumatic stress. I've seen it before.' He hesitated. 'You've had help for this?'

She nodded. Months of therapy. But she didn't want to tell him that. She didn't want to tell him anything of how she had suffered.

'Can I get you a drink or something?' he said gently.

She shook her head and took a deep breath, firming her resolve. 'No, thanks. I'll be fine in a minute.' And she found that she was. When her thoughts calmed she said, 'Even if you didn't know about the bomb, it's clear you were involved that day. The police can't have been wrong about that.'

To her disappointment, again he didn't deny her accusation. 'Sure I was involved. But the police investigating didn't know all the facts.'

Her gaze held his. 'But you do, don't you?'

He nodded, his face wary.

She rushed on, 'I hoped it would all be a big misunderstanding, perhaps even a mistaken identity. That you'd be proved innocent. You used me. But for what reason I don't know. All those times you told me you loved me, it was just pretending, wasn't it?'

She knew she had hit a nerve when she saw his jaw stiffen.

'All right. I did use you in the beginning,' he admitted, 'but . . . you were wrong about that.'

She stared at him, unsure. What was he saying? That he really had fallen in love with her?

He exhaled. 'You have to believe me, Katrina. If I could tell you everything I would, but I'm under oath.' He shook his head adamantly. 'You have to forget about it. Let it all go.'

No, she vowed, that was the last thing she would ever do.

★ ★ ★

Mid morning, Ross found Sean in the stable saddling up his horse. 'What's going on? I heard raised voices earlier. You and Katrina.'

Sean shrugged, attempting a smile. 'Oh . . . nothing to worry about. Just getting to know each other.'

Ross gave a frown. 'Huh, didn't sound like that to me. Whatever you were talking about sounded very serious.'

'Yeah, well, we were just catching up on old times. We had some unfinished business to discuss.'

'You what?' Ross's mouth fell open.

'Katrina and I knew each other a few years ago. Back in London.'

'Is that so? She never mentioned anything. And I'm pretty sure Dad doesn't know either. He would have told me.' Ross studied Sean carefully. 'Wait a minute. There's more to this than you're letting on. Some dark and deep secret from your past, perhaps?'

Sean gave a low laugh, feeling uneasy. 'You know something? You're right. And if I had my way, that's how things would stay. But that's not going to happen now.' Sean led his horse forward. Ross followed.

'Ever heard of Pandora's box?' asked Sean.

Ross thought for a minute. 'Isn't that to do with Greek mythology? Something about Pandora opening a box containing the evils of mankind?'

'That's right. And the only thing she didn't let out the box was hope.'

Ross felt bewildered. Hope? What exactly did Sean mean? His gut instinct told him something was going on. Yet, somehow he knew it wasn't the time to question him. Katrina suddenly turning up at Glenroy had to be more than coincidence. Maybe, he'd have a talk with her and find out what it was all about.

'I've got plenty to do today so I'd better get on with it. See you down at the river later for a swim,' shouted Sean over his shoulder as he urged his horse forward.

'You're on,' replied Ross. 'Don't work too hard.' He was joking, of course. Sean was one of the hardest workers he'd ever known.

★　★　★

A couple of hours later, Ross made his way to the homestead. No time like the present, he thought. Besides, he was hungry and it was lunchtime. With a bit of luck Katrina might have rustled up some muffins she'd promised earlier. He was right. He found her in the kitchen busy baking. Steam rose from the spicy muffins just out of the oven, sitting on the bench. He grabbed one and tossed it in the air from one hand to another.

'Phew . . . too hot to handle . . . '

Katrina handed him a plate, unable to resist a smile. 'Here . . . use that.'

'Thanks.' After placing the plate on the table, he opened the fridge to find a cold drink. John had stocked up on beer and, although he was tempted to have one, he knew perfectly well the alcohol would slow him down in the afternoon. Playing safe, he grabbed a bottle of orange and took a long swig. Then he pulled out a chair from beneath the table and sat down.

He said casually, 'Sean mentioned that you knew each other before. Is that right?'

Katrina stiffened. 'Actually, I'm surprised he even told you.'

'He didn't exactly. At least, not until I asked him.' Ross surveyed her carefully. 'So is that why you're here?'

She swung around to face him. 'Partly. I'm sorry. I was going to let you know eventually. But when I arrived, Sean asked me not to say anything yet.'

Ross looked thoughtful. 'I see . . . ' He took

another bite of the muffin, then swallowed it. 'It's Sean's business. And yours, I guess. As long as it doesn't interfere with the work around here.' He gave her a puzzled look. 'Is there something between you?'

Katrina avoided his gaze, reaching for the basket of vegetables. 'Like what?'

'You know what I mean.'

Katrina shrugged. 'There was. There isn't now.'

Yeah, sure. Ross didn't press the issue. He'd find out more all in good time. 'OK. If you've got anything to sort out with Sean, you'd better do it quick. We'll be away mustering soon. Probably leaving tomorrow.'

Katrina whirled around. 'Tomorrow? But . . . ' Her voice trailed off as she considered what that meant.

'That's just the way things have worked out,' he said wryly. 'If you're worried about being on your own, don't be. Dad isn't going with us. There'll be a couple of farmhands around as well.' Ross hesitated. 'Dad would go if he could but his old bones can't stand the pace on the top run. He'd never admit it though. Ever since he had his heart attack, he's been told to ease off a bit. As usual he ignores everyone.' He gave a grin. 'It's going to be pretty hard work even for us fit blokes.'

Katrina hadn't reckoned on this. Sean

59

being away would delay her plans. In a daze, she listened carefully as Ross gave his instructions on the housekeeping.

'Think you can clean out the shearers' quarters? It badly needs it. The shearing gang will be here soon, so it would be good to have everything ready,' he informed her.

'Yes. I can easily do that. But . . . but . . . when will you be back?'

'Oh, in about a week's time' He leaned back in the chair, a teasing look in his eyes. 'Why? Will you miss us?'

In spite of her dismay, she found herself replying in the same vein. 'More than you ever know.'

Ross leaned over and grabbed another muffin. He took a bite. 'These are pretty good. Must admit when you first arrived, I had my doubts about whether you could cook. Seems like I was wrong. I guess I owe you an apology.'

'Apology accepted. You know the old adage . . . looks can be deceiving.' If anyone knew that, she did, she thought wryly. 'Still, at least, if you're away, I won't have you sneaking into the kitchen and eating all the baking I've just made.' Her words were tinged with laughter. She pulled herself up with a jolt. What was happening to her? Playing housekeeper wasn't so bad after all and to her surprise, she was enjoying it.

Ross grinned. 'Well, you'd better make the most of our quiet time because when the shearing starts you won't know what's hit you. I guarantee it.'

No way, she thought. Surely, she'd be out of there before then.

And Sean would be behind bars.

★　★　★

Ross wiped his forehead with the back of his sleeve and led his horse towards the stables, a brown wooden building some distance from the homestead. The sun had already dropped behind the mountains. It was hot and humid and insects buzzed in the long grass. After he'd rubbed his horse down and fed her some oats, he shut the stable door.

Walking along the trail to the river enabled him to think about Sean. When his cousin had first arrived on the station, Sean had stated he'd come to look up his long lost relatives. Since Sean had never been in touch much before, Ross didn't know what to make of it, but Sean was kin, after all, being his cousin. And his father was pleased to see him. So with the typical hospitality of those in the high country, they'd invited Sean to stay.

Later, after Sean had started helping out with the chores, they realized that he was keen to learn about life on the station. He'd say one thing about him: Sean was a crack shot with a rifle and that counted for a lot in his estimation. When questioned about how he had learned to shoot so well, Sean would just shrug, smile and say he'd done some training in the armed forces. What armed forces they were, Ross hadn't probed any deeper, but he wouldn't have put it past Sean to be involved in something. Whatever Sean was hiding, he was keeping it to himself and Ross didn't press him any further. A man had a right to keep his life to himself. That was one rule at Glenroy: people who came to work for them were judged on their day's work not for any deeds they'd done in the past. If they didn't pull their weight, they were out pretty fast.

Ross sighed. Living on a farm wasn't easy; the weather played an important part in their life. Too much rain meant flooding and not enough meant a drought. They ran sheep and cattle and things had been going along just fine these past few years especially latterly with Sean's help. He had done more than his fare share so if he was in any trouble, and it was catching up on him with Katrina being here, Ross wanted to know about it.

Sean was already in the water when he reached the swimming hole. Ross unzipped his shorts and threw off his work shirt. He climbed up to the rock and dived in quickly. When he finally surfaced, he trod water for a few minutes and then swam over to where Sean was already drying out, lying flat on his stomach on top of the smooth, grey rocks.

Ross spoke first. 'River's down low. Looks like it's going to be one of the driest summers we've ever had. You know what that means?'

Sean nodded. 'Sure do. Not enough grass for the stock to feed on. Maybe we'd better buy more feed. The sooner, the better.'

'Not that simple. Things are a bit tight financially. Dad went over our accounts again last night. If this drought doesn't end soon, it could break us.'

'Then use the money I offered you,' urged Sean. 'There's plenty there, sitting in a bank account in Ireland. I don't need it yet. So you might as well put it to good use for now. You can repay me later, when things settle again.'

Ross looked thoughtful. 'I'm tempted. I'll talk to Dad again about it.' Then he added, 'That money you've talked about, you earned it legally?'

Sean's head jerked up. 'What the bloody hell is that supposed to mean?'

Ross shrugged. 'Just asking.'

Sean stared at him. 'It's legal. And it's mine.'

'OK,' said Ross. He shifted to a more comfortable position, and decided to change the subject. 'We might as well start shearing the hoggets and wethers next week, after the muster. The shearing gang arrive soon, so I hope Katrina will be able to cope with the cooking.' He gave a laugh. 'She's a nice girl. I'll give Dad top marks for finally choosing a housekeeper who isn't for once two axe handles wide across the backside. You know, I've been thinking some. Thought I might take Katrina out one day, show her about the station.'

Sean's mouth set tight. Ross noticed it. He pushed harder. 'Hey, Sean, if you've still got some feeling for her, best you tell me now. I wouldn't want to step on your toes.'

Sean swore under his breath. 'Back off, Ross.'

'Ah . . . thought so,' said Ross, a grin sliding across his face. 'You can't blame me for asking. But you know something? What I don't like to see is Katrina's miserable expression every time she thinks I'm not watching. I'd hate to think you were responsible for that.'

Sean's shoulders stiffened. 'Things are a bit complicated. Like I said, I'm still trying to sort it out with her. That won't happen overnight.'

Trying to gauge Sean's depth of involvement was proving difficult. Maybe there was much more going on here than Ross realized. Still, it wouldn't do any harm to ask. 'So what did you do to upset her?'

A nerve beat at Sean's temple. 'You really want to know?'

'You bet.' Ross gave a chuckle.

Sean turned to face him fully. 'OK. I asked Katrina to marry me, but something went wrong and I left without saying goodbye.' His voice had the edge in it that Ross had detected earlier.

Ross's jaw dropped. 'You bastard . . . you mean you jilted her?'

3

London

Danny Maguire stood at the dingy flat window looking out onto the street. The place he was staying in suited him fine, thanks to Jessie. She'd spent a week finding him the flat, somewhere that he could come and go easily without attracting attention. Brixton was ideal. Many of the residents in the terraced houses on the street were from the West Indies. Easy-going, smiley sort of people. He couldn't even walk down the street without Bob Marley wailing out of an open window. Every so often he got a whiff of something spicy, something frying in hot oil. It made his mouth water.

There were a few Irish in the street as well, from the south. He'd heard their accents when he'd bought some fags at the corner shop.

He'd made a point of going out every day to get the layout of the place. It was a habit he'd picked up from living in Belfast. You never knew when the police — the bastards — were going to do a raid. He'd always had an escape plan, no matter where he'd lived.

Sometimes he'd go out in the dead of night. London was a different city then. Shadows everywhere. Night was when the daily grind, the bustle and rush were forgotten. The darkness attracted the criminals and the terrorists, ideal for plotting and scheming. Just like him, he thought. He'd always felt comfortable walking in the dark. It gave him a sense of power. It helped he carried a weapon, a Luger, under his jacket. The flick knife he kept in one of his pockets.

The day before, a street hawker had come up to him in broad daylight. He was Jamaican by the looks of him. Lean and colourfully dressed, dreadlocks flowed down his back. He had a sly grin on his face.

'Hey, man, you wanna buy something?' he'd said.

Maguire was tempted to tell him to get lost but his curiosity got the better of him.

'Why? What have you got?' asked Maguire, edging closer.

The hawker opened a small box where several pieces of jewellery and three gold watches lay nestled against velvet. Nice looking pieces too. It was tempting.

Maguire pointed to one of the watches. And a necklace of fine gold. 'How much for those?'

'Forty quid. For both of them.'

'OK,' said Maguire. He made a move to lift them out the box, but the hawker suddenly clapped shut the lid, nearly taking off his fingers, and stepped backwards.

'Money first,' the Jamaican said gruffly.

Maguire looked both ways, making sure no one was watching. He counted the notes from his wallet and handed them over. The hawker opened the box again, grabbed the items and shoved them into his hand. Maguire slipped them into his pocket. With a nod, the Jamaican blended into a dark alleyway and when Maguire looked again, he had gone.

You could buy anything you wanted in London, thought Maguire. Business brought him here at least several times a year. So there were a few bonuses to be had.

Maguire drew himself back from the window as dusk set in. The streetlight came on, flooding the street in amber. He drew the curtains, then sat down on the couch that Carrie had purchased from a second-hand shop. Flicking open his cell phone, he texted a message to Hannad Khalis that he'd meet him later that night about nine o'clock. Khalis replied promptly, confirming the time and address. It had been months since he'd last seen his friend in Paris where he'd been procuring weapons. They'd made plans to work together. Years ago he'd stayed with Khalis in Afghanistan where they'd both been undergoing training in bomb-making and warfare techniques. An alliance had been forged between him and Khalis, both having in common their hate for the British Government. Even then he knew that someday they'd both be working together. The time had come, Maguire thought with a smile.

Maguire went through to the kitchen to make a cup of tea but swore when he realized he'd run out of milk. He was tempted to buy some at the corner shop but then decided to wait. Carrie would be back any moment. He was right. By the time he'd boiled the kettle, he heard the door open. Within seconds, Carrie walked in, breathless.

She threw her bag on the couch and kicked off her black high heels. 'Sorry to be so long. Got caught up in a damned animal rights demonstration so couldn't get past the crowd.'

Maguire took a second look at his wife. Today she wore a blonde wig, bob style, her hair reaching to her shoulders. Normally her hair was dark, almost black and short, which she preferred. She was also dressed in a grey silky suit. The black and silver high heels added another three inches onto her five foot five frame. He gave a whistle. 'Nice outfit.'

She laughed. 'Have to look the part, right?'

'You always look the part, sweetheart. How did you get on?'

'Fine. The lawyer says everything is going through. The land contracts have been signed.'

'No problems with the money coming through?'

She shook her head. 'None. Khalis must know some very wealthy people.'

'He does. Al-Qaeda make a lot of their money from the poppy fields. He'll be rolling in it.'

'You think this will work?' she queried.

'Don't see why not. We have to be inventive. Think ahead.' He gave a short laugh. 'A good job I saved some of those weapons and Semtex from the Provos' arms dump. They were mad to decommission them. We'll need to get them moved from that farmhouse to our new place as soon as we can.'

'What about Sean O'Riley? Knowing the bastard is still out there gets to me. What are we going to do about him?'

'Nothing. Forget him. For now anyway. Once we move back to Ireland, we'll think of something. We'll see what the Army Council think. He won't get away with what he did.'

* ★ *

Frustrated at Sean's attitude, Katrina still hadn't got the answers to all her questions no matter how much she tried. Even her threat to call the authorities hadn't fazed him. She couldn't understand it. He admitted carrying the bomb, but he stuck by his story that he hadn't known it was in the briefcase.

'I can't tell you any more. You'll just have to be satisfied with that,' Sean told her adamantly.

She still didn't know what to make of him. 'So what where those documents in the briefcase?' It was a question that had been driving her mad ever since he'd mentioned them.

'Intelligence reports. All top secret.'

'And did you read them?'

He nodded.

Things were becoming more drawn out than she had anticipated, realized Katrina. What was Sean doing carrying the briefcase anyway? He gave her some information, but not enough for her to get a clear picture of what had been going on, and what role he had played exactly. It wasn't any more than she had read about in the newspapers. He baffled yet intrigued her all in one breath.

The thought that he could silence her by

killing her still occurred, and yet some inner sense told her he wouldn't do that. But she wasn't going to rely on her intuition, not when she'd made so many mistakes about him before.

Later on, after she'd fed the dogs in the kennels, she heard the thump of an axe. Sean stood by the woodshed, a pile of wood stacked neatly. He flashed a smile. 'Just keeping up the supply of logs. It can still get pretty cold at night.'

'I thought you might have been packing for the muster tomorrow? Ross mentioned you were going.'

'I wouldn't miss it for the world. I've got plenty of time to pack. Besides, we travel light. The other farmhands see to the supplies. The only thing I need to worry about is my own gear.' He stepped closer, the axe swinging in one hand.

Katrina glanced at it uncertainly. His closeness had her heart beating faster. The words came out before she knew it. 'I just want you to know, I've left a letter with my lawyer, so if anything happens to me, they'll know where to start looking.'

Sean's jaw dropped. 'Surely you don't think — '

'It's not that. But it makes me feel safer.'

'Safer?' he queried, an angry light entering

his eyes. 'What the hell do you think I'm going to do? Murder you?'

She didn't answer.

He took a step forward, his mouth tightening. 'That's what you're thinking, isn't it?' His tone was flat. 'You don't trust me.'

'I . . . I did once. And look what happened. Maybe if you'd answer more of my questions, I might consider it again.'

He fell silent, a broody sort of silence that unnerved her. Had she done the right thing in telling him about the lawyer?

Later, in the evening, she made her way to the study. Dusk was falling, casting dark shadows. She switched on the table lamp which added a cheery golden glow. Earlier on, John had invited her to look at the rows of books on the shelves whenever she had time. It might take her mind off things for a while, she thought.

'Borrow anything you want,' he'd told her. 'There's plenty to choose from.' John had already retired for the night and Ross was busy organizing the supplies for the muster with the other farmhands down at their quarters. As for Sean, she suspected he'd be outside still. She'd noticed he'd already brought in a basketful of logs.

Katrina crossed the room, drawn to a large oil painting hanging over the stone fireplace.

Even through the isolation, the artist had captured passion and wildness. The colours were vivid, earthy, the peaks almost blue, casting long shadows in the valley.

'It's powerful, isn't it?'

Jolted, she whirled around, not realizing Sean had been sitting there all the time in the corner of the room. 'Sean . . . '

He gave a brief smile. 'The painting belongs to John. His wife bought it for him for his birthday. The year before she died.'

'It's beautiful,' she murmured, turning back to the painting. 'A real gift of love.'

Sean came to stand beside her.

'Do you still draw?' she asked, interested.

'Sometimes, when the mood takes me. Pen and ink drawings mainly.'

'So you are an artist, after all,' she commented.

He shrugged, his gaze enigmatic. 'Amongst other things.'

'Other things?' she repeated, curious. He's so full of secrets, she thought. He didn't answer. 'Sean?' she prompted.

He turned to face her.

They were standing close together, too close, she thought with alarm, sensing something but not knowing what. Yet, somehow she couldn't step away.

He murmured, 'Katrina.'

The way he said her name turned her fear to an ache, so deep it hurt. She almost cried out. Instead, she whispered, 'Yes.'

He bent forward slowly, his hand curving around her jaw. His mouth covered hers. It had been so long since she'd been touched like this. It brought back memories between them. Memories she had *no right* to remember. Memories he had *no right* to evoke.

Her hand fisted, pushing at his shoulder. 'No, Sean,' she managed to say. But it was herself she was fighting, she realized, not him. Further protests were drowned under the assault of his mouth.

Gathering strength, she pulled back hard. 'Why did you do that?' she almost shouted as she stepped back.

'Because I had to,' he said. 'So you wouldn't forget how it was between us.'

Her breath came out in gasps. How dare he? No way could she forget *that*.

★ ★ ★

Katrina drew the white calico curtains in her bedroom. The old sash window was already open wide and she could hear the distant whinny of a horse drifting toward her. She paused to look at the night sky, absorbing the stillness. The moon had risen above the mountains, casting an unearthly silver glow over the land. Somehow the light gave her strength.

So what if Sean had kissed her, she suddenly thought? She could handle it. For all she knew he had done it to unsettle her. Perhaps, even to distract her from her purpose. Well, if that's what he intended it had certainly worked, she admitted.

She continued to stare out of the window, absorbing the night, wondering what tomorrow would bring.

I'm in a land at the bottom of the world. How crazy is that?

It was a far cry from Boston where at night she could hear the low hum of traffic, shouts and snippets of conversations from pedestrians on the street below and cats wailing as they scrapped in the alleyways.

A shadow suddenly fell across the veranda, startling her. She stepped back from the window, her breath catching in her throat. The lean profile in the moonlight was unmistakably Sean's. He started to whistle an old Irish ballad. And suddenly, against her will, her thoughts skipped back in time to when she'd first heard the tune. It was mid-summer and London was heaving with tourists. She hadn't been working at the bookshop for very long when Jessie had asked her to go to an Irish evening at a local pub.

'Come on, you never know who you might meet,' teased Jessie. And so she had gone.

The pub had been full, but they had managed to get a couple of seats near the band. About halfway through the evening, Katrina had noticed the stranger leaning against the bar. He was alone. Something about the sensual way he moved attracted her. She caught his gaze once or twice and he smiled back.

After a while he made his way towards their table. 'Mind if I sit down?' His tone was friendly, unmistakably Irish.

Katrina shook her head. 'Not at all.'

His dark eyes looked into hers. 'You come here often?'

Katrina smiled. 'No. Not really. This is the first time. I haven't been in London very long. And you?'

'Just passing through.'

She hadn't realized she had been holding her breath until her next words came tumbling out. 'So what's an Irishman doing in England?'

'Oh . . . this and that,' he mused. 'But somehow I think I'm going to be here longer than I anticipated.' He held out his hand. 'I'm Sean O'Riley. And you are?'

'Katrina Jones. Yorkshire born and bred.' She took his hand, noting his grip was firm, very strong. She liked the feel of his skin against hers.

'Yorkshire? I've been there once. Liked it a lot.' He moved closer. 'So now that we know each other's names, and since we're both new in the city, how about dinner tomorrow night?'

He didn't waste any time, she thought, flattered. All the same she ought to be careful. Jessie had warned her that being in a city had its dangers. Not that she needed warning. She was quite capable of looking after herself. But he was a stranger. She hesitated. 'I'm not sure . . . '

Sean glanced at Jessie. 'Your friend knows who I am. Why don't you tell Katrina?'

Jessie laughed. 'That's right. I do. Sean's a business associate of Danny's, my brother.'

'Oh,' was all Katrina could say. 'I hadn't realized.'

Sean turned back to her. 'So there you are then. What do you say? Do you like Italian food?'

Her mouth curved. 'Love it.'

'Good. How about a movie afterwards?'

She couldn't help but laugh and feel flattered at his persistence. 'OK. Sounds great.'

'We'll choose something romantic.' He inclined his head, a teasing light in his eyes.

She laughed again, deciding on the spur of the moment, she really liked him. He was charming, she thought. She hadn't needed much persuasion to see him again. That was the start of their relationship which had her falling head over heels in love with a man whom she had thought felt the same about her.

★   ★   ★

The next day Katrina stood on the veranda watching the men get ready for the muster. She caught sight of Sean packing his gear on his horse. She had to speak to him before he left. For a fleeting moment she felt guilty, hounding him like this. Then she reminded herself, if anyone should feel guilty it should be him. He was the fugitive.

She edged closer until she stood right behind him. 'I hadn't expected you'd be going away. It's not some ruse to leave the station, is it?'

He looked up. 'No, it damned well isn't. If I could stay, I would. But if I don't go on the muster, John will go instead. He's got a heart condition and it would put a lot of strain on him.'

Katrina felt foolish. 'I'm sorry, I hadn't realized.' Then she added quickly, 'John mentioned something about losing a bottle of tablets last night. I found them on the floor where he must have knocked them over.'

'He's a bit forgetful sometimes,' remarked Sean.

'In that case, I'll keep an eye on him while you're away.'

Sean nodded gratefully. 'Thanks.' He stood looking at her. 'Things will have to wait until I get back then.'

'I'm booked in here for a month. So if you think I'm going to change my mind and leave before then, you're wrong. I'm not one to give up when the going gets rough, Sean. Being here proves that.'

'I never thought for one moment you would.' He paused slightly. 'Why don't you stay on longer?'

Katrina's heart did a somersault. Did he mean he wanted her to stay? She hadn't counted on him asking her that. She bit her lip, unsure. 'I've got commitments back in Boston,' she said coolly.

His gaze held hers. 'So?' he said with an underlying edge that had her pulse jerking.

★ ★ ★

Afterwards, silence descended in the farm-yard. It was a strange feeling. Only the sound of the cicadas backing the morning chorus of birds, and a cow protesting in the distance, reminded her there was still some life left around the place. John had left earlier on to check some stock down by the river.

Katrina decided to phone Jessie in London. Now was a good time to speak to her, to reassure her friend she was all right, and to keep her up to date on what was happening. She dialled Jessie's number quickly.

Jessie answered. 'Thank God you've rung, Katrina. I was going out of my mind with worry. Is everything OK?'

Katrina told her briefly the events so far. 'Things are going fine. But I have to wait until Sean returns from the muster. I'd hoped to be out of here within a week but it hasn't worked out like that.'

'Leave there while you've got a chance,' urged Jessie. 'Someone came to see me the other day. They said they were from MI5. They'd had a tip off that you'd gone to New Zealand to find Sean. They asked me if I knew anything about it. Of course, I denied any knowledge. Said you hadn't mentioned it to me.'

'MI5?' repeated Katrina, stunned. Then it occurred to her. Could Jessie's phone possibly be tapped? She'd heard about things like that.

It was almost as if Jessie read her mind because she said, 'Stop worrying. An electronic expert friend of mine checked the line out. It's safe.'

Katrina wasn't convinced. 'Do you think they could track me down?'

'I don't know. But eventually they might. You found Sean, didn't you? So what's stopping them finding you?'

Katrina turned over in her mind what Jessie had told her. If MI5 were on to her, they surely would have turned up by now, thought Katrina, worried. The only unusual thing that had happened so far was the phone had rung earlier, but when she had gone to answer it, no one was there. Perhaps MI5 were establishing she was at Glenroy? She didn't know what to think.

* * *

Jessie hoped what she had said to Katrina would scare her enough to make her leave the station. It wasn't true about MI5. They were the last people that Jessie would even speak to. No doubt, MI5 would have her on file though, and Danny and Carrie. She had to be careful every time she contacted her brother and his wife in case they were tracked down by the authorities. They'd be arrested on terrorism charges. Jessie could only be thankful the two of them had escaped after the explosion and gone into hiding.

'You talk with her?' asked Maguire.

Jessie nodded.

'So what did she say?'

Jessie shrugged. 'Nothing much. But she's determined to get to the truth.'

Maguire gave a short laugh. 'Maybe you should have just told her. Saved her the journey to New Zealand.'

'I was tempted. But if I had, she would have wanted to know how I knew. That would have given me away.'

Maguire grunted. He brought out a small box he'd kept hidden in a drawer. 'Here, got something for you.'

'What is it?'

'Something I picked up. Thought you'd like it.'

Jessie opened the box. A fine gold necklace lay nestled amongst the velvet material. 'For me?'

Maguire nodded.

'Oh, Danny, it's lovely. Thanks.' She went forward and gave him a hug.

'Here, let me fasten it for you,' he offered.

It was at that moment Carrie walked in. As

soon as she saw them, Jessie could see the irritation in her eyes. She came up to Jessie, and lifted the necklace, fingering it. 'Nice little trinket. Doesn't look like real gold though.'

Jessie scowled. She knew Carrie was jealous. She didn't like Danny giving her things. That was just tough, thought Jessie. She wasn't going to let Carrie's jealousy spoil the gift.

'It's the thought that counts. And it is gold, isn't it Danny?' She smiled at her brother. 'I'll always wear it. Honest I will.'

'Good,' he said, pleased. 'Now that we're all together, we'd better get down to business. What did you think of Khalis?'

'He seems very nice,' replied Jessie.

'Nice?' Maguire gave a chuckle. 'Never heard him called that before. Ruthless, fanatical, maybe even crazy, but never nice.'

Jessie flushed. 'You know what I mean. At least he is respectful to women.'

Maguire gave a short laugh. 'Sorry, Sis, I'm just teasing you. As long as you think you can carry out the role OK.'

Danny was testing her. She knew that. 'A piece of cake,' she replied confidently. 'Do I have to wear a burka or something?'

Maguire shook his head. 'Nah . . . let's not attract any attention. Ordinary clothes are fine.'

'What about learning Arabic?'

'You can if you want, but Khalis speaks fluent English.'

Jessie nodded. 'I was always good at languages when I was at school. I can still remember French.'

'Good. But let's just keep it simple. So here's what we'll do.'

★ ★ ★

Later that morning, Katrina entered Sean's bedroom. While the men were away, John had asked her to go through the house and clean it thoroughly. The hot dry conditions outside blew in dust where it settled on all the furniture.

Taking a damp cloth, Katrina wiped the dressing table, lifting up a photo of four men; Ross and his brother Brent, John and Sean. Sean hadn't changed much, she thought, although his skin was deeply tanned. He was leaning over the fence, in blue jeans, his hat tilted backwards at a casual angle. The three other men stood nearby laughing.

She put the photo down and scanned the room. Sean was still untidy, clothes scattered everywhere. He had never been fond of housework, she recalled. She picked up his clothes, folded them and put them away.

After she had started making Sean's bed, she noticed the folder lying halfway underneath the table. Unable to resist a peek, she opened it to see some sketches of the high country; men on horses, shearers, a dog. They were very good, she had to admit. She flicked through them until she came to some scenes of London.

There was a drawing of her. Stunned, she could only stare at it. A dreamy look was on her face as she sat in the park on a wooden bench. Sean had signed his signature at the bottom along with the date three years ago. So he was telling the truth about being an artist, she realized.

He must have drawn the picture of her from memory because she certainly didn't recollect him drawing it. It was before the explosion, she remembered, as if that event had measured another time and place.

★   ★   ★

It had been a productive day, Sean decided, as he gathered up the reins of his horse and urged the animal forward. Following the track he made his way along the ridge keeping a watchful eye out for any sheep lurking in the gully below. The dogs were only a whistle away and could still run with enthusiasm even after being on the go since the break of day.

The sun had dropped from the sky, leaving a golden light teasing the tops of the mountains. Soon it would be dusk. Knowing there would only be a few more minutes of daylight left, he dismounted and led his horse over to the river. A brown wooden hut stood a few yards away. Several of the stockmen congregated nearby.

Ross made his way over to him, leading his horse, a broad smile on his face, 'I hope Dinger's got some tucker on. I'm starved.'

Sean glanced at the camp-fire. 'Whatever he's cooking, it smells good.'

Dinger, the oldest of the shepherds did the easy runs, and minded the camps. He was stirring a pot of stew vigorously.

When they reached the camp-fire, the crackle of the flames rose higher as Dinger piled on more wood. Sean wiped his forehead with his sleeve, then decided he had time to do a few sketches. Fetching his drawing pad, he sat down on the hard ground watching the scene unfold in front of him. The scent of sweat and dust from the horses and men drifted widely. Ross flopped down lazily beside the fire and lifted a mug of tea to his mouth. Lyall, the head shepherd, and Ross, were sitting by the fire on a log bench. They were laughing at a joke, someone was telling. Lyall was tall, lanky and wore tattered clothes. His brother was a younger version but slightly heavier. They were hardcases but good men and had both been at Glenroy for years.

Someone brought out a harmonica and the sound mellowed over the land, drifting in and out of the tall, tussocky grass before coming to rest beside him. Sean's pencil flew over the paper capturing the images like a moment in time.

Mustering had been like this since the first Europeans had come to this land and would never change, he thought. Irish immigrants had built this station over a hundred years ago. Apart from a spell in winter during the great snow of 1867, when the owners were declared bankrupt, the farm was still going strong. Sean wanted to be part of its future. But he also knew with an uneasy feeling that sometimes life didn't always go the way you planned it and, if ever he had to leave New Zealand, it would be memories like this which he would take with him, and the comradeship of the men he worked with.

Satisfied with his drawing, Sean put his sketch book down and made his way to the river. Shadows were springing up everywhere. After his quick dip, he leaned against a rocky ledge listening to the water tumbling over the stones. Tension eased from his shoulders. An unbidden picture of Katrina sprung into his mind no matter how much he tried not to think of her.

If she had found him, there was a high possibility that others could too. He knew it would come eventually. He just wasn't sure what to do about it. A perverse part of him wished she would contact the police straight away and that would have been the end of it. The only trouble was, if and when she did, life wouldn't be the same at Glenroy.

After he'd eaten, Sean got up to stretch his legs. He walked slowly back to the hut to get his bedroll. Even though he could have slept on one of the bunks inside the hut, he chose to join the other men who slept outside.

He picked a spot near the glowing red fire and settled down for the night, gazing up at a sky studded with silver. A warm wind whispered along the ground, winding its way through the blades of tussocky grass, until it reached him, skimming across his hot skin like a lover's kiss. He said Katrina's name under his breath. He could almost imagine her touch, the way she had once felt in his arms. She made his blood heat. If only he could have her beside him now.

It was late before he slept.

Five more days passed. The shearers' quarters needed to be cleaned. Katrina made her way to the wooden building after slipping on a striped apron that had seen better days, collecting her bucket and some cleaning gear.

By the looks of it, the living quarters hadn't been cleaned for some time. She threw out the dog-eared magazines of scantily clad women, brushed the cobwebs from the ceiling, and washed the floor thoroughly. The shearers had their own showers and kitchen and, although it was fairly rough, it was adequate for their needs. By lunchtime she was finished and decided to take the afternoon off.

It was while she was sitting on the veranda writing a letter to Jilly and the rest of the staff at Parisiana that she heard horse's hoofs. She put her hand to her forehead to shield her eyes from the sun as she stared. She couldn't quite make out who it was. A rider was approaching, moving fast.

'Sean?' she murmured, somehow knowing it was him. But where were all the others? Within moments, he'd reached her. Dismounting quickly, he gave her a slow, easy smile, leaving her heart hammering resentfully. He hadn't shaved for days and his clothes were dusty and creased. His face was thinner but deeply tanned adding to his dark looks. He raked a hand through his hair. 'I'm back early.'

She nodded. 'So I see.'

He tied up the horse. 'Things went well. We've got most of the stock.' He turned, heaved the gear from the back of his horse, then placed it on the veranda with a thump. 'The others are on the way. They'll be wanting food and drink.'

'It's all ready. Fridge is filled with cold beer too.' Perhaps, she'd better make some sandwiches, and cut up the fruit cake she'd baked yesterday. While Sean unpacked some of his gear, she turned about and headed into the kitchen.

A few minutes later, Sean appeared, frowning. 'You've been in my room.'

Katrina whirled around, disliking the hostile tone in his voice. 'That's right. I cleaned it. And I didn't go searching your things, if that's what's entered your mind.'

His jaw tightened. 'Cleaning is one thing: it's not your job to go picking up after me.'

Maybe she had overstepped the boundary, but he didn't have to sound so ungrateful. Her voice was defensive. 'I was just trying to be helpful.'

'Sure, and maybe I'm just not used to having a woman run after me.' He paused slightly as if it was an afterthought. 'Thanks anyway.' Within seconds, he'd returned with a roll of paper which he laid down on the table. 'Here, take a look at this.'

Still smarting, she said warily, 'What is it?'

'Why don't you open it and see?'

She did. 'Oh . . . it's a drawing,' she remarked, surprised. She took it in fully, absorbing the flow of lines, the lightness of pen. Several men, salt of the earth, sat around the camp-fire after a hard day's mustering. Most of the men she recognized, including Ross with his lopsided grin. She glanced at Sean, saying nothing. Not even knowing what to say. Finally, the words tumbled out. 'It's wonderful. If I had a gift like that, I'd be earning a living from it. An honest living,' she emphasized.

Something flickered over his face, then it was gone. 'I sold my art gallery back in Ireland some time ago. Put my own drawings into storage. Maybe someday I'll send for them.' His eyes met hers. 'Keep this one, if you want. I've plenty of others.'

Her voice came out sharp, resistant. 'No . . . I can't possibly take it.'

'Why not? It's only a drawing,' he said drily. 'Not a kiss. Not even a damned wedding ring.'

She gasped, appalled. 'How can you say

something like that?' She couldn't figure him out sometimes. She looked down at the drawing again, torn between accepting it, and refusing. If she was honest with herself, she wanted to keep it. But she couldn't. To accept something so personal from him like this was like saying she had forgiven him. She hoped forgiveness would come later. But she wasn't ready quite yet. Her chin lifted. 'No. I don't want it, Sean.' Then hated herself for saying it.

His voice hardened. 'Right then, if you don't want it, then neither do I.' He lifted it up, scrunched it into a ball and threw it in the bin.

Shocked, she said, 'You didn't have to do that. It's a fine drawing.' Hot tears blurred her eyes at the violence of his actions.

'Don't cry on me,' he said flatly.

She shook her head. 'I'm not,' but couldn't hide the sob in her voice.

She watched him walk towards the door, his face furious. He paused, his hands fisted at his side, then he hit the door, shocking her even further. She hadn't even known he had a temper.

'Damn you, Katrina.' He whirled around, the intensity of his gaze searing her.

She'd hurt him, she realized, with a jolt. Badly. Regret filled her. She took a step forward, unsure, wanting to make amends but not knowing how to.

'Sean,' she murmured, but it was too late. He'd already gone.

★ ★ ★

Still John hadn't returned. He'd phoned to say he was spending the night in town with some friends as he had an appointment first thing the next day for a check-up at the hospital. He also told Katrina he hoped to see the bank manager about extending the overdraft for the farm.

The next day, still smarting from the incident over the drawing with Sean, Katrina made her way to the shearing shed with flasks of coffee and muffins for break time. The shearers had arrived that morning and were a rowdy lot but easy-going. Five men stood in a row on a shearing platform, each with clippers, their shirts peeled off because of the heat. Sweat slicked their bodies.

Ross moved forward to greet her. 'Come to see what's going on, huh?'

'Just a bit curious,' she admitted.

He pointed. 'You see those blokes over there, they're damned good shearers. The best. They can sheer about two hundred sheep a day.'

'That's amazing,' she replied, fascinated.

She noted how everyone moved in natural rhythm and harmony. She could hear the friendly banter between the men.

Then, as if she couldn't help herself, her gaze scanned the shed for Sean. She spied him straight away. His shirt had been stripped off and his tanned, gleaming body was bare to the waist. His muscles flexed as he lifted heavy bags of wool and deposited them on the floor. He turned to pick up the next bag, caught her gaze and stopped, straightened his back and stared at her. For a few seconds she was unable to look away. How could she forget the curve of his jaw, the darkness of his eyes and the way he had once looked at her, just as he was looking at her now. Her breath started to come in faster. The wanting was still there, she realized.

Trembling, she pushed her blonde hair back from her face saying, 'I'd best get back to the kitchen. I've got a tray of scones in the oven.' She turned quickly, her heart hammering wildly.

Once outside, the fresh air hit her, clearing her thoughts. Since their argument about the drawing they'd hardly spoken to each other. It had shocked her that Sean could have such an effect on her. For the rest of the day, she avoided going into the shed and left food and drinks outside on the table.

One of the young Maori girls, Tui, called out to her in the afternoon, 'Come back later on, when we finish. We talk for a bit, if you want.'

Katrina smiled, warmed at the girl's offer. 'Thanks. I will.'

Three hours later, Katrina found Tui sitting outside her quarters. The girl smiled, though Katrina couldn't help but notice her worried frown. She indicated for Katrina to sit beside her.

'Is there something wrong?' Katrina asked, sensing a depressed atmosphere amongst the men sitting nearby. They were talking in low tones amongst themselves.

Tui flicked back her waist length black hair. 'They're worried. It's this drought. Some of the farms in the region are in trouble, so the army is going to move in to help transport feed and water. It's not looking good.'

'I hadn't realized things were so desperate,' replied Katrina.

Later on, while serving dinner to John and Ross, Katrina thought she'd ask more about the farm's affairs. 'Is it true about the drought? Are things difficult?'

John looked up grimly. 'It is. We have the river nearby, so we'll be OK for water for now, although the level has dropped drastically these past few weeks. It's the feed I'm worried about.'

Ross added, 'We're hoping the army will deliver a supply of hay. Then we'll have our work cut out for us, making sure the stock get fed. But it's nothing we can't handle.'

Katrina nodded. 'Sounds like you've got it all under control.'

'We can only do our best,' said Ross, 'and put in more working hours until things settle again. That reminds me, where's Sean?'

'He finished shearing early and went into town, I think,' replied John. Just after he uttered the words, Sean's footsteps could be heard in the hallway. 'Sounds like he's back already.'

Katrina made a move towards the kitchen, anxious to avoid him. 'I'll dish up dinner.'

Sean walked in. 'Sorry I'm late. I gave Anna Reid a lift into town while I picked up some supplies. Things took longer than I thought.'

'So Anna's still got her sights set on you, huh?' asked Ross.

Jaysus. Where did that come from? thought Sean. He tried to keep his voice casual. 'What made you think that?' asked Sean.

Ross flicked off the top of his beer and took a swig. 'Phil, her brother. He told me that you and Anna were holed up in a new café for a couple of hours. Looked real intimate. He even saw you kiss her.'

Sean almost groaned aloud. He tried to recollect every move he and Anna had made, and how her brother would have perceived things.

Sean spoke calmly. 'Phil's got it wrong. Anna and I are only friends. She was upset about something, we hugged and I gave her a peck on the cheek. That's all . . . '

Sean's voice trailed off as realization hit him. Katrina was listening to every word. The mirror in the dining room, hanging on the wall opposite him, reflected her image clearly as she stood under the doorframe clasping a bowl of steaming vegetables. Sean turned to greet her but the hurt in her eyes froze the words in his throat.

★   ★   ★

After the meal, Sean wondered how to explain to Katrina about Anna. She was their closest neighbour, about the same age as Katrina, who'd lived on a station all her life along with her brother Phil and their parents. She jumped whenever she got a chance to go into town though, admittedly, this time she had sought him out, asking for a lift.

Things were already shaky between him and Katrina since the incident with the drawing, now, this had made things worse. He had to get Katrina on her own, make her understand. He found the perfect opportunity when she was in the kitchen finishing up.

'We need to talk about Anna.'

'What you do in your private life has nothing to do with me,' she said coolly.

He gave a wry smile. 'I thought that's why you were here: to find out about my life.'

She snorted. 'That does *not* include past lovers. Or even current ones.'

'Is that what you really think?'

Katrina could feel her cheeks flushing.

'It is, isn't it?' he added softly. 'You're so determined to see the worst in me. It never even occurred to you that I might have been helping Anna.'

'Helping?' she said uncertainly. 'What do you mean?'

'She came to me with a few boyfriend problems. Thought maybe I could give her a male perspective on things. So I took her for a coffee to calm her down.'

'Look, Sean, I . . . ' Her voice faltered. Perhaps he was right. Maybe he really was telling the truth about Anna and she *wanted* to think the worst of him.

'And while we're at it,' he added, 'about that drawing. I'm sorry. I lost my temper. Mustering has a tendency to do that. Too many broken nights, I guess.' He gave a quick smile. 'It doesn't matter. There're plenty of other drawings. If you change your mind later, you can pick out another one.'

But it did matter, she thought. It mattered to her very much. And now he had apologized over the whole drawing incident when it had been she who had thrown the gift back at him in the first place.

She felt so confused. 'I'm sorry too. I really did want to keep the drawing. It was just that . . . ' Her voice trailed off again. How could she explain something she didn't even understand herself?

'Sometimes we do the opposite of what we really want to,' he finished for her.

He was being so understanding. Aware of his close proximity, a tight knot within her begged for release. She tried to take a breath and relax but it was impossible. All she could think about was the touch of his warm hand on her arm, her skin tingling wildly from the contact.

Chemistry. That's what it is. She couldn't help but be attracted to him. No matter what he had done.

'I'd like to choose another drawing,' she found herself saying.

He flashed a smile. 'Sure. I'll look some out for you. So is this a truce then?'

She nodded. 'As good as it gets for now.'

After he'd gone, she sank down onto the

kitchen chair, still reeling from what had occurred, and what he had said. For a moment there had been a closeness between them, brief yet so intense. She'd have given anything to hold on to it.

★ ★ ★

The next morning, Sean pulled on jeans and a tattered sweatshirt. He ought to shave, but for once he'd give it a miss. He'd promised to meet Katrina at seven for her riding lesson and he was already a few minutes late. When he entered the kitchen, she was frying bacon and eggs, humming softly as if she hadn't a care in the world. Her hair hung down her back in a plait. An image of her exactly like this in his flat in London, all those years ago, caught at him unexpectedly.

She whirled around to face him. 'You're up at last. I thought you'd forgotten about the riding lesson.'

'Ross wouldn't let me,' he replied drily. 'He banged on my bedroom door earlier on. Threatened to drag me out of bed if I didn't make a move.' He chuckled. 'Don't worry, I'll get my own back, preferably after he's had a night in town at the local pub.'

'Would you like breakfast now or after-wards?' Katrina asked.

'Afterwards. I'll just have coffee, thanks.' He poured himself a mug from the jug on the stove, then turned to face her. 'Are you almost ready? It would be good to get started, before the sun gets too hot.'

'OK. In a minute. Once this is cooked.'

He couldn't help but study her as she moved around the kitchen at ease in her surroundings. He'd forgotten how competent she was. How she could conjure up a meal in no time at all. Cooking had always been something he'd hated. But Katrina had always made it seem like fun. She'd even cooked meals for him at his flat in London.

'So you took up cooking professionally,' he remarked. 'Quite a change from working in a bookshop.'

'I combined both. I own a café and bookshop in Boston. One of my life's ambitions fulfilled.'

'I'm impressed.'

She shrugged. 'I must admit I didn't do it entirely on my own. I had help from Jessie initially with a loan. I guess I owe her a lot. Parisiana — that's the name of the place — is doing so well, I paid back the last instalment a month ago.'

'So you still keep in touch with Jessie?' he asked, frowning.

'I do. We're good friends. She comes to

Boston several times a year. Sometimes she even stays with me. It gives us a chance to catch up with each other.'

He looked thoughtful. 'So what does she do in Boston?'

'Mostly looks for rare books to sell in her bookshop.'

Sean's mind ticked over. 'Her bookshop? I thought the bookshop belonged to a Mr O'Donnell?'

'It used to. But he retired. So she bought it off him.' Katrina slipped off her apron and hung it on the peg at the back of the door. 'I'm ready now.'

He nodded. 'Good. Then let's go.'

Katrina walked by Sean's side towards the stable. Since he'd apologized, she'd felt something had changed between them.

'What's life really like on the station?' she asked, trying to make an effort.

He gave a smile. 'Hard work. Long hours, little pay. In spite of that, I've always enjoyed working outdoors.'

'So you're a terrorist turned farmhand,' she remarked, then immediately regretted her choice of words. They sounded so flippant.

He grimaced. 'If that's how you see it. A lot of those fighting for a united Ireland are people just like you and me. They're not all thugs and killers like they're made out to be.

My mother taught me life was sacred. She was Catholic. She wasn't religious in the conventional sense, but she instilled in me certain beliefs.'

Katrina studied the strong planes of his face, noticing the wariness in his eyes. She couldn't resist asking, 'You've never talked much about your family, apart from telling me your parents died when you were a child.'

He shrugged. 'Somehow it didn't seem important at the time. They died when I was thirteen. So I was adopted out to a family in Connemara. I still keep in touch with them.'

Katrina was tempted to ask him how his parents had died, but the way his face shadowed when he mentioned them, made her hesitate.

He turned to her. 'What about you? Are your parents still in Yorkshire?'

'Yes, retired now. My father still lends a hand at the local vets when they need him. Somehow I don't really think he wanted to retire. He enjoyed his work too much. My mother is still involved with her charities. I think she thrives on it.'

'Having a job you love makes all the difference,' replied Sean. 'When I first left school, I thought about coming out here to work for the summer. But in the end I opted to go to university to study law. I guess I wanted to follow in my father's footsteps. He was a criminal lawyer. But after a while, I got tired of studying and wanted some action. So I joined the Garda.'

Katrina stared at him. 'Wait a minute. Are you saying you were a police officer?'

'Ten years' service,' he replied proudly. 'I joined as a uniform and then transferred to the Special Detective Unit in Dublin. Later on, I joined the Metropolitan Police in London. That's when I went undercover.'

'An undercover cop?' she repeated, stunned. 'Are you kidding me?'

He gave a smile. 'No. Is that so hard to believe?'

'Yes and no.' Katrina shook her head in bewilderment. 'None of this makes sense. The police officers in London never told me any of this. As far as they were concerned, you were heavily involved in the IRA.'

'That's because I was. I had become another identity. Sean O'Riley in the Provisional IRA. The whole undercover operation was top secret.' He hesitated. 'You seem to think that because I had a part in what happened that day, I'm some sort of monster. Did it ever occur to you I was a soldier in a war? But the difference is I tried to save lives.' Wearily, he rubbed a hand over his eyes. 'After it was all over, I just wanted to live like a normal person again, so I came out here.'

No way was she going to let him justify his actions that easily. 'You carried that briefcase, Sean McKinlay. I don't care whether you were a cop or not: the bomb went off because of you. Is that what you call saving lives?'

'Hard words, Katrina. You've changed.'

She wasn't hard, she wanted to shout at him. But she wasn't the young, vulnerable girl who had fallen in love with him. And yes, she had changed. He was right about that.

She couldn't help the sarcasm in her voice. 'What about that ten-year-old boy who died in the explosion? Do you ever think of him?'

Sean's mouth tightened. 'I see his face every time I pass a kid about his age walking along the street.' It might have been the way he'd said it, or even the inflection in his voice, but afterwards, she realized, it was the regret in his eyes that convinced her.

He added quietly, 'Even if I'd said I'm sorry a million times over, it would never be enough for you after what happened.'

She fell silent. Was he right? He confused her in so many ways. Finding out he had once been a police officer had completely thrown her. Not just any police officer either but an undercover cop. She needed to probe more deeply, but something told her to go easy. Too much pressure on him wouldn't work. She knew that instinctively. Maybe, given time, she pondered, he might just open up and give her the key to what she was looking for.

The riding lessons had gone well, Katrina thought. At first, she had been anxious about spending so much time in Sean's company, but gradually she had relaxed, and concentrated on the task. For two days Katrina had practised, under Sean's supervision, in the paddock. She now knew how to saddle up as well. On the fourth day, just when her confidence was growing, the horse reared up unexpectedly after it was spooked. She slid off, landing with a thump on the hard ground.

Sean sprinted over to where she lay. 'Are you all right?' He knelt down beside her, his face full of concern.

Katrina's head was bowed, her blonde hair cascading over her face. Her riding helmet had slid down her back. He gently drew her hair back. 'Are you hurt?'

At first she couldn't speak. Her eyes met his. 'No, I don't think so. Just winded.'

'Can you stand up?'

'I'm not sure,' she said shakily. When she gathered her senses, she was only too aware of his arms around her waist as he helped her gently to her feet. The warmth of his body infused with hers as she leaned against him. She tried to take a step forward. 'Ouch . . . my ankle.' She winced. 'I must have twisted it when I fell.'

'Let me take a look.'

'No . . . no . . . I'm OK. Really, I am.'

He ignored her protests, and bent down on his haunches, smoothing his hands over her leg. She'd forgotten how gentle he could actually be.

'There's nothing broken, probably just bruised. Still, best you rest up for a while.'

She tried putting her weight on it again, but stumbled. Before she knew what was happening, he had stood up and slipped his arm around her waist again. 'Here, let me help you.'

She felt close to tears. The pain and his close proximity was creating havoc with her senses. 'No, I'm OK. I can manage.'

'Don't argue, Katrina.'

Giving in gracefully, she let him help her to the homestead. Once seated on the couch, he said, 'Don't move,' and disappeared into the kitchen. He returned with a bag of ice and placed it on her ankle. 'This should take the swelling down. Keep your feet up, and you should be fine by tomorrow.'

He gave her a reassuring smile that sent her heart skittering all over the place. Damn you,

Sean McKinlay, she thought. He hadn't lost one ounce of his charm. She tried to concentrate on anything but the touch of his fingers gliding over her leg.

He was right. She had no trouble walking the next day, though her foot was a little tender when she put her full weight on it.

Sean found her in the kitchen. 'Seeing your ankle is better, we'll ride further into the hills today. Be good practice for you.'

'I'm not so sure. Why do we have to ride so far?'

'I need to measure the rainfall gauges. We keep a record on the station. Besides, it will do your confidence good if we try somewhere a little more challenging.'

She tried to put him off, though she knew her excuses sounded lame. 'Can't we do that another time? I'm a bit busy in the kitchen right now.'

As if he guessed her thoughts he said, 'Are you worried about being alone with me? Or are you afraid to get back on the horse? You needn't be on both accounts. Ross will be working nearby; he'll be within hollering distance.' His voice firmed. 'And if you don't get back on that horse, you never will.'

It wasn't the horse she was afraid of. Even admitting it sent a quiver through her body.

'I'll think about it,' she replied carefully.

Just to make sure Sean was telling the truth about where Ross would be she checked with him when Sean was out of hearing. 'Sure I'll be around,' Ross had replied. 'You two go on ahead. Do you good to ride a bit further.' Seeing her hesitation, he added, 'Everyone falls off sometime; it's just one of those things.'

★ ★ ★

Katrina shaded her eyes as she looked down into the valley, the parched brownness of the pasture evident. So far so good. Getting back on the horse hadn't been so bad after all. She took a swig of water from her flask. The coolness soothed her parched throat.

Sean was busy writing in his notebook. 'Only ten millimetres of rain have fallen.' He shook his head. 'It's just not enough.' He bent down and picked up some of the grass. 'Look at this. Soft crumbling dust. Everything is so dried up. And the worst of it is, we can't do anything about it.'

It was heartbreaking, Katrina thought sympathetically. The farmers in the region worked so hard.

'Is drought common?' she asked.

'All depends on the weather pattern. It's been a problem for the last couple of years.'

Turning her horse back the way they had come, the wind in her hair and against her face brought a flush to her cheeks. Katrina enjoyed the longer ride. She could so easily get used to this life, she realized with a pang, looking around her at the bleak wilderness.

Later that night, as she lay in bed, the norwesterly wind blew making conditions worse. It screeched like a howling banshee at night and all of the following day. She lay there thinking of Sean and how far she had progressed in her quest to find out the truth. She believed him when he'd said he'd been an undercover cop. To take on an identity of a terrorist would have meant living in it twenty-four hours a day, seven days a week. She couldn't help but wonder what had driven him to undertake such a role?

* * *

Ross told them all over dinner, 'If we don't get rain by early next year, we'll be in trouble.'

John shook his head despondently. 'You're right. The ground is so bare, I could see a mouse at forty yards.' He leaned back and lit his pipe, the smoke drifting lazily across the room.

'Then sell off some of the stock,' Sean

suggested. 'It's the only way.'

Ross leaned back against the soft sofa. 'I just don't know.' His face was serious. A worried frown settled across his brow.

Katrina cleared the empty cups, listening carefully to their conversation. She knew it was really none of her business, but even so, she couldn't resist finding out more. 'So if you have to sell off the stock, what happens then?'

It was Sean who answered, explaining patiently. 'The farm loses money. The only option is to borrow from the bank to buy more stock next year. The farm could end up bankrupt.'

'Bankrupt?' Katrina exclaimed. 'All this hard work for nothing? Are you saying one bad season of no rain and it's all finished?'

'That's right,' answered Sean. He turned to John. 'Why don't we make a decision after Christmas? The shearing will be finished in a couple of weeks and we should get a premium price for the merino.'

John agreed.

★ ★ ★

After dinner, Katrina was conscious of Sean watching her from the kitchen doorway, his arms folded. The broody look on his face unsettled her.

'Is something the matter?' she asked.

'I've been thinking.'

'Oh, what about?'

'Those letters. And why someone would pretend to be you. The letter was typed out. But it had your signature at the bottom.'

'It would be easy to forge a signature,' she pointed out.

Sean frowned. 'Seems to me that someone had a reason for us not to meet again.'

Katrina jolted. 'But that's stupid. Why would anyone want to do that?' The idea was too ridiculous to even think about. 'Since you're so busy thinking, you can give me a hand. Or I'll be stuck in the kitchen for hours.'

Sean surveyed the dishes piled high on the bench. He gave a groan. 'I knew I should have headed outside to chop more logs.'

Katrina gave a smile. 'We could do with a dishwasher. It would save a lot of time. I also noticed John still does his accounts by hand. He asked me to help him. If he had a computer, he'd speed up the process.'

Sean agreed. 'He's still of the old school. I don't blame him in some ways. Life seems to be getting faster all the time. We even had a sales rep calling in to sell us mobile phones. We're thinking about it. Could be handy on a station this size though coverage could be a problem way out here.' He gave a grin. 'We could even text you when we'd be home for dinner.'

Katrina considered his words. 'That's not a bad idea. Yet, in a way it's the opposite of what this place is all about. I'd have thought people come here for the very reason there is no technology. They want to get away from the fast pace of life.'

'I suppose that's true enough. Must be quite different here from your life in Boston.'

'It is.' She shrugged. 'City life is OK, but I prefer the wide open spaces. Always have done. Maybe it's because of where I grew up in Yorkshire. The wild moors. All that space. Looking back at my childhood, my parents were both great believers in plenty of fresh air and exercise. Now, when I go back home we walk the moors whether it is rain or snow. I love it.'

Conscious of his gaze on her, and that she had revealed a little too much about herself, she turned away to wipe the bench. Eventually she said, in as normal a voice as she could muster, 'I can see why you call this place home. It has a nice feel about it.'

'I know. And I don't want to leave,' he replied firmly.

She faced him. 'Meaning?'

'That the only way I will leave is if I'm forced to.' His eyes shadowed. 'You haven't phoned the police,' he stated. 'Why?'

'Simple. Because you haven't answered all my questions yet.'

'Was that the only reason?'

Disconcerted by his question, she said vaguely, 'What other reason could there possibly have been?'

He caught her wrist gently. 'I thought that maybe . . . ' His voice tailed off as he looked at her intently.

'Yes?'

' . . . you felt something between us still.'

Her heart started to beat faster. 'No,' she said vehemently. 'The past is in the way. Can't you see that? You promised if I stayed on, you'd tell me more. So I could, at least, come to terms with what you did. But so far you haven't told me anything more than you were an undercover cop.' Then it occurred to her. Had he been corrupt? That would explain his refusal to talk and the reason he'd disappeared.

Sean's mouth set tight. 'Katrina, I just can't tell you any more than that. Already, I've told you more than I should have.'

Her chin lifted defiantly. 'I don't want to argue with you, Sean. But the truce is up tomorrow. I've decided to return to Boston. But before I go, I want you to give yourself up to the police.'

'Katrina — '

Ross walked in to the room. 'Whoa . . . ' he said, giving them both a strange look. 'Would you mind telling me what the hell is going on?'

4

Katrina spoke first. 'I hadn't meant you to hear that. But now that you have, I might as well tell you, Sean isn't who you think he is.'

'Isn't he now?' replied Ross, carefully. He turned to face his cousin. 'Mind explaining?'

Katrina waited for Sean to continue but she could see his mouth had clamped shut. She couldn't back down now. Perhaps, it was time everything was out in the open. She had kept the secret to herself for long enough. She took a deep breath. 'If Sean won't tell you, I will. He's on the run. He's wanted by the authorities in Britain for terrorist activities.'

Ross caught Sean's gaze, saying slowly. 'Is this true?'

'Some of it,' replied Sean tightly.

'This had better be good,' said Ross, his glance settling on Katrina then on Sean. He pulled out a chair from underneath the table and sat down. 'Right then, let's get this over and done with.'

Sean grimaced. 'Looks like I might not have a choice. Katrina has threatened to involve the police. And that's the last thing I want.' He hesitated. 'I know what it looks like

. . . but it's a complicated story.' He formed his words carefully. 'When Katrina and I met, I was on an undercover mission. Operation Pandora.'

Ross raised his brows. 'For who?'

'The Metropolitan Police in London. Anti-Terrorist Branch.' Sean's glance fell on Katrina. 'I was playing the part of an IRA operative named Sean O'Riley. To do that, I had to spend months living in the role. We were after a splinter group that had been set up in Belfast. They had plans to set off a campaign of bombing in London. Everyone knew it would ruin any chance of a peace settlement if a rogue element was out of control. They were causing havoc, leaving no room for negotiation between the IRA and the Brits. My mission was to identify the leading members and liaise with MI5.'

Katrina stared at him in amazement. 'My God. So that's why you were in London.'

A shadow passed over Sean's face. 'Only things went wrong. A bomb went off. Unknown to me, it had been planted in my briefcase. As far as I knew the briefcase was supposed to contain only papers identifying the top two leaders of the splinter group. I suspect the bomb was meant for me. Maybe' — his eyes narrowed — 'because I was getting too close.'

'You mean, someone tried to kill you?' Katrina responded, her fingers curling into her palms.

'I guess that sums it up, but instead of killing me, they killed Joe MacNeill instead. MacNeill was a colleague of mine in MI5. He was the one who took the briefcase from me in the bookshop.' He gave Katrina a long, level look. 'After the bomb went off, I was in hospital for a few weeks, injured. It was all kept highly confidential. That's why I couldn't get in touch with you straight away even though I wanted to.'

'I hadn't realized you were hurt,' replied Katrina aghast.

He shrugged. 'It was nothing major. I guess I was lucky.'

'The police never said anything to me.'

'They wouldn't have. Everything was classified. As far as they were concerned I was a terrorist. Very few people know what goes on in the covert section of the police. That day I turned up at the bookshop to see you, I was going to tell you the truth. Only I never got a chance. I never meant you to be caught in the middle of it all. You have to believe me.'

Sean swallowed hard. 'Anyway, the police made it pretty clear to the media I was the guilty party and no-one was going to inform them otherwise. It established my credibility that I was in the IRA. After I got out of hospital, I resigned my undercover role. Arrangements were made for me to disappear discreetly. It wasn't too difficult. The intelligence services can work miracles when they want to. I was offered a chance to change my identity, but I refused. Instead, I opted for New Zealand, willing to take my chances.' He paused slightly. 'The rest you know. I turned up here, at Glenroy, looking for a job.'

Katrina said softly. 'I just don't know what to say.' The situation hit her. She had disrupted everyone's lives just to satisfy her obsession for finding out the truth. But something told her it was more than that. Sean had tried to contact her after all; he hadn't abandoned her like she'd always thought he had. Her hopes rose.

'All the time I thought you were guilty,' she murmured.

Sean spoke quickly. 'None of this was your fault. I'd probably have thought the same thing given the circumstances.'

Ross spoke up. 'And the splinter group? Did you get them?'

Sean looked thoughtful. 'No. They're still out there somewhere. I can identify them though. I'm probably the only one who can.'

'Sean, there's something I have to tell you,'

said Katrina. Taking another deep breath, she launched into her story. 'One night, about a month after the bomb went off, I arrived home at my flat. I had just opened the front door when someone attacked me. There were two people. A man and a woman. But what they really wanted was you, Sean. It was dark and they wore balaclavas. One of them held me down with a gun at my head. I was terrified out of my wits. But when I convinced them I didn't know where you were, they let me go. Thankfully, my friend Jessie turned up soon afterwards.'

Sean shot out, 'Christ . . . I didn't know about this. Did you inform the police?'

Katrina bit her lip. 'I was going to. But they threatened they'd come after me again if I did. They told me to leave London at once. That if I didn't, they'd kill my parents. So that's what I did, with Jessie's help. I went to Boston.' Katrina shook her head. 'I don't know what I would have done without her.'

'And these people who attacked you . . . had you seen them before?' questioned Sean.

'No, never. But they were Irish. I could tell that from their accents.'

'It's possible they could have been part of the splinter group,' suggested Sean, his mind ticking over frantically.

121

'Oh Sean . . . ' Katrina murmured, looking at him. Now she had found out he was innocent, the years of betrayal faded away.

His gaze locked with hers. Something was happening between them again and she was powerless to stop it. And did she even want to?

★ ★ ★

The clock in the hallway chimed midnight. Sean took a seat in the living-room thinking about the night's events. Katrina had gone to bed and he'd been tempted to head for his room too where he could think in peace, but he knew he wouldn't sleep. Not after what Katrina had told him about being attacked. That was twice he'd brought her into danger. How could the undercover mission have gone so wrong? He'd always suspected there had been an informer. But who?

Ross brought through a bottle of Bushmills and poured two glasses. 'Phew. I think I need a strong drink after tonight,' stated Ross. 'That's some confession, Cousin.'

Sean agreed. 'Make it a large one.'

Ross sat down opposite him. 'What do you think we should do about this?'

'Nothing. What does it matter now? My home's here, in New Zealand. Everything

122

that's happened is long past. As far as I'm concerned it can stay that way.' Sean took the glass of whiskey Ross offered him. '*Slainte.*' He took a gulp, the liquid fiery against his throat. It made him feel better, sharpened his senses.

Ross frowned. 'You know, I might be half Irish, with our mothers being sisters, but I've never even been to Ireland. My mother talked about the place a bit though. She was pretty cut up when your parents died.'

At the mention of his parents, Sean tried to stop the images reeling through his mind. His parents might have died over twenty-two years ago, when he was thirteen years old, but that horrific day had been imprinted on his mind for eternity like an oil painting on canvas. The two IRA gunmen had burst into the cottage, firing their weapons as they sat around the kitchen table having dinner. When Sean finally crawled out from under the table, sobbing, moments after the gunmen had fled, it was to see his mother lying dead across his father as if to protect him. His father had died on the way to the hospital. Even now, dwelling on it, brought him out in a sweat.

'From what I've heard tonight, you've been a part of something over there, Sean. Something important,' said Ross.

Sean shrugged. 'I was just a cop doing my

job.' Deep in thought, he downed another whiskey and shoved the images from his mind.

★   ★   ★

A couple of hours later, Sean tossed about in bed. He punched his pillow for the tenth time but, as he lay looking up at the ceiling, he still couldn't sleep. Somehow, talking about his time in the police force tonight made it seem as if it had all happened yesterday.

After dropping out of university, he'd joined the Garda in Dublin with the best intentions of helping the community. It had only been a matter of time before he decided to apply to the Special Detective Unit. His skills in investigative work had been welcomed. A joint operation between the Garda and the Metropolitan Police had him moving to London where he was taken on the Met Police payroll permanently. It had been Detective Sergeant Andy Davis of the Anti-terrorist Branch who'd taken him under his wing and encouraged him to consider working undercover. He had all the right qualifications as Andy Davis had told him, when he'd applied for the undercover programme.

He could still remember Davis saying to

him, 'You're in a unique position, Sean. Your mother was Catholic from Dublin, and your father was Protestant from Belfast.' He gave a short laugh. 'Talk about having a mixed family upbringing, eh? You'll be seeing the political situation from both sides too.' He'd stared at Sean. 'So tell me. Where do your loyalties lie?'

'You mean in a religious sense?'

'That wasn't exactly what I meant, but we'll start with that.'

'That's a tough question.' Sean thought hard. 'I suppose you could say I'm a lapsed Catholic.' He didn't tell Davis that after his parents had been murdered, he decided that there wasn't a God. How could there be when the only two people he'd loved had been so cruelly taken away from him? As he grew up and later joined the Garda, he met many people from all walks of life and began to change his mind. Rather than believing in any traditional religion he felt drawn to spirituality and how it affected humankind's nature and purpose. He'd seen a lot of evil and a lot of good.

'And politically?' added Davis.

'That's difficult. A grey area.' Sean shrugged. 'I can see the sense of a united Ireland, but I'm against the IRA: they've caused nothing but misery.'

'Why did you become a police officer?' added Davis, settling back in his chair.

Sean answered straight away. 'To protect the everyday people on the street. Whatever it takes.'

How could he explain to Andy Davis the hate he felt against the IRA for what they had done to his parents? That was one of the main reasons he'd joined the Garda. To stop the violence. To stop *any sort of violence* no matter who was responsible for it. Kids had every right to grow up in a safe world, and to enjoy their childhood. Unlike what had happened to him. The day his parents had been shot had taken away his childhood forever. That information was in his file though Davis hadn't brought it up yet. He'd wait until he did. *If he did.*

'And how would you do that?' continued Davis.

'I'm under oath. That means putting my personal opinion aside for the job. Keeping the law. Making arrests if I have to.'

'So if your father broke the law, what would you do then?'

'My adoptive father,' corrected Sean. Jaysus, could he arrest him, thought Sean? Somehow he didn't think so. He could either answer Davis directly or play for time. 'Come on, Andy, what kind of question is that?'

'It's something we need to know. It's only a hypothetical question. This interview for the undercover programme is pretty rigorous. Only the best qualify. After you've finished with me, you've got to undergo a psychologist's evaluation. Believe me, my questions are pretty tame compared to the shrink's. So you'd better start getting used to them.'

'That's just great,' replied Sean sarcastically.

Davis rose a brow. 'Well?'

'All right. I suppose that depends on what he did to break the law,' said Sean carefully. 'I don't believe in following procedure blindly. I'd like to think using my common sense would come into it.'

Davis pursed his lips. 'OK. Here's one for you. Say, for example, your adoptive father joined the IRA. Would you dob him in?'

This was a question Sean had been dreading. 'He wouldn't do that. He's a peaceful man. He adopted four kids who lost their parents to violence. I'm one of them.' Then Sean added for good measure, 'For Christ's sake, Andy, you and I know the politics in Northern Ireland have never been clear cut. Everyone knows there are some families here in the South and in the North with mixed loyalties. You can't hold me responsible for my family, their religion or

127

their politics. Just like they're not responsible for me. We all choose what path we want to follow.'

'You mean we reap what we sow.' Davis gave a short laugh. 'You know the saying, 'blood is thicker than water'.'

Sean's voice firmed. 'Like I said, I'm a police officer, so I'll do whatever it takes. If any of my family break the law, then I'll cross that when it happens. I want to help bring back peace to Ireland. It might not be much but, at least, it's something I can do. The undercover role will be a challenge. To be honest, I was getting bored anyway. I'm needing something different.'

'Very noble,' commented Davis, looking impressed. 'But did you stop to think you might have to use violence yourself to do that? You think you can shoot someone, if you have to?'

'If my life depended on it and there isn't any other way, I guess I'd have no choice. But I'll make that call when I have to. No point in thinking about it now.'

Davis studied him, his eyes narrowing. 'Working undercover means you're going to have to make split second decisions about the people you meet. No matter who they are. Family, friends, enemies.' He paused briefly. 'You think you're up to it?'

'I wouldn't be here if I wasn't.'

'Good.'

And that's exactly what Sean had done. He'd used his own initiative, a prerequisite of going undercover. He might have made some mistakes, but that was the nature of the job and he'd long accepted that.

He might not be able to forget his past, but he could live with it, if he had to. The question was, could Katrina?

⋆ ⋆ ⋆

The meeting with Hannad Khalis had gone well, Maguire decided, feeling pleased with himself. It was arranged that Jessie would act as Khalis's wife when accompanying him into Ireland. Maguire had bought two fake passports for a few thousand pounds which would do the job. The forger was the best in his field and Maguire had met him in Paris a few years ago where he'd set up shop. Only the man had to leave Paris in a hurry and so decided to set up in London. It wasn't the money the man worked for, it was the craftsmanship. Maguire had to admire him for that. Even more, he understood it. Making bombs was a craft too and Maguire had learned his craft in the Provisional IRA as a teenager in Belfast. He'd worked hard, risen in the ranks through hard work.

He'd given Khalis the gold watch as a present and as a symbol of their friendship. He'd had it engraved on the back with Khalis's name. The Afghan had been very pleased. The necklace he had already given to Jessie in appreciation of the task she would undertake for him.

Maguire locked the flat and lifted his suitcase intending to head for the tube. He'd catch the train to Liverpool and then the ferry to Dublin. Carrie had already gone ahead of him a few days before. They figured it would be safer to travel separately in case any of the authorities were watching out for them. Both of them had taken every precaution, from using different identities and fake passports and changing their looks physically, so the risk was low. Even so, it paid to be careful.

Maguire's mobile phone rang. It was Carrie.

'Hello, darling,' she said.

'I'm just heading away now,' he told her.

'Good. I'll meet you in Dublin. Got ourselves a car. A cheap deal. We can drive to Clifden together. Take in the sights.' She gave a sigh. 'We've been away from Ireland too long.'

'Don't I know it?' Maguire smiled. 'You've been busy then.'

She laughed. 'I have. You know me, Mrs Efficiency. I don't muck about. Everything is going ahead as planned. Any word from Khalis?'

'He's already left with Jessie. She'll ring you when she gets to Dublin.'

'Good,' she said.

He hesitated slightly, not wanting to say too much over the phone but he wanted to know how she had got on in Belfast.

'Did you make those arrangements we talked about?' he asked.

'Everything is all set. We hired two men in New Zealand.'

'Who are they?'

'No names. All I know is they belong to a gang over there. They were keen on the money and sounds like they're a good shot. So I took their word for it they can do the job.'

'It's risky involving others. We could send some of our men.'

'No,' said Carrie sharply. 'The Army Council is against that. Our men would stick out like a sore thumb. Best to hire local men. They'll know the area.'

Maguire could see the sense in that.

5

'Don't make a sound or you're dead,' said a voice sounding like the devil himself. His fingers dug into the back of Katrina's neck.

Katrina bit back the scream threatening to choke her. If he was going to kill her, let it be quick, she prayed silently.

A woman stepped out of the shadows. She was slim, athletic looking, and dressed in a dark track suit. She moved with stealth. On her head, she wore a woollen balaclava. Her hand lifted to strike Katrina as she lay on the floor.

Katrina automatically curled into the foetal position.

'Where's Sean?' the woman demanded.

Katrina sobbed, 'I don't know. Please . . . '

The man gripped her harder. Katrina braced herself, her body going rigid. A hand grasped her hair and pulled it cruelly, forcing her head to jerk to the side. Cold blue eyes stared down at her and no matter how hard she tried, Katrina couldn't look away.

The barrel of the gun was raised in front of her and he lowered it slowly, touching her once on the cheek. Cold metal against warm skin. She shivered. He pointed it to her head, pressing the end to her scalp. A click sounded.

Katrina screamed.

Sean threw open the door. 'Katrina, what the — ' Light flooded the room as he took in the scene in front of him.

Katrina was sitting up in bed shaking uncontrollably, the covers dragged up to her neck. 'They were here . . . in this room. They were going to kill me.'

He moved forward. 'No . . . no. There's no one here. It was just a nightmare.'

'Oh Sean, it was so real. Those two people who attacked me back in London. I can still see them.'

Something in her eyes got to him. And then he knew. This wasn't the first time she'd had this particular nightmare. If anyone ought to know, he did. He'd had his own demons to face.

'No one is going to hurt you,' he said softly. 'You're safe here. I promise.'

But still her eyes were desperate. 'I can't get them out of my mind. Don't leave me, Sean. Please, stay for a while.'

He hesitated. 'Katrina, I'm not so sure that's a good idea.'

She held his gaze, whispering, 'Why?' But even as she asked the question, she knew the answer.

He sat down on the bed next to her and held her. After a few moments, his mouth found hers. She gave in to the heady sensation and the warmth of his touch. Unable to help herself, her arms slid around his neck pulling him down beside her. It felt so good to be held like this, she thought.

When he pulled back, he said softly, 'That's why I shouldn't stay.' He disentangled her arms. 'Katrina, I should really go.'

'Wait, Sean, there are some things I need to tell you. To make you understand what it was really like for me after you left.'

'I can imagine,' he said quietly.

'Can you really?' She drew in a shaky breath. 'Sometimes I felt like I'd go mad. If it hadn't been for Jessie, I think I would have. She helped me a lot.' She hesitated slightly, 'But always there was this underlying obsession to find you.' She shook her head. 'It's hard to explain. Even now I still don't understand it.' Her voice lowered. 'I had to come here. It was the only thing I could do. I'm sorry if I upset things for you.'

'I'm glad you did.' He swallowed hard. 'After your letter arrived — the fake letter — I convinced myself I didn't deserve you. Even so, I never gave up hope. I thought that maybe if I gave you time, let your anger cool, you might change your mind. Somehow the weeks turned into months. Before I knew it, three years had gone. And still I never heard. It was easy to throw myself into working on the station from sunup to sundown. When night came, I'd be too exhausted to think about it all.'

So he'd suffered too, she thought. More than she had ever realized. Hearing him talk about his feelings so openly surprised her. Yet, it somehow drew her to him. She had wanted Sean for so long, even though she'd convinced herself that she hadn't. Now he was here, sitting right beside her. His close proximity brought a flush to her face. She couldn't pull back now. She wouldn't allow herself to.

'I'm sorry I woke you,' she offered.

'Doesn't matter. I sleep very lightly. Mostly from habit,' he explained. 'I never knew when someone was going to make a move on me.' He didn't tell her about the sleepless nights where every shadow could possibly have been a threat.

'That sounds terrible. I wouldn't have liked to live like that.'

His voice deepened. 'I don't now. That's why I came here to Glenroy. This station is the safest place on earth.' His face turned thoughtful. 'I've been thinking. Those two people who attacked you in London. It still

135

bothers me who they were. Maybe they had something to do with the letters.'

She stared at him. 'I don't know, Sean, but even if they did, why would they do that?'

'To find out where I was. Draw me out. I never disclosed my whereabouts in my letters to you. I had a post office box number in London, and a colleague of mine forwarded my mail on to me from there.'

'But I don't understand. If they wanted to draw you out, they wouldn't have written to you saying I didn't want to see you again. They would have done the opposite. Arranged a date and time to meet.'

He grimaced. 'You think I haven't thought of that? That's the really bizarre thing about it.' He looked down at her. 'I guess it's a mystery we'll never solve.' He gave a reassuring smile. 'Why don't you try to get some sleep?'

'Sleep? That's the last thing I feel like doing.'

He lay beside her. Eventually though she must have dropped off. When the first rays of daylight filtered through the window, Sean woke first. He whispered in her ear,

'Katrina, I've got to go.'

She stirred, opening up her eyes sleepily. 'What time is it?'

'Just before five o'clock. I'm heading up the

mountain. But I'll be back before nightfall. Think you'll be all right until then?'

She nodded. 'I'll be fine. Honestly I will.' She gave a soft sigh. 'Thanks for staying with me.'

His smile had her heart skittering along again. Then his lips skimmed across hers in the gentlest of kisses, before he left. His touch had been almost unbearable in its tenderness. There were so many sides to him, she thought.

Katrina lay in bed thinking over the events of the night. It had never once occurred to her Sean had been an undercover police officer. But who was Sean really, she wondered? Was he the artist she met in London, or the man she was beginning to know now? Confusion filled her again.

All her questions had now been answered. Except for one: who had written the letter to Sean pretending to be her?

★   ★   ★

Within a few hours, Sean reached the summit, climbed off his horse and led her over to the ridge. The whitewashed homestead below was like a welcome beacon amidst the golden tussocks. Further along the valley, not far from the river was his own land

and cottage, nestled at the side of a hill. He'd ordered some building supplies the day before, so he'd need to go into town to collect them. He couldn't wait to start. He had almost been tempted to tell Katrina about the cottage but decided he'd wait a little longer, perhaps even surprise her.

Drawing his thoughts back to the task in hand, some of the stock needed checking, so he'd better get on with it. He was about to climb back on to his horse when, in the distance, he saw a large army truck, its dark green canvas billowing, make its way along the winding valley road. Sean felt a flicker of unease, then shrugged it off. They would only be dropping off feed.

He glanced at a mob of sheep nearby. They had no extra body weight, their thin ribs poked out, making them look ungainly. They hadn't been able to hold off any longer asking for help from the government to feed their stock. The army delivering the feed would save the haulage fees from the local trucking firms.

A low humming noise in the distance caught his attention. A Hughes 500 helicopter, splashed red against the sky, swooped down low towards him.

Sean waved, seeing the two men aboard. The helicopter lifted up again, veering left before it gained more height and flew off.

Helicopters were common in these parts and they were probably some tourists out for a ride — or even some hunters. He just hoped their only quarry was deer.

★　★　★

Now that Katrina knew the truth, she was free to leave. And yet, she realized, she couldn't. Ross had told her they needed every hand they could get. No bookings had come in for the homestay so they'd be short of help. And there was the end of shearing season dance too; they'd need someone to organize the food. But after that she'd be free to go. If she wanted to. Only now, because of Sean, she wasn't sure she did.

The day was hot. Katrina's clothes were sticking to her while little beads of sweat broke out on her forehead at every exertion. She examined the temperature gauge on the wall. It was thirty degrees centigrade.

She turned around making a mental list of all the chores she had to do. The cooking took up a great amount of the day and in between she did the washing and cleaning. Now it was time to feed the chickens and collect the eggs. The list was endless. She would fall into bed exhausted at the end of the day. And yet, she felt a part of the place now.

The sound of an army truck roaring up in front of the homestead had Katrina glancing out the window. Ross hadn't said anything about them delivering more stock feed. She noticed, however, that there were no hay bales on the deck. She hurried outside to find out what the soldiers wanted.

Katrina watched a tall man in army khaki overalls get out of the truck and make his way over to her. 'Gidday . . . I'm looking for Sean McKinlay. Is he here?' His manner was friendly and put her instantly at ease.

'He's up in the mountains checking on the stock,' Katrina replied. 'Did you want to speak to someone else? Ross is down at the river, rounding up cattle.'

The soldier shook his head. 'No, that's OK. When are you expecting Sean back?'

Katrina frowned. 'Tonight, I expect.'

'Right.' He smiled. 'See you later.'

Katrina watched the truck turn. The soldier waved and they were gone. She wondered why they were looking for him?

When Sean finally returned she told him about the visitor. 'He knew your name.'

'It's probably nothing,' he answered with a shrug. 'Perhaps someone I met at the pub.'

It was then Katrina remembered what Jessie had told her. 'Wait, Sean. I completely forgot. When I spoke to Jessie on the phone, she said MI5 had paid her a visit. They were asking questions. They wanted to know if I'd found you.'

Sean frowned. Unease slid down his spine again. MI5 knew exactly where he was. So why were they questioning Jessie?

* * *

Ross walked into the kitchen. 'Been thinking some. Since it's nearly the end of the shearing season, let's have our party this Friday. What do you say?'

Katrina responded warmly 'That sounds great.'

'Good. I'll give our neighbours, the Reids, a ring. Mrs Reid is a dab hand at Pavlova as you've probably already heard, so she won't mind helping. Besides, I don't want you spending all night cooking. I want you to have a good time, too.'

Ross decided to ride over to the Reids' place instead of ringing. It had been a while since he'd been there anyway, so was long overdue for a visit. He'd known the Reids for years, and had gone to school with their son, Phil, and daughter, Anna. Then, later on, Phil had gone to the same university, at Lincoln, even taking similar classes since they'd both specialized in agriculture. Mr and Mrs Reid were in their sixties and Phil planned to take over their farm some day, just like he'd take the station over from John. So they had a lot in common.

He wondered what sort of reception Anna would give him. Last time they'd talked to each other they'd had words. What it was about he couldn't even remember now, but he'd asked her out to the movies and she'd turned him down flat saying she was going out with someone else. He had suspected Sean. But when he'd questioned her further, she wouldn't give him a straight answer. Damn it, she stirred him up at times. The trouble was he couldn't get her out of his mind.

It would have been quicker to take the truck and follow the road, but he wanted to ride his horse. Besides, if Anna was out riding as well, he might even see her. He was in luck. By the time he reached the river, she was galloping along the other side of the bank and pulled up sharply when she saw him.

'Heading over your way,' he shouted across the river. She nodded, waiting patiently until he waded through the shallow water, then made his way across the shingle.

'Just heading over to see your folks,' he told her. 'We're having an end of shearing party.

142

Thought I'd let them know.'

She tossed her mane of red hair back from her face. Her eyes sparkled. 'Sounds good.'

Conversation lapsed while they negotiated difficult ground. 'How's the new homestay lady working out?' she asked, once they reached the flat again.

'Better than I thought. Katrina sure knows how to cook. We're lucky. You ought to come over to meet her.'

Anna's head jerked up, interested. 'Maybe I will. How long is she staying for?'

'Not sure, but if I had my way, I'd employ her long term. We could do with someone like her around the place.' Ross gave a chuckle. 'She's one of the prettiest girls I've ever seen. All blonde hair and long legs.' He gave a wolf whistle.

Anna said in irritated tones, 'You mean a blonde without brains?'

'She no dummy. She's bright. Got her own business in the States. But she's taking a break from the fast pace of life.' Then, because the Devil made him do it, and he knew it would stir Anna up, 'Half the guys on the station are falling over themselves to take her out. But she's turned them all down. Seems like Sean's got a thing about her.'

'Sean?' she repeated, frowning.

'Yeah.' He waited a few seconds for his

143

words to sink in, then added, 'I think she feels the same way about him too.'

'Oh, really? I didn't think that kind of woman would be his type.'

'It will be interesting to see what happens.' Ross gave a satisfied smile. Anna wasn't going to get it all her own way. He'd chased her long enough, and she'd been playing hard to get, so now he was going to turn things around a bit. Before she could question him anymore about Katrina, he threw at her, 'Race you to the farmhouse.'

'OK. You're on.' She dug her heels into the horse's side.

He let her win, of course.

Two hours later, after staying for lunch, Ross caught Anna outside where they could talk in private. 'So what about it, Anna? Are you going to come to the movies with me?'

'Nope, but thanks anyway.'

Ross's mouth tightened. 'If you've set your sights on Sean, forget it. Like I told you, he's got his sights set on someone else.'

Her eyes flashed. 'Quit telling me what I can or can't do. You've done that since I was knee high.'

Ross exhaled. 'You're so stubborn — you just can't see what's in front of you.'

Her voice turned frosty. 'I can see perfectly well. And what I see is you, Ross Forrester, bossy and arrogant, who expects me to go out with him. I don't like being taken for granted. And the answer is still no.'

After he'd gone Anna took a seat on the veranda feeling annoyed with herself. She knew she'd handled Ross's invitation badly. The trouble was, she just didn't know what she wanted.

★   ★   ★

Friday morning came sooner than expected. It was going to be a big end of shearing party that night. Other neighbours from nearby farms had been invited. Katrina wondered if she'd made enough food, although she still had more dishes to prepare. She was busy in the kitchen finishing off the salads, when she heard a female voice behind her. Whirling around, she saw a redheaded woman in her mid-twenties, standing there, a hesitant smile on her face. She had a beautiful complexion, a smattering of freckles and friendly eyes.

The woman stepped forward. 'Gidday, I'm Anna.' She held out her hand and Katrina shook it. Anna added quickly, 'I thought I'd turn up early. See if you need a hand.'

'Oh,' said Katrina, surprised. 'Ross never mentioned — '

'He didn't know,' cut in Anna. 'But I'm

145

sure he wouldn't mind.' Her gaze flitted around the kitchen. 'Looks like you need someone to scrub those potatoes. Here, let me. I'm a fast worker. We'll have these done in no time.'

She was right. Within twenty minutes, the potatoes were simmering on the stove while Katrina made up the mayonnaise. Satisfied that everything was under control, Katrina poured them two glasses of orange juice.

'This seems like a good time to take a break,' suggested Katrina, handing one glass of orange to Anna. 'Come on. Let's take a seat outside and get some fresh air.'

'Fancy coming all the way from Boston to work here,' said Anna, shaking her hair back from her face. 'Don't you miss the bright lights?'

'No,' said Katrina, and found she meant it.

'Imagine all those boutiques,' added Anna dreamily, 'and the latest fashions. Sipping cappuccinos, and visiting art galleries.' She sighed wistfully. 'And here's me stuck here, right in the middle of nowhere, wasting my life away.'

Katrina gave a smile. 'The city can get tedious too. It's not all it's made out to be. If I had a choice I'd rather live here. You don't know how lucky you are.'

'The only luck I've had lately is meeting

Sean McKinlay,' shot out Anna. 'Now I wouldn't mind being holed up in the middle of nowhere if he was around.'

Katrina jolted. 'Oh?'

'Mmm, those dark eyes of his, and that deep voice.' Anna laughed. 'Pure Irish charm.'

Katrina stared at her with dismay. 'You're in love with him?'

Anna pursed her lips. 'Huh, who wouldn't be?'

'He'd break your heart,' Katrina found herself saying.

Anna chuckled. 'It would be worth it.'

No, it wouldn't, Katrina thought with an old pang. Was there something going on between Sean and Anna, or was it just wishful thinking on Anna's part?

★ ★ ★

Katrina covered the tables with bright blue check tablecloths adding to the festive occasion. The conversation with Anna had dampened her cheerful feelings. She tried to shrug them off.

Sean had just arrived back with a keg and several crates of beer. He'd also bought several bottles of champagne. As Katrina was laying out the food, he came up behind her and whispered in her ear. 'Don't forget to save a dance for me.'

She whirled around. 'Dance?'

'A couple of the shearers play guitars and another plays a harmonica, so once the meal is over, we'll have some music. That's when the fun will start.'

Katrina hadn't danced for ages, not since Sean had been in her life. She never had time when she was running Parisiana since she was always working in the evenings. A sense of excitement shot through her.

'You do remember how to dance, don't you?' teased Sean.

She gave a laugh. 'I think so, but don't ask me to do the tango.'

He laughed. 'Actually, I had a slower dance in mind.' He said the words so sensuously, a flush raced across her cheeks.

When the guests arrived, the women lent a hand in dishing out the food, and that enabled Katrina to take a break and have her meal. An hour later, she saw the shearers get out their musical instruments and start to play. Katrina watched, fascinated.

Ross came up to her and grabbed Katrina's hand, pulling her up. 'Come on, let's dance.'

At the same time, she saw Sean take Anna's hand to dance with her. There were half-a-dozen couples who joined the dancing amidst the clapping and stamping of feet. Ross whirled her around until she was feeling dizzy. After ten minutes, she protested, laughing. 'Stop. I'm out of breath. Let me sit down a minute.'

Ross grinned widely. 'You can't give up now, we're only halfway through this dance.'

'Have a heart. I've been on my feet since early this morning.' After a few more whirls, she added, 'For a man well built, you are certainly light on your feet. So where did you learn to dance like this?'

'Student parties at university,' he stated. 'We raved all night long and attended classes during the day. I needn't tell you the parties were pretty debauched.' He rolled his eyes. 'And I'll leave that to your imagination.'

'Hmm. And obviously you've not forgotten a thing from the amount of dancing you've done tonight.'

'Some things never change,' he remarked light-heartedly, pulling her even closer, 'especially if the spirit's willing.'

When the music stopped a slower song was played — a haunting folk melody about the pioneers forging a new life in New Zealand. It caught everyone's attention.

'One more dance?' whispered Ross, hopefully.

She was just about to refuse when Sean

came up to them. 'Looks like my turn, I think.'

Ross let her go quite willingly, though couldn't resist a parting shot. 'It took you long enough, Cousin.'

Amusement entered Sean's eyes. 'I've been waiting for the right song. Seems like I just found it.'

'Do I get a say in this?' laughed Katrina.

'Nope.' Sean's arms encircled her, one hand in the small of her back. The mere touch of his fingertips sent a warming shiver through her. 'If I remember rightly, you loved to dance,' he added.

'I still do. When I get the chance, that is.'

'Then we'll do it often.'

Her head jerked up in surprise. Sean was talking like he expected her to stay. 'Sean, I — '

He put his fingers on her lips briefly. 'No, don't say anything. Let's just enjoy tonight. Live for the moment and forget the past.'

Perhaps, he was right, she thought. Tomorrow would take care of itself.

'You know Anna well?' she asked casually.

'We're good friends. Anna's brother, Phil, and I go hunting occasionally.'

'Seems like she's very fond of you.'

He arched a brow. 'Jealous?'

She pulled back sharply. 'No, of course not.

What made you think that?'

He pursed his lips. 'Oh, the way you spoke.'

'It's been three long years,' she stated, her heart lurching. 'A lot has changed since then.'

Too much, she thought. Somehow, she wasn't quite ready to leave herself wide open again. Yet, she couldn't deny her attraction to Sean was even stronger than before.

* * *

The next morning, Katrina was sitting on the veranda drinking coffee when she saw Anna galloping towards her on her horse. Within moments, she dismounted.

'Hi, just stopped in to say hello. Thought you might need a hand to clear up after last night.'

Katrina shook her head, smiling. 'I didn't have to do a thing. Sean and Ross did it all before I even woke.'

Anna's eyebrows rose. 'Wonders will never cease. I've never known them to offer to clear up. What did you put in their food?'

Katrina laughed. 'Nothing, I promise. But since I organized all the food, it was the least they could do. Come on, you're just in time for morning tea. I baked a tray of scones, so we might as well get our share before the men turn up.'

Anna smiled. 'Glad to know someone else thinks like me.' She took a seat at the table. 'Where is Sean anyway?'

Katrina shrugged. 'Not sure. Down at the stables, I think.'

'Well, if he doesn't appear soon, I'll head down there. I'm hoping he'll give me a lift into town today. He's picking up some supplies for that cottage of his.'

'Cottage?'

'Hasn't he told you?'

Katrina shook her head bewildered.

'He owns some land up the valley. It's pretty run down, but he's keen on the place. Next thing we know he'll be getting married. A man living in a house all by himself in these parts won't last long, that's for sure. Some female will snag him.'

Katrina's heart plunged. 'You think he has someone in mind?'

Anna's tone turned wistful. 'If he has, he's keeping quiet about it. Lucky girl, whoever she is.' She leaned forward, speaking in a whisper. 'He treats you like a woman. You know what I mean?' She winked. 'Unlike someone else I could mention.'

Katrina caught on fast. 'You mean Ross?'

'Uh-huh. He treats me like one of the boys. Maybe because I've known him all my life. That's the trouble. He knows me too well and vice versa. There are no surprises. I don't think he would know what moonlight and romance is if I hit him over the head with it. Whereas Sean is different, don't you think? One broody look from him makes my knees go all weak. Must be the Irish blood in him.' She paused slightly. 'Something tells me when Sean gives his heart it will be forever.'

Katrina thought over Anna's words. Had Sean once given his heart to her?

'Ross has Irish blood in him as well,' replied Katrina. 'Maybe you ought to give him another chance. Seems to me he's a bit rough on the outside, but I think if you dig deeper, you could be in for a surprise.'

Anna flashed a smile. 'I suppose so. Hmm. Maybe I'll give it some thought.'

'Perhaps he needs some encouragement.'

Anna shook her head. 'No, it's not that. He's not shy in asking me out. It's just that he's so used to getting his own way.' Anna gave a dreamy look. 'Maybe I'll meet someone special when I go travelling. I wanted to go overseas, but Mum got ill and I didn't want to leave her. Not that I minded staying. I'll go sometime, but it won't be until next year now.'

Katrina gave a laugh. 'Isn't that strange? All I want to do is to settle in one place. I could make my home here, if I had the chance.

There's something about Glenroy that draws me.'

It was true, Katrina thought, she loved it here. She could spend ages gazing at the mountains, never tiring of them and the way the light shifted and forged shadows later in the day. The thought of returning to Boston somehow didn't seem to appeal any more.

Nor did leaving Sean.

★ ★ ★

Early next morning, Sean was repairing the fence near the back of the homestead. He saw Katrina walk outside carrying a basketful of washing. He lifted his foot and placed it on the first rung of the wooden fence, whistling an old Irish ballad as he did so. He saw her pause briefly as the sound reached her on the morning breeze. She turned and smiled. His heart slammed up against his chest. If he could only go back in time, he thought suddenly, it would have been so different for them both.

Her smile reminded him of the day he'd turned up at the bookshop, just before the bomb went off. The whole scenario had been imprinted on his memory; the two men waiting to accost them, the desperate attempt to leave the mall, and then Katrina's scream.

He remembered lying in the hospital bed racked with worry that Katrina was dead. When the news came through she was OK, he had made a pact with himself: he'd live life straight from now on. Katrina's life had nearly been taken through his actions.

Later, when he had arrived at Glenroy, he hadn't known what to expect. The simple everyday life on a station of working, eating and making real friendships with people whom he knew had no ulterior motive other than to earn their keep, had done wonders. Ross's good natured bantering had lightened things up whenever he'd lapsed into bouts of depression at losing Katrina. He'd trust Ross with his own life. He couldn't remember thinking that about any other person before.

It was the luck of the Irish, he murmured. Nothing was straightforward in love. Hadn't the Irish sung songs for years of tragedies, wars and women? Maybe that's why they had to fight for what they believed in.

He watched Katrina go back inside. 'Now or never,' he murmured, making his way to find her. When he reached the kitchen, he stood there in the doorway, just watching her for a few moments. Her face was deep in concentration as she iced a cake sitting on the table. She turned, reached over for a spoon and, as her gaze lifted, she caught him watching.

'Hi,' she said, her eyes uncertain.

All those words Sean had rehearsed beforehand suddenly flew out the window. What the hell was wrong with him?

'Are you hungry?' she asked.

He shook his head. 'No . . . just watching you.' The sweet fragrance of her perfume drifted over to him, making him unexpectedly want to pull her into his arms.

Eventually, he said, 'I've been thinking. Let me take you out tomorrow. Away from here, somewhere we can be alone. There's a place I want to show you, down by the river.' He saw her hesitate but he'd gone too far to turn back now.

'And then what?' she asked, her gaze level with his.

He gave a smile, his eyes full of promise. 'And then we'll go for a swim.'

★　★　★

Katrina had completed the chores by eleven o'clock. The picnic basket was packed and she'd slipped in a bottle of Chardonnay and two wine glasses. Now all she had to do was wait for Sean to turn up. His suggesting they spend time together had surprised her — thrilled her if she was honest, but it was only a picnic, she convinced herself. Even so, her stomach fluttered as if she was on her first date with him all over again.

Sean appeared. 'All set?'

'I think so.'

Sean picked up the basket and she followed him outside.

'I hope John doesn't mind me taking some time off,' she ran on. 'There is so much to do.'

'I've already checked it with him. You've worked pretty hard these last few weeks. You can take time off whenever you want to.'

'Fine. So where are we going?'

'Mystery tour. About twenty minutes' drive from here. Take your swimming togs with you,' he reminded her.

'They're already packed,' she confirmed. Reaching for her sunglasses, she slipped them on, grateful at the relief from the strong light.

Within minutes they had set off. Black cattle grazed contentedly, every so often staring at them with a blankness as they passed. Along the edges of the road, wild flowers grew in abundance, blue borage to match the sky and yellow buttercups adding desperate colour to the already scorched landscape. Further up on the hillside, matagouri, and briar with their small pink budlike flowers. Their prickly branches provided a stark contrast to the reed-like leaves of the tussock-grass. For the thousandth time, Katrina marvelled at the scenery all around her.

A couple of times, Sean braked suddenly to avoid white boulders lying in the middle of the road, and swerved around them. He pointed upwards to a couple of large areas of scree, small brittle sandstone in an area too unstable for much vegetation to grow.

'Ross told me that when he was a kid he used to climb to the top and skate down the fine stones, picking up speed as he went,' Sean mused. 'Do you want to try it? Looks like fun.'

'Hmm . . . maybe on the way back. At least, if I break my leg, I can do it after the picnic and swimming.'

A couple of times during the journey Katrina glanced at Sean wondering what he was thinking. His strong hands that had once caressed her skin so lovingly gripped the steering wheel. The years fell away all of a sudden.

'Do you remember the time we went away for the weekend to Wales?' she said.

He smiled. 'How could I forget? We had a puncture in the middle of nowhere and then after I fixed it in the pouring rain, we finally found a bed and breakfast place. The owners thought we were on our honeymoon.'

'They certainly made a fuss of us, didn't they?' She paused reflectively.

'Do you remember that romantic dinner by candlelight?' he added.

Did she ever? She flashed him a look of surprise. 'You mean you can actually recall that?'

His shoulders lifted as he smiled again. 'Some things never fade.'

Katrina couldn't deny they were special memories. 'We might have known each other only for several months, but really we didn't know each other at all.'

His fingers tightened around the steering wheel. 'Maybe. But that was then, this is now.'

Sean was right, she thought. 'I always thought that undercover agents were hard, ruthless, the way you were portrayed in the newspaper. But you're not like that, Sean.'

A hint of steel came into his voice. 'It takes all sorts. You don't know what I'm capable of.'

'No, I suppose not.' She hesitated, unsure whether to bring the subject up. Not wanting to spoil the close rapport that had developed between them, yet, somehow wanting Sean to know she understood what had driven him to do the things he had done as an undercover agent. 'The way your parents died, it must have been terrible for you. You were only a kid.'

'You know?'

'Ross told me.'

'I should have guessed.' He hesitated. 'I would have told you eventually. I was just waiting for the right moment.'

She added quickly, 'It explains a lot of things about you.' And then she realized with a jolt, it was *the key* she had been looking for all along.

'What do you mean?' he asked curiously.

'You keep things hidden within yourself. Sometimes shutting people out. Consciously or unconsciously.' She shrugged. 'I just don't know. Maybe that stems from being an undercover cop. Or maybe it stems from the trauma you suffered as a kid. Perhaps, a little of both.'

He laughed. 'I'm not sure I like being analysed like that.'

'Sorry, I didn't mean to. But you did ask.' And that was what attracted her to Sean. The deepness. She just couldn't get enough of it.

★ ★ ★

Soon they turned off the gravel road to follow a rough track down to the river. When he pulled up outside the small cottage, Katrina gasped. 'Is this yours?'

He nodded. 'It is. What do you think?'

She walked up to the veranda, taking in the flaking paintwork on the walls. 'Needs a bit of work, but it looks sound.'

'Nothing that can't be fixed with time and money. I've got plenty of both. Been saving for something like this for a long time.'

'It's nice,' she said finally. 'There's a real charm about the place. Can I go inside?'

'Sure you can. Take a look around.'

She didn't just like it, she loved it. It wasn't as big as Glenroy but there was still plenty of room. The floorboards creaked as she walked. There was a huge fireplace, the mantelpiece made of rimu. She could imagine the flames roaring up the chimney when the snow lay thick on the ground outside. The kitchen needed replumbing, and the bathroom sink was cracked. The old-fashioned bathtub had giant brass taps and lion claw feet. It was deep enough for two people. Her cheeks flushed at the thought. She whirled around and let her fingers glide over the walls.

'Looks like the original wallpaper. Perhaps early 1900s.'

'You're right, it is. The house has been rented out to farmhands for the past fifty years. Before that it belonged to the manager of Glenroy Station. Originally an Irish family built it.'

'What happened to them?'

161

'They moved. Built a bigger house after they made some money. Glenroy.'

She turned to face him. 'Know something? I prefer this place. It might be smaller, but it's cosier.' Entranced she stood on the veranda taking in the view to the river. A light wind tossed her hair. 'Imagine how it must have been for them,' she said dreamily. 'The Irish family. Nothing but silence. Only the stirring of wings as birds fluttered by. And over there,' she pointed, 'the raging river.'

'You've a poetic soul,' remarked Sean, moving closer to her. 'Do you still read poetry?'

She smiled. 'Sometimes, when the mood takes me. Occasionally I even write it.'

He arched a brow. 'Now there's something I didn't know.'

She laughed, then said daringly, 'There are still a few surprises left. Like you said, that was then, this is now.'

A devilish smile lurked around his mouth. Before she could say another word, he pulled her towards him. He started with a kiss, deep and purposeful. She melted. By the time she pulled away she was breathless.

'Well?' he mused. 'Does that surprise you?'

She pursed her lips teasingly. 'Hmmm . . . passable. But I recall you can do much better.'

Before she knew what was happening, he had scooped her up into his arms.

'Hey. What are you doing? Put me down, Sean,' she exclaimed.

He gave a laugh. 'Shouldn't tempt Fate, Katrina. You of all people should know that.'

He carried her towards the river, across the short red tussock and stumpy grass, scattering small moths like white petals. When he reached a small clearing, he put her down gently. Then lay down beside her.

Katrina's throat went dry at the tenderness in his eyes. 'Oh Sean, I've got so many regrets. Forgive me for doubting you.'

He pushed back her blonde hair, smoothing it behind her ears. 'No, don't even think that way. Whatever you do, don't look back . . . never look back,' he told her. 'When I first came out here, it was difficult. What happened between us haunted me. I had been on special operations before but that one was different. I knew it was because of you.'

His honesty made her resistance slip away like a tide on the turn. A gust of wind blew, making the branches of the willow trees wave back and forward, as if whispering that two lovers were in their midst.

Her breath quickened as he whispered in Gaelic, something unmistakably loving. The heat began slowly at first, a touch here, a touch there. She lay back gently against the soft grass, his hand slipping through the strands of her silky hair, then curving around her neck. His lips brushed hers in the tenderest of kisses.

'You can never pick a right moment to make love,' he told her, 'it just happens.'

'Then show me,' she replied softly, her hand lifting to caress his jaw.

'Katrina,' he murmured. It was all the encouragement he needed. He gave her an intense look, then slipped the straps of her top over her shoulders.

It had been so long since she had been touched like this, and even longer since she had wanted a man. Suddenly, what she was doing hit her and she pulled back a little.

He lifted her chin with his finger. 'Afraid?'

'Yes,' she admitted. 'I'm afraid of myself though. Not you.'

He shook his head. 'Don't be. We have to finish what we began. Let me show you how it should have been. Would have been, had there been time for us both.'

'You broke my heart,' she accused. 'The lies, the deceit. The way you disappeared like that.'

'Guilty,' he said, without hesitation, his gaze level with hers. 'But I never stopped loving you.'

Her heart danced. He'd loved her. He'd

just told her so. Everything was moving so fast, she thought with excitement, and yet while he lay beside her, she wanted it no other way. She needed to touch him like he was touching her. Her hands smoothed around his back, fingers playing over rippled muscles. The sheer force of wanting him finally chased away any lingering doubts.

His body half covered hers, his hand moved downwards tracing a path across the flat planes of her stomach. Yes, he was stripping away her defences one by one and she was going to let him. The kisses spun out. Soft, eager and wanting.

His eyes focused on her, drawing her in to another place. A secret place where he reassured her no harm could come . . . and this time she had to believe him.

Would believe him.

He held her tightly, so tight she couldn't breathe.

'Katrina,' he murmured again. 'It's been so long. Too long.'

Tenderness was so seductive, she thought, as she let his hands stroke and arouse her. He'd always been like that, she remembered. So patient, so willing to love her. And yet, she knew there was still a darkness within him still. It attracted and disturbed her all in one breath.

'No matter what, I'll never let you go. Not now, not ever,' he promised.

The force of his words sent her hopes spiralling. Nails scraped against skin as her fingers slid from his shoulders, then reached upwards curling into his hair. She hungered for him. It was a hunger that consumed her. There were sobs, her body tensed and again a desperate sound but this time, she realized, it came from Sean.

The first wave hit her and almost dragged her under but she held on, wanting more. His mouth slammed onto hers, making her gasp with pleasure. He devoured, plundered and took as much as she was willing to give. Then, as if that wasn't enough, he claimed her with an unleashed wildness that thrilled and shocked her all at once. She matched him readily, every movement, her fingers digging deep into his back. When he neared the end, their gaze locked, and their breath held, he arched.

'Sean,' she cried out aloud, and surrendered to an ecstatic release.

★　★　★

Afterwards, they both lay still, too stunned to move. Katrina couldn't speak, her thoughts warm like mellow honey. The sound of the river had changed, she noticed. It was louder, almost musical, true and distinct. Her gaze fixed on the wide blue sky reflecting a never ending promise. Sean had told her he would never let her go . . . never leave her. She believed him completely.

A soft sigh escaped her. 'I keep thinking I'm in a dream. If only this one could last forever. But things don't work out like that in real life, do they?'

'Oh, that depends.' He paused slightly, his eyes enigmatic. 'So if you had a wish, what would it be?'

'If I told you, it might not come true,' she teased.

'I'd still like to know,' he answered seriously.

'Well, let me think.' She thought hard. 'I'd like to hold onto this moment forever. Just you and me here beside this river. No matter what happens.' She paused slightly. 'And you?'

He gave a laugh. 'That's easy. That you'll stay here with me at Glenroy. Forever.'

'Oh Sean . . . I will. It's what I want. More than anything.'

Sean watched her, not saying anything else, just watching. Katrina's eyes had turned another shade of green, soft with love and it made him feel humble. He knew then, at that precise moment in time, she had finally forgiven him. The guilt eased from his body readily as he lay beside her, his hand curved over her breast where her heart lay. He felt three heart beats, one for each year they had been apart. Then a thousand more for every year their souls would be together.

When he saw the solitary tear slip down her cheek, his smile faltered. He propped himself up on one elbow. 'Katrina? What's wrong?' When she didn't answer, he added, 'Is it something I've said?'

Her eyes flickered. 'No . . . no . . . it's not that.'

He stared at her thoughtfully. Something wasn't right. 'What is it? Tell me. No secrets between us now, right? We've come too far this time.' His fingers skimmed across her cheek tenderly, wiping away the last of her tears. His mouth brushed hers, coaxing her to tell him what was wrong.

'There's something you need to know,' she started to say, conscious of her voice trembling.

'Sounds serious,' he replied, his forehead creasing.

She had to tell him. Now.

She swallowed hard, forcing out the words. 'I . . . I . . . I'm married.'

Sean jerked. 'You're what?' A deep

disturbing light entered his eyes. 'Why didn't you tell me?'

'I know. I should have. But I didn't know how to.'

'So where's your husband?'

'He's in the States. I left him. Things hadn't been right between us for a while.'

'Do you love him still?' said Sean, his eyes intense.

She gasped. 'How can you ask me that after what we've just shared?'

He grabbed her by the shoulders, repeating. 'I haven't heard you say no. Answer me, Katrina, damn it. Do you love him?'

A sob rose in her throat but she pushed it down. 'No, I don't. I married Scott because I liked him.' She tried to explain. 'I thought that was a good basis for a marriage. Seems like I was wrong. I didn't love him. After what you and I had, I didn't want to feel that deep again. I thought by marrying him it would help me forget you. I was wrong on that account too.' She shook her head. 'I can't believe I made such a mess of things.' She paused momentarily, wondering whether she should tell Sean any more. Somehow knowing that if she didn't she couldn't move on. 'You want the truth? When things started to go wrong between us he'd get into these terrible rages. He started seeing other women. When I challenged him about it, he hit me. I walked out on him that day and never went back.'

I've got to put it all behind me now.

He stared at her, then his voice gentled. 'Oh Katrina, I'm so sorry. I had no idea.'

'I don't want your pity,' she threw at him.

'You're wrong. You'd never have that.' His arm reached out for her to hold her close. 'Listen to me. This is a new beginning for us both. We'll live in the cottage. We could even run some sheep and cattle. God damn it . . . I know we could have a good life together. We have another chance now. Don't you see? We have to take it.'

She nodded. She felt such a hypocrite. Sean wasn't the only one who had deceived, and now she had done the same to him.

He picked up her towel and wrapped it around her. 'Here. You're shivering.'

She didn't resist, leaning her cheek against his shoulder, feeling his warmth. She knew it was going to be a rollercoaster ride into the unknown but it was one she was more than willing to take.

Her voice steadied. 'I've been thinking, Sean. I can sell the café. Tom and Jilly mentioned to me they'd be interested in buying it. With the money I get, I can invest in our farm. I'd like that.'

'No regrets?'

She smiled. 'Only one. Just that I didn't find you sooner.'

Sean looked thoughtful. 'If only I'd questioned that fake letter. It's possible the security intelligence services had something to do with it. Yet, they had nothing to gain. It just doesn't make sense, no matter how many times I go over it.' He paused briefly. 'The first thing I'm going to do is contact them, see if they know anything about it. If they don't, they could look into it for me.'

'No,' said Katrina sharply. 'Please don't. It doesn't matter now. Let's leave the past alone. I just want to put it all behind me.'

Sean's eyes narrowed. 'I'm not so sure I agree. Someone has gone to a lot of trouble. I'd like to know why.'

'But if we stir things up, it could cause complications. Please, Sean.'

He gave a reassuring smile. 'OK, let's not worry about it just now.' Sean lifted his head slightly. A movement in the sky had caught his attention. He saw a helicopter in the distance, moving towards them, its black outline distinct against the hazy sunlight. It followed the ridge of the mountain before sweeping down into the valley, all the time drawing closer.

'What is it?' asked Katrina.

He frowned. 'A helicopter. An Iroquois — nothing unusual in these parts. The army or police are probably out on exercise, or searching for cannabis plantations. We'd better get dressed, it's starting to lose height.'

Katrina slipped on her clothes quickly. 'It looks like it's heading our way.'

Sean pulled on his jeans and fastened his belt, all the time keeping his eyes focused on the helicopter gradually coming closer. A shadow enveloped them like a bird of prey as it hovered above, cutting out any sunlight. The tree branches whipped around them buffeted by the force of the air current as the two huge rotor blades thudded through the air. Then it gradually moved forward, landing on the white shingle flat about fifty metres from where they stood.

Katrina put her hands to her ears. The heavy repetitive beat of the rotors seemed ominous and threatening like a heartbeat in trouble.

Katrina glanced at Sean fearfully. 'What do you think they want?'

'I'm not sure, just keep calm,' he murmured reassuringly. He put his arms around her protectively, drawing her to his side.

The blades of the helicopter finally slowed down and stopped. The door slid open.

Katrina recognized the man in front as the one in the army truck who had come to Glenroy asking for Sean. Two other men followed close behind him wearing dark clothing, black bullet proof vests and black helmets. They both carried short stubby guns with long magazines held across their chests.

'Looks like an anti-terrorist squad, probably out on manoeuvres,' Sean told her, but his senses screamed out a warning.

'Are you Sean McKinlay?' the man demanded, moving forward quickly.

Sean's eyes narrowed. 'I am. What is it you want?'

There were metallic snapping sounds as the other two men in black cocked their weapons.

'You're under arrest. I've got a warrant here.'

6

Sean took a slow breath as he heard the police officer read him his rights. Keep calm and think, he told himself, and do exactly what they want. All they needed was an excuse to shoot him.

'What's this all about?' asked Sean.

'You'll find out more at headquarters. So get a move on.' The police officer jerked his head toward the helicopter.

'There must be a mistake.'

'I don't think so. You're wanted by the British Government for connections to a terrorist group. Entering New Zealand under false pretences is a crime.'

'I'm not guilty of any of those charges,' retorted Sean. He shot a quick worried glance at Katrina.

She whispered, 'Sean, I don't know anything about this, please believe me. I didn't tell them you were here.'

Sean's face was strained as the seriousness of the situation sunk in. Had Katrina betrayed him in spite of her denial?

Sean surveyed the men facing him. 'Wait a minute, Katrina can't drive the truck back to the station. She doesn't know the road.'

The police officer in charge signalled to one of his colleagues, a younger man in his twenties, fresh-shaven with blond cropped hair.

'Drive the truck back to Glenroy, will you? We'll follow and pick you up there.'

Sean knew there was nothing he could do. He grimaced as he handed over the key to the truck. One of the officers came up to Katrina waiting for her to follow him. She looked pleadingly at Sean. 'Let me go with you.'

Sean shook his head. 'No, it's safer you leave now. Wait for me at Glenroy. I'll have all this straightened out as soon as I can.'

Katrina stepped in front of him and faced the man in charge. 'Please, let me go with him. I won't be any trouble.'

The police officer hesitated, then nodded his head. 'All right. But you can only go as far as Glenroy. We'll drop you off there.'

Katrina grabbed her bag and followed Sean as he climbed into the cargo bay of the Iroquois.

One of the men in black followed her. He indicated a place for her to sit on a long bench seat. 'Belt up,' he ordered. He told Sean to sit on another seat opposite.

The police officer sat beside Katrina, the muzzle of his gun pointing at Sean. The second man joined him. He had handcuffs and snapped one end to Sean's right wrist, the other to the pipe frame of the seat. The officer in charge, Detective Inspector Dennis, was the last inside and he sat to Sean's left. He gave a signal and the chopper lurched upward.

Katrina had never been in a helicopter and she would have enjoyed it, if she hadn't been so worried about what was happening. When they took off, she felt giddy as the ground was suddenly left behind. A smell of kerosene filtered through making her feel slightly nauseous. Through the open cargo bay door, she could see the tops of the trees below like green webs. She leaned back in the seat and took a deep breath, conscious all the time of the man sitting beside her.

There was no end to it, Katrina thought with dismay. Sean attracted danger and, once again, she had been caught in the middle. It was up to her whether she wanted to stay with him.

The question this time was, would they let her?

* * *

For the past few hours, Sean had been trying to explain why he had a right to be in New

Zealand just like any other immigrant who wanted to make a new life in another country.

The man interrogating him had sandy hair, cut short, and was in his early forties. He wore his trendy pin stripe suit with the air of someone who followed fashion. However, appearances were deceptive. Sean had a feeling that this man was sharp, not easily duped. Sean studied the man's name badge: Stephen Powell, New Zealand Security Intelligence Service.

'You can make this easier on yourself by answering our questions,' said Powell.

'Fire away,' answered Sean, bracing himself.

'So, you worked for the Metropolitan Police?' said Powell, raising a brow.

Sean nodded. 'That's right. Undercover work. I was a police officer, a Detective Constable, attached to a special anti-terrorist unit in the London Metropolitan police. We liaised with MI5.'

Powell's gaze dropped to the document in front of him. 'According to our information, when you entered New Zealand, you lied about your occupation. It says here you worked for an art gallery in London before immigrating. There's nothing written here about the police.'

'Like I said, I was working undercover,' Sean said calmly. 'Everything was top secret.'

The SIS agent rustled the papers in front of him. 'You've also stated you have had no previous convictions. Our report from Interpol says you were involved with the IRA. You planted a bomb in London three years ago. And you've also done time in prison.' His tone was accusing.

'I know what it looks like, but I'm not guilty. I'll admit I was there but I was gathering intelligence, not planting bombs. The brief prison spell beforehand was to give me credibility that I'd gone over to the IRA.'

'Hold on. You admit you were at the scene of the bomb explosion?' Powell repeated.

Sean swallowed. 'That's what I said, didn't I?'

Powell exchanged looks with Detective Inspector Dennis leaning against the wall. The police officer's large frame stepped in front of the window, casting a shadow over Sean. Sean knew it was meant to make him feel intimidated. He ignored it.

Powell stared at him. 'And what exactly happened that day in London? Who were you meeting there?'

'A contact. I had some papers to deliver to him. He was in MI5. Only he got killed in the explosion.'

'I see.'

'How many times do I have to go over

this?' said Sean, losing patience.

Powell's mouth tightened. 'Until I'm satisfied with the answers. You do realize it is an offence to make a false declaration, McKinlay? I have your original immigration documents right in front of me and your signature is very clear. You've ticked the box stating no criminal convictions.'

Sean damped down his temper. There wasn't any advantage in losing his cool. If anything, it would go against him. 'I haven't made any false declarations, I've only omitted giving information,' he stated. 'And that's simply because I was under oath.'

Powell shook his head. 'That's not good enough. You should have come clean.'

Stalemate. Sean exhaled. 'You're wrong. I couldn't break the Official Secrets Act. If I had, I would have been arrested. Surely you of all people can understand that.' Sean paused briefly. 'I'm not a terrorist. I was in prison playing an undercover role.'

'Irish paramilitaries have long sought refuge in other countries, McKinlay. We're only too aware of that. If you can prove that you really were involved with the police and intelligence services, then you might just have a chance of staying in this country.' Powell looked thoughtful. 'Who was your commanding officer? I can get in touch with the

London Metropolitan Police. See if they'll verify your story.'

Sean nodded. 'Detective Sergeant Andy Davis. I reported to him during the operation.'

Powell wrote something down on the pad in front of him. 'Right. I'll get on to him straight away.'

Powell turned to the detective inspector. 'Any questions?'

Dennis nodded. 'A few.' He took a step forward and pulled up a chair. There was something about him that Sean didn't trust. 'Sean, that's a nice-looking girl you've got . . . Katrina's her name, isn't it?' The police officer's voice came over as friendly, but his manner was smarmy.

At the mention of Katrina, Sean's stomach clenched. 'She's got nothing to do with this, so let's just leave her out of our discussion.'

The detective inspector chewed his lip slightly. 'Seems like you've got something going with her. She's been calling us all day, asking when you're going to be released. Sounds pretty upset at what's happened.'

'I met her at Glenroy Station a few months ago,' explained Sean. 'We're just friends.'

'Really? That's not the impression I got when we picked you up. I'd say it looked real cosy by the river. She's pretty keen on you, isn't she?' He turned to Powell. 'I ran a check on her — she's a Brit, but she lives in the US and she's married.'

Sean's fists bunched at his side. He tried to hold down the urge to punch the Detective. 'So what's that got to do with things?' retorted Sean.

The detective inspector stared at him. 'I bet you knew her American husband is sympathetic to the Real IRA and God knows what else.'

Sean froze. The Real IRA? Katrina hadn't said much about her husband. Did she even know what he had been up to? If she did, why hadn't she told him?

'So?' answered Sean. He shrugged, trying to feign indifference. 'That's nothing to do with me. Besides, there are thousands of people in the US sympathetic to the Real IRA. That doesn't mean Katrina is.'

Dennis spoke quickly as he turned to Powell. 'Maybe we ought to pull her in. Find out what she knows.'

Sean's heart sank. That was the last thing he wanted.

'You say you met Katrina at Glenroy Station,' Powell added, 'about two months ago?'

Sean nodded. 'That's right. She tracked me down.'

'Isn't that a bit odd? After all this time,' remarked Powell, frowning. 'You're sure she's not involved with the Real IRA in any way?'

'I'd stake my life on the fact she's innocent.'

A knock at the door interrupted the proceedings and Powell rose, pressed the pause button on the recording device. 'I'll be back in a moment.' He went outside, keeping the door slightly ajar with his hand.

Seeing Powell leave, Sean took the opportunity to stretch his legs. He got up and walked over to the window. He wasn't sure what to think. He'd answered all their questions as best he could without breaking confidentiality, but even so, he had a feeling that things might end up being unpleasant. Sean's gaze settled on the detective inspector.

'I've told you everything I know,' Sean said quietly. 'It's up to you to check it out.' He turned back to look out the fourth floor window at the city street below. Wellington in the rush hour. Red trolley buses buzzed around picking up people finishing work for the day. It was windy, blustery. A sidewalk sign cart-wheeled across the road causing traffic to stop suddenly while someone rushed over to pick it up.

Suddenly, he wondered what Katrina would be doing. Probably she'd be in the kitchen preparing the evening meal. A sudden longing to be back at Glenroy shot through him.

The detective inspector's voice sliced into his thoughts. 'Sit down, Sean.'

Sean's jaw tightened but he obeyed. He looked at Sean with disdain and his mouth twisted. 'We're going to nail you . . . you bastard, and your girlfriend, Katrina.'

Sean stood up, kicking back the chair. It fell on to the floor with a crash. Grabbing the man by the collar, he wrenched him forward over the table, half choking him. 'You touch her and I'll see you in hell, you hear me?'

The police officer gurgled. At the sound of raised voices Powell and two other police officers rushed in, grabbing Sean and forcing his arms back. Sean struggled for a moment but he was outnumbered. They dragged him into the chair and handcuffs were snapped on, immobilizing him.

Dennis backtracked slowly, straightening his tie and smoothing back his hair. 'The man's an animal,' he said distastefully. 'I guess we'll have to add assaulting a police officer to the charges, won't we?' He threw Sean another smarmy look.

The SIS agent took command of the situation immediately. 'What the hell happened?'

'Nothing,' Sean replied, breathing heavily. 'I was just teaching this cop some manners which he obviously lacks.'

Sean cursed himself for playing right into the detective inspector's hands. There was only so much he would take and the jibe had made him lose control. He had never responded well to authority. But at least he had worked in an area which suited him and in which he got results. For that, they were willing to overlook his insubordination at times. Violence never accomplished anything, least of all on a man like Detective Inspector Dennis. It would only end with him in the slammer — and that was the last place he wanted to be.

Powell's face was strained as he took a seat back at the table. 'Like I said, McKinlay, we'd appreciate your co-operation.' He flicked open the folder in front of him. 'Right, let's start again.'

'Get these handcuffs off me. You've no right to hold me. I've done nothing wrong.'

Powell's head jerked upward, his eyes stony. 'We've every right, especially if it's a matter of national security.'

The two men glared at each other, each testing, weighing each other up. Powell was the first to speak. 'Right, let's start again. We've tried to contact your commanding officer, Andy Davis, but we've been informed he died about a month ago.'

Sean gasped. 'Christ ... Andy's dead? What happened?'

Powell looked sympathetic. 'He was shot in an Irish pub a few weeks ago.'

'Shot? Who did it?'

'The Real IRA. They're targeting police officers.'

'But why?'

'They're opposed to Northern Ireland's new policing deal. Rumour has it they've formed an assassination squad aimed at dissuading Catholics from joining the police force.'

'But I don't understand. Andy was in the London Met, not the police force in Northern Ireland.'

'He left the Met about a year ago. He got divorced and remarried a girl from Belfast. So they moved there and he joined up.'

Sean shook his head disbelievingly. 'Andy was a good man. He wouldn't let anyone else take a risk, he wasn't prepared to.' He didn't tell Powell that Andy had taught him everything he knew. To be murdered like that just didn't bear thinking about. Andy had always been so careful, so precise in everything. 'But there are records, there has to be.'

'We've contacted someone else in London. Detective Inspector Andrew Harvey of the Metropolitan Police, Counter Terrorism Unit, SO15.'

Sean frowned. 'SO15?'

'There's been a few changes since you left the Met. The Anti-Terrorist Branch and Special Branch have amalgamated. Now known as SO15.' Powell looked at his watch quickly. 'Harvey will be here in exactly three days.'

Sean groaned. That meant he'd be in custody for at least another week.

'I'd like a lawyer,' said Sean. A bit of legal advice wouldn't go amiss.

Powell agreed. After a moment's hesitation, he said, 'Look, Sean, if you tell us the truth, something might be salvaged from all this. We're not a nation of squeaky clean immigrants you know, but we need to know what's going on. Things have been pretty tight since the scenario with Jimmy Dunne — a refugee from Ireland. He came here because a death squad in Ireland was after him. He was refused residency and it all hit the headlines in a big way. When it came to the crunch, he barricaded himself in his home and the police had to drag him out. Then he was deported. No one won. And, what's more, the authorities don't want to get into that again. So, if you've got anything to hide, it's better you tell me now.'

Sean stared at him. Yes, he remembered the Jimmy Dunne case and during all the time he'd followed it on the news, he'd never thought for one moment he'd end up following in his footsteps. It didn't have to be that way, if he was careful. Realistically, Sean didn't have much choice. The security intelligence services were all powerful in any country and Sean didn't want to leave New Zealand. Not now, especially when there was Katrina to think of. He'd promised her a life at Glenroy. He was going to keep that promise if it was the last thing he did.

'OK, I'll talk,' Sean conceded, his face grim. 'But I want that recording device switched off and what I say is between you and me.'

Powell looked at him thoughtfully, making a quick decision. 'Alright. Take off the handcuffs,' he ordered the police guard standing nearby. Powell leaned back, loosened his tie and ordered another two coffees. When they had been brought in, Detective Inspector Dennis said, 'I'll be outside if you need me.'

Powell nodded, closed the door and sat down again. 'Right then.'

Sean leaned forward placing his hands on

the formica table and told him what had happened in London before the bomb went off. 'That's how Katrina and I met. After the explosion she ended up in Boston and I came out to New Zealand.'

Powell drummed his fingers on the table, his face thoughtful. 'Alright. I'll tell you what we'll do. We won't make any decisions until this Detective Inspector Harvey arrives.' The SIS agent consulted the notes in front of him. 'I guess that's the best we can do for now.'

Sean felt relieved. At least he wasn't going to be thrown out the country like some criminal. If that happened, he'd be a sitting target for anyone who held a grudge in Ireland, no matter what the faction. Undercover agents could play many roles and it would be easy to attribute blame, make him a scapegoat in retaliation for some political move. Sean's mind worked frantically. Stephen Powell was clever but he suspected any decision made would have to have New Zealand's interests in the forefront. Sure enough, Sean couldn't blame him for that. He was only doing his job.

Left alone for a few minutes, Sean stood again, then walked around the room. He flexed his muscles to relieve the cramps from sitting too long. He strode over to the window again wishing he could just walk out and put the whole thing behind him.

Night was falling, lights were coming on. His mind drifted. He thought of Glenroy. Sean had spent some of the best years of his life on the station and he'd like to think that the stability and effort he'd put into his life there would help his case. He was known in the farming community and had helped out in the community when it had been needed. Now, owning his own land and cottage confirmed he'd serious intentions to make his home here. Surely things had to go in his favour?

Now that Katrina was back in his life again, they'd both been given a second chance. He wasn't going to let her go, he vowed. No matter what.

Powell returned. He stood in the doorway. 'I'll make arrangements for you to use the phone before you leave. You'll want to ring your family at Glenroy. After that, you'll be escorted back into police custody and held for further questioning.'

Sean nodded. It wasn't over yet.

★ ★ ★

Once outside the room, Dennis came up to Powell and said, 'What do you think?'

Powell rubbed a hand over his chin. 'I don't know. There's something different about him. Let's just keep an open mind, shall we? McKinlay could be telling the truth but we won't know for definite until Detective Inspector Harvey gets here.'

The detective inspector's lip curled. 'I still think he's lying.'

Powell's brow lifted slightly. 'Well, if he is, he's doing a good job of it. I've been interviewing people for twenty years and something tells me he's straight up.' He paused thoughtfully, thinking about some of the cases he'd reviewed. 'It's unbelievable the lengths or excuses people go to in order to gain residency in New Zealand. It's a desirable country.' He paused again, shaking his head. 'But Sean McKinlay . . . I don't know.' He shook his head. 'He isn't motivated by money, I can tell you that now. No, it sounds to me like he really did come out here to forget his past and make a new life.'

Dennis snorted. 'Yeah, but he's clever with words . . . a smooth talker. I wouldn't put it past him to have planted that bomb in London.' He shook his head as he shifted his weight onto his other foot. 'I don't know how he managed to slip through immigration. Still, we can't be too careful after the Rainbow Warrior bombing,' he reminded

Powell. 'And since 9/11, terrorists are everywhere, so why not New Zealand? How do we know he hasn't been hired by some terrorist group to set up a base here? I think you should deport him now before he gets hold of a lawyer.'

Powell spoke sharply. 'If Sean McKinlay is telling the truth, his only crime is omitting to give us information on his immigration forms. It's hardly big time.'

Dennis didn't like his answer. 'Get rid of him. This could cause more trouble than it is worth. And I've got a nasty feeling about the whole thing.'

The SIS agent firmed his voice. 'No. I say we'll hold fire until Harvey arrives and then we'll make a decision.'

7

Katrina stood in the kitchen. Four pans were simmering on the stove, the lids clattering with the steam. The smell of roast beef drifted in the air. She adjusted the oven temperature and put the plates in the warming tray. It was hard to concentrate. Her heart just wasn't in preparing the meal but she knew she had to make an effort.

'No word from Sean yet?' asked John.

'No. Not for a few days.' Sean had spoken to her only briefly and he had been close-mouthed as to what was happening to him. She had rung the police department and immigration, but they had fobbed her off, saying that Sean would call her as soon as possible and that he wasn't able to receive any incoming calls right now.

She didn't know what to think. Worry gnawed at her. She wanted to do something to help Sean, but what?

Moving forward, and trying to focus on the task in hand, Katrina took out the bright red table mats she had bought last time she was in town and set the table.

Then she peered at the rain pounding at

the window pane. The sky looked black. Clouds rolled over the tops of the mountains like angry gods going to war. Stormy weather, she thought. She hoped it wouldn't last long.

She glanced at her watch and frowned. There was no sign of Ross finishing for the day. Usually, she could see him riding towards the homestead around this time. Tonight he seemed to be taking a long time but then again, she reminded herself, he'd been working long hours since Sean had been taken away.

'Just had the weather report,' said John worriedly. 'It's turned southerly. More heavy rain and cold winds are expected. I would have thought Ross would be back by now. It's not like him to be so late for dinner. I'd better go fetch him.'

Katrina made a quick decision. 'No, I'll go. He can't be that far away. Dinner's almost ready anyway. And I could do with some fresh air.' She turned off the stove, removed her apron and hung it up behind the door. 'I know you aren't feeling well and the last thing you need is to be riding out in this downpour. You'll catch pneumonia.'

John smiled, rubbing his aching head. He sat down wearily on a chair. 'I guess you're right. My blood pressure must be up again. All this worry over Sean. Always knew that his past would catch up with him eventually.'

Katrina put on her weatherproof gear and boots and made her way to the stables to saddle up one of the horses. She noticed Ross had taken Sean's horse as the animal had needed the exercise.

The regular riding lessons had improved her riding ability. She was quite happy to go riding on her own although she had never been out of view of the homestead. When she mounted, she wondered which way she should go but decided to follow the trail up to the shepherd's hut. Ross had mentioned at breakfast-time he was going up there to check on the building.

She made her way up the mountainside trail slowly. The horse slipped once or twice, sending showers of stones hurling down the scree. Gripping the reins tighter, she kept her eyes focused ahead. As she was approaching a gully, she thought she heard a horse whinny. Perhaps Ross was somewhere near. She listened carefully.

'Ross,' she called out, her gaze skimming the area. There was no answer. All Katrina could hear was the sound of a sheep coughing as it scurried from behind a bush. She couldn't get over the niggling feeling something was wrong. Maybe it was the stormy weather unnerving her, she thought.

She tried to shrug off the uneasiness.

At a grumble of thunder in the distance, her horse shied to the left, stumbling slightly. She reached forward and patted his neck. 'Easy now,' she said softly, wondering if she should continue.

Lightning flashed across the sky in a silver zig-zag blinding her for a second. Her horse jerked its head back, catching Katrina unaware and nearly throwing her.

'It's all right,' Katrina said in her calmest voice, even though her heart thudded with fear. That had been a close call. They both could have ended up rolling down the mountain. The mare was a gentle soul and if she was unsettled, maybe it would be safer to walk beside her. Katrina climbed down and led her by the reins, talking to her softly.

When Katrina reached a small plateau, she scoured the land below for Ross and the horse. Still nothing.

A crack of a rifle, sharp and vicious over the wind, rang out. Both Katrina and the horse started. 'Easy, girl, easy.' She had to haul on the reins to steady her spooked mount. Katrina knew instinctively the shot was a signal, but where had it come from?

Still leading her horse carefully, she moved across the plateau calling as she went. She would circle through the area listening for another shot trying to see through the scrub and rocks.

A few minutes later, she found him. There, lying propped against a rock under a bluff, was a hunched figure. 'Ross!' she called, as she ran towards him dragging the horse after her. She knelt on the wet ground. 'For God's sake, what's wrong? Are you hurt?'

At first he didn't answer. His head lifted, his eyes looking glazed. 'Get out of here . . . Katrina . . . someone's trying to kill me.'

It was then she noticed the blood on his heavy jacket. She gasped. 'You're bleeding. Oh my God.' Katrina gazed at him in disbelief. 'What do you mean, someone's trying to kill you? There's no one here.' She lifted her head and swept the area. Nothing. Though it was difficult to see more than a few yards ahead. The mist clung to the sides of the mountain like a shroud. If there was someone lurking around, where were they?

A stone rolled down the hillside below them and away to the right. It was then she spotted two figures scrambling down the scree, making their way to where a ute was parked, half hidden in scrub.

'Don't let them see you,' uttered Ross.

Katrina crouched down low, her heart pounding. Who were the men? Katrina turned her attention back to Ross. His eyes were closed, his head slumping forward slightly on to his chest. He tried to move but was in too much pain. She wrapped his arm around her neck intending to lift him to his feet but he was too heavy. She just wasn't strong enough.

If she rode back to get John, she would lose valuable time and Ross might die from loss of blood.

Ross whispered hoarsely. 'The rifle. Over there.'

Katrina followed his gaze. Ross's horse was standing nearby, waiting patiently like a well-trained stock horse. The rifle was in a scabbard hanging under the saddle.

Katrina realized now that the shot she had heard earlier hadn't been a signal, it had been fired by the men who had tried to kill Ross. She approached the horse, careful not to spook it and pulled the rifle from its leather sheath. It was heavy and cold and wet. She hadn't fired any sort of gun before, but she had watched them shooting at the station and she'd been out rabbit shooting with the men. 'Three shots, a minute apart,' Sean had once told her.

She walked away from the horses to a place under the bluff as close to the station buildings as she could get. She worked the handle. Sean had explained it was the bolt, and a fat brass cartridge was pushed into the breech. She held the rifle away from her, the muzzle pointing in the general direction of the farm buildings and pulled the trigger. The noise was deafening. She worked the bolt, counted to sixty under her breath and fired again. A minute later she repeated the process, then she ran back to where Ross lay and dropped the rifle beside him.

'Someone will be here soon,' she reassured him as she knelt down and took his large hand in hers. His skin was cold, clammy. His face was white, his lips tinged blue. She didn't even know if he heard her. He had already lapsed into unconsciousness. The hood on his jacket had fallen back, showing his hair, like darkened gold, wet from the rain. She knew he was still breathing because she had put her hand on his chest to feel his heartbeat.

Salty tears ran down her face but she wiped them away with her sleeve. She huddled down beside him.

'Please . . . please . . . don't die, Ross. You can't die. I won't let you.' Her arm slid around him, her head bent on his shoulder. She held on to him tightly as if trying to breathe some life into him.

Suddenly, Katrina thought of the last few weeks. Ross had been kind to her, making her feel welcome at Glenroy. He'd been like a brother to her. He had been patient, caring and tolerant. Ross was all these things and more.

She leaned back against the rock, feeling the cold stone and dampness seeping into her back. Ross was a good man and he wouldn't have harmed anyone. So who could have done this? And why? Suddenly she heard herself mumbling a prayer, bargaining with God. If only Sean had been here, she thought desperately, he would have known what to do.

She just felt so helpless sitting there, watching the life ebb out of him.

A voice called out, faint, but she was sure it sounded like John. Katrina scrambled to her feet and waved frantically. 'Over here,' she cried. 'Quick . . . we're over here.'

The two men, dark figures, galloped quickly towards her from the other side of the ridge. One of them was Philip Reid, Anna's brother, and the other was John. Philip dismounted quickly, and crouched down beside Ross, checking for a pulse.

Katrina swallowed hard. 'I found him here like this. He said that someone tried to kill him. I don't know what happened exactly but I saw two men running over there.' She pointed. 'They made their getaway in a white ute.'

'Could be sheep rustlers,' suggested Philip.

'But why shoot someone?' replied John. 'No, I can't see it. That wouldn't make sense.' John looked down at his son. 'Ross,' he called out, 'can you hear me?'

There was no answer.

Philip looked grim. 'It's no good. He's out cold.' He turned Ross slightly, so he could get a better look at the wound. 'We've got to get him to a doctor before he loses any more blood.'

Within minutes, they had lifted Ross on to his horse and were heading quickly down the trail. Katrina's hands were shaking. She started to shiver.

John shouted against the wind. 'The rescue helicopter won't come out in this weather. Visibility is down to only a few yards.'

'We'll take him to hospital in the truck,' replied Philip. 'It's the only way.'

When they reached the homestead, Katrina rushed inside and grabbed some towels and blankets from the cupboard. Ross had already been placed in the back of the truck. She climbed in beside him, tucking a cushion gently under his head. After she wiped his face, she gently put towels around him to staunch the flow of blood from the wound in his side. Philip put a large weatherproof canvas cover over all of them and tied it down to the sides of the truck. 'Hold fast,' he said. 'It will be a bumpy ride.'

Once in the truck, Philip took out his mobile phone and handed it to John. John dialled the emergency services.

The medics were waiting with a stretcher when they arrived at the local hospital. Within minutes, Ross was transported into the emergency room.

★ ★ ★

Detective Inspector Andrew Harvey of the London Metropolitan Police Counter Terrorism Command, stood at the reception desk of the Security Intelligence Services in Wellington. The receptionist was busy talking on the phone. When she finally hung up he introduced himself and said, 'Stephen Powell is expecting me.'

The receptionist gave him a warm smile. 'If you'd like to take a seat, he'll be with you shortly.'

'Thank you.' The detective inspector returned the smile. The gesture transformed his face, softening the harsh lines around his eyes. It made him look ten years younger than his fifty years.

He made his way over to a row of comfortable seats. No one else was waiting.

He flicked through a couple of magazines on the table, then checked his watch. It was a quarter to nine and the man he was meeting was exactly five minutes and forty seconds late.

Another ten minutes passed. Harvey flicked through the documents in his briefcase familiarizing himself with the profile on Sean McKinlay. McKinlay had been one of their best undercover police officers in the Met. Educated at Trinity College, Dublin, he'd studied law, but had dropped out after two years, choosing to join the An Garda Síochána — the National Police Force of Ireland — at twenty-two years old. After five years as a constable, he transferred into the Special Detective Unit. After a joint operation with the London Metropolitan Police, where he'd met Detective Sergeant Andy Davis, he'd resigned from the Garda, and moved to London joining the Met. There, he'd been based in the Anti-Terrorist Branch, then known as SO13 where he'd undertaken covert duties. His conduct as an undercover police officer had been exemplary.

His personal details were a little sketchy. Few relatives, his parents had died when he was young. McKinlay had never married, but he'd got involved with a woman, Katrina Jones, who had been hurt in an explosion during his last assignment, Operation Pandora.

The psychologist's evaluation undertaken by all undercover operatives, after the completion of an operation, showed him to be suffering from exhaustion.

The document went on to say that McKinlay had resigned a few weeks later after he'd recovered from physical injuries, refused the offer of a new identity, though he accepted a resettlement fee before leaving for New Zealand. No contact had been made with him since.

A door opened. Harvey glanced up, snapped shut the briefcase. The man who walked towards him was taller than most men, solidly built and exuded an air of confidence. Detective Inspector Harvey was keenly aware of it, recognizing an equal.

Stephen Powell held out his hand, saying warmly, 'Sorry to keep you waiting. I got held up unexpectedly.'

The detective inspector stood and shook hands. 'That's no problem at all. These things happen.'

'Please, won't you come this way?'

Harvey followed the man, every so often getting a whiff of aftershave as they walked down the corridor.

'Did you have a good flight?' Powell asked,

turning slightly. 'I understand you were delayed in Tahiti.'

Harvey nodded. 'Yes. Some problem with the radar on the plane. Spent one night in Los Angeles but even so the jet lag is catching up with me now.'

Within seconds, Harvey stepped into Powell's office. The room was large, the carpet a rich blue, and the walls a pale cream. A large rimu desk was placed near the window to take advantage of the natural city light. Harvey noticed a small antique lamp sitting on the corner of the desk along with a gold ink stand which glinted as it caught the sunlight. Obviously Powell believed in working in comfort and pleasant surroundings.

'Please, won't you take a seat,' Powell said graciously, indicating the leather bound chair facing him.

'Thank you.' Harvey saw a man already seated on the black leather couch, dressed in dark blue jeans and a white T-shirt. He recognized him from the photos as Sean McKinlay.

After the initial introductions were made, Harvey balanced his battered briefcase on his knee, unlocked the combination lock and took out some documents. Making sure they were the right ones, he handed them to Powell.

'There you are. I'm sure you will find these in order,' Harvey said in clipped tones.

Powell didn't say anything straight away but his face was serious as he read through the papers stamped with the official golden seal of Her Majesty's Government.

'I can assure you everything has been checked and double checked,' added Harvey.

Powell glanced up. 'So I see. Certainly this explains everything and backs up what Sean's already told us.' Powell's gaze settled on Sean. 'I'm sorry about the arrest and the interrogation. But you realize we had no choice at the time. We were only acting on information passed to us.'

'It could have been handled better but I enjoyed the helicopter ride,' Sean replied drily. 'Something's been bothering me though: you never did tell me how you tracked me down.'

'A private investigator, Rick Caruso, who's worked for us in the past, alerted us. He'd been paid by Katrina Jones to find you. Once we received his report on your background, we needed to check it out. An army officer discreetly confirmed your whereabouts while they were delivering feed to the valley farmers. Afterwards it was just a matter of picking you up.'

Sean recalled the soldier Katrina had mentioned who'd been making enquiries about him. So that's what it had been about.

Powell leaned back against his chair. 'Anyway, apart from that, we still have the problem of your immigration status. Now that these documents confirm your identity, and you've lived here for three years, you could be granted New Zealand citizenship. Considering the circumstances, I'll put a good word in for you.'

It was what Sean had been waiting for. He breathed a sigh of relief. 'Thanks.'

Powell continued. 'There is one other matter though. The British Government have a special request.'

Sean's eyes narrowed as he looked at both men. 'A request?'

'I'll leave it to Detective Inspector Harvey to explain.'

Harvey coughed slightly. 'Sean, we'd like to know if you'd consider an assignment to go back to Ireland and do some intelligence work.'

Sean stared at him. 'What? No way. I've been out of action for three years. I wouldn't know where to start. All the contacts I had originally have been killed or are on the run.' He gave a short laugh. 'Besides, what's the point? The peace agreement is underway. It's just a matter of time before the violence stops.' Sean knew the moment he said the words he was only kidding himself. The violence wouldn't stop completely. There would always be some who wouldn't agree to the ceasefire and the terms of the peace agreement. As Powell had pointed out the Real IRA were strengthening. Sean shook his head firmly. 'No . . . I'm sorry, I'm not interested.'

'I can't emphasize how important this is to us.'

Sean frowned. 'In what way?'

Harvey continued. 'We've had intelligence reports that al-Qaeda are linking up with the Real IRA.'

Somehow, that didn't surprise him. Terrorist organizations had been known to work together. 'Al-Qaeda? But why?'

'They both want to destroy the British Government for a start. It's no secret that some of the Provos trained in the Middle East military camps. Alliances were forged.'

'So have many other terrorist groups,' Sean pointed out.

'But this is different,' said Harvey seriously.

'Different?' repeated Sean.

'A bomb factory in Southern Ireland has been set up. We need to find out how well equipped they are. If you can get us the information we want, we'll take over from there.'

'Why me? You've got other undercover officers who can do the job. Ones who are specialized. Things have changed since I was in the field.'

'That's true. We do. But there are certain factors which point to you being the best person. For a start, you're the only one who can identify the two leaders of that splinter group we were after three years ago. We think they're the ones who have set up this terrorist base in league with al-Qaeda.'

'Where is the base?' asked Sean, interested.

'We've reason to believe it's in Connemara. Cardell Castle.'

'Cardell Castle,' repeated Sean, surprised. 'I know the place well. I was brought up near there by my adoptive parents when I was a teenager.' Sean thought quickly. 'But didn't the castle belong to the Gallagher family for generations?'

'It did. But was sold off. Just like many other large estates because the owners didn't have the money to keep them up. A foreign investor from the Middle East has bought it. They've turned it into a bed and breakfast. No doubt a ruse to cover up their illegal activities.' Harvey hesitated, swopped glances with Stephen Powell. 'There's something else.'

Sean detected the change of tone in

Harvey's voice. He began to feel uneasy.

'It's about Andy Davis,' continued Harvey.

'What about him?' asked Sean.

'After he died, a letter arrived at our office, sent by his lawyer. It was in Davis's handwriting. He confessed that he was an informer for the Provisional IRA during Operation Pandora. That's why everything went wrong on that last assignment.'

Sean was stunned. 'You can't be serious.'

'It turns out that he did it for money, paid to him by the Provos.'

Sean shook his head. 'No, I don't believe it. That doesn't seem like the Andy Davis I knew. There has to be some mistake.'

'There isn't. It makes sense when you know why. His teenage son had serious medical problems. Something wrong with his bowel. He needed an operation that cost thousands of pounds. It was a new, pioneer operation. The only place he could get it done was in Canada.'

'Jaysus.' Sean's mouth went dry. He'd liked Andy. Trusted him. They had worked together closely for years. 'I can't believe he'd go to those lengths. His betrayal cost the life of a ten-year-old kid and injured many others. That's some sacrifice for his son.'

'That's why he left the letter for us. He said that if anything happened to him, he wanted the truth to come out. That he had lived with the guilt for the last three years. He also said he hadn't known a bomb was in the briefcase. He particularly asked us to pass that piece of information on to you.'

'And what about his son?' asked Sean, still reeling.

'He survived. The operation was successful.'

Sean let the information sink in. It all made sense now. Why the two men had turned up in the shopping mall ready to accost him and Katrina. No doubt, ordered to kill them both if the bomb hadn't done the job. The briefcase had been checked earlier on by Andy Davis and had been out of sight from Sean for half an hour. Davis had cited that they needed to attach a tracking device. It had been time enough for someone to plant the bomb. Davis must have given the briefcase to Danny and Carrie Maguire, the leaders of the splinter group.

'So Maguire and his wife found out I was an undercover cop. That's why they planted the bomb,' muttered Sean.

Harvey nodded. 'Looks that way. Only you survived.'

'And you never caught Maguire and his wife?' asked Sean.

'We tried. But they went into hiding. We've

had some recent intel about them. Rumour has it, from one of our informers, that Danny Maguire has set up an assassination unit, under the Real IRA. They're the ones responsible for targeting police officers in Northern Ireland and killing them.'

'Did they kill Andy Davis?' asked Sean, his jaw hardening.

'It's a possibility. But we don't know for sure.'

Harvey leaned forward in his seat like a salesman delivering his best pitch. 'Look, all we want you to do is to find the bomb factory and confirm the link with al-Qaeda. I won't pretend the assignment isn't dangerous. We all know it is. But there is a limit to the role we want you to play.'

'You make it sound easy.' Sean shook his head. 'But the answer is no. I don't want anything to do with it. I've been away from that world too long.'

'Will you at least consider it? You'll be well paid for your efforts.'

It wasn't the money, thought Sean, even if the detective inspector was using it as an incentive. He just wanted to be left alone. To be able to get on with his life. Their life. His and Katrina's.

Sean had to make them understand. 'You expect me to leave Glenroy and go back to

Ireland to play your war games. I turned my back on the place long ago because I was sick of the corruption and the killing. Good people died back there . . . friends. Do you know what that feels like?' He shook his head as he stared into space. 'I left because in the end nothing made sense any more. Sure I thought I was doing some good but it just wasn't enough. And now you tell me Andy Davis, the one who trained me, whom I called a friend, a man I would have trusted with my life, was an informer.'

'It happens, Sean. It's no reflection on you. Your work in London was invaluable. We know you were under intense pressure at the time. You shouldn't have been on that last assignment for so long. From reading your reports, it's obvious you were pushed too far . . . and you got involved emotionally with one of the suspects.' Harvey looked grim faced. 'You suspected Katrina in London, didn't you? Wasn't that why you introduced yourself to her in the first place?'

Sean flinched. 'That was in the beginning. The bookshop she worked in was under suspicion. It was thought the owner was harbouring IRA men. I needed to know what was going on, but I've told you Katrina was just a pawn in the game. An innocent employee. She never even knew what was going on.'

Powell cut in sharply. 'You used her?'

'I had no choice at the time. It seemed the best option. But things didn't turn out as planned. I got involved with her on a personal basis.' Sean shrugged. 'Well, you know the rest.'

'Mistakes were made. Not by you, that much is clear. You should have been monitored more closely. But at least you got out when you'd had enough. I know it was hard, but your work during Operation Pandora saved many lives both in Ireland and out of it. You have to remember that.'

'The cost was too high. I lost Katrina. She was almost killed.' Sean shook his head. 'No. I'm not going through that again,' added Sean emphatically. He looked directly at Powell. 'Katrina and I are getting married. Soon as her divorce comes through. So you see, I've got other plans.'

'And you're sure Katrina's innocent?' asked Harvey.

'I'd stake my life on it.'

'She has connections with a woman called Jessie Quinn. That's Maguire's sister,' pointed out Harvey.

'I know,' replied Sean carefully. 'But that doesn't mean Katrina is guilty of anything. They're just friends.' Sean wasn't about to tell them how close Jessie and Katrina actually were. Jessie had even loaned Katrina money to start up her café. If the men in front of him knew that it might incriminate Katrina in some way.

'We're going to have to pull Katrina in for questioning. We need to find out what she knows,' stated Harvey.

Sean's voice steeled. 'I've told you, Katrina's innocent of all this. I won't let her be brought in.' He took a quick breath. 'Why can't you arrest Jessie Quinn? She might talk under interrogation.'

'No. If we arrest her, they'll know we're on to them,' Harvey replied. 'And they and the equipment would disappear in a flash. We can't afford to take the chance. We're almost a hundred per cent sure the bomb factory is at the castle. But we need to get someone inside to take a look around. More importantly, confirm that al-Qaeda are also involved.'

Powell interrupted. 'Listen, Sean, before you make the final decision I advise you to listen to what else Detective Inspector Harvey has got to say.'

Sean considered his words. 'Go right ahead.'

'You're still on the hit list,' Harvey announced.

'I'm what?' said Sean in disbelief. 'But why?'

'For sabotaging their plans. Sounds like someone has got it in for you. Have a listen to

214

this.' The police officer produced a micro cassette and gave it to Powell to play.

Sean listened to the voices, one of them a woman.

'We've got everything planned,' she said. 'Khalis is arriving in Ireland in a month's time to rendezvous with us. He'll meet us in Connemara.' There was a muffled noise, then, 'By the way, here's a turn up for the books. We've found out that Sean O'Riley's in New Zealand. I want you to find him. Kill him.'

Sean's heart slammed against his chest. 'Who are they?' But even as he asked the question he knew.

'We think it is Danny and Carrie Maguire.'

'And Khalis?' asked Sean.

'His full name is Hannad Khalis. He's a friend of Maguire's. They first met in the Middle East a few years ago. Maguire saved his life during one of their operations. Since then Maguire's been a regular guest at Khalis's home in Afghanistan and vice versa.' Harvey leaned forward slightly. 'The CIA have been following Khalis for some time. So has MI6. They've even taped interviews with him and some colleagues. He's suspected of designing and manufacturing bombs. Drawing up plans for high tech rockets. Rockets that can destroy a helicopter a second or two after take-off, before the pilot can even blink.

215

He's even developed an advanced computer programme which could revolutionize terrorism.'

'Fairly high-powered stuff,' Sean remarked.

'He's clever all right. But now he's in league with Maguire and his wife, there's no telling what they will do.'

The phone rang at that moment and Powell answered it. 'I thought I told you I wasn't to be disturbed . . . ' His gaze lifted and settled on Sean. 'He's what? When? Yes . . . I'll let him know right away.' Powell slammed the phone down, his face serious. 'You'd better brace yourself for this, Sean.'

Sean's head jerked up. 'What's going on?'

'It's your cousin, Ross. I'm afraid he's been shot.'

Sean's face paled. 'Shot? What the hell do you mean?'

'He's in hospital; they don't know if he'll pull through.' Powell explained what had happened. 'Katrina was the one who found him in the mountains.'

Sean gripped the arms of the chair. 'Was it an accident?'

Powell shook his head. 'No. They don't think so. It looks like the bullet was meant for you.'

★ ★ ★

Sean knew his fate was sealed the moment he'd heard about Ross. It was a dilemma he'd rather not face but he had no choice now. Ross had been shot because of him. The long arm of terrorism had finally stretched all the way to New Zealand. It was incredible, and yet, terrorism knew no boundaries.

If Ross died, Sean would never forgive himself. As for Katrina she had been through enough. If they pulled her in for questioning because of her connection with Jessie, it wouldn't be pleasant. Interrogation never was. Now, he just hoped like hell Katrina would understand what he had to do.

He had to go back to Ireland: to finish off what he'd begun.

Sean stood at the window, absorbing the blueness of the sky, unmarred except for a jet trail. After a few seconds he turned, his gaze fixing on the two men sitting in front of him. 'All right. I'll go. I'll find your bomb factory. If al-Qaeda are involved I'll get the evidence. But I'll do it my way.'

Powell swopped glances with the detective inspector. This was the leverage they needed.

Sean moved forward. 'I don't want you touching Katrina. Keep her out of this. No questions. No interrogation. Is that clear? And she's not to know where I'm going. I don't want her following me.'

'You think she would?' asked Powell, raising a brow.

'It's highly likely. She found me in New Zealand, didn't she?'

'We won't allow her to leave the country,' Powell promised. 'As for bringing her in, we'll hold off until you return from Ireland. That's the best we can do, I'm afraid.'

'Agreed,' replied Sean. 'Before I go, I need to return to Glenroy. I can't leave without seeing Katrina. And there's Ross too.'

'Two days enough?' offered Powell.

Sean nodded. He rubbed his chin thoughtfully, already making plans. 'Right then, you'd better brief me on what's been happening and what resources I've got.'

Harvey drew his chair closer and took out some more papers from his briefcase. Powell rang through for a pot of coffee and a bottle of brandy.

Five hours later, Sean walked out of the office a free man in body but not in spirit.

★ ★ ★

Katrina stared out the hospital window. Dawn had now come, bringing with it the first rays of sunlight. The storm was finally clearing.

It had been a long night, one Katrina would never forget. Glancing at the clock on the wall, she realized she'd been there for several hours. Already, the nursing staff were changing shift from the sound of voices at the reception desk.

Katrina turned to see John still asleep on the couch. Hesitant to wake him, she wandered into the foyer to get a hot drink from the coffee machine. She had just lifted the foaming brew to her lips when the doctor appeared from around the corner, lines of tiredness ingrained on his face.

He smiled with the reassurance of one who had dealt with life and death often. 'You can see Ross now, but he's still unconscious,' he told her.

Katrina's lips parted, not wanting to ask the question but knowing she had to. She wanted to be prepared. 'Is he going to be OK?'

The doctor's gaze levelled with hers. 'He's stable. So at least that's something. The bullet has been removed. He's fairly tough. I'd say he's going to pull through OK.'

She heard John behind her breathe a sigh of relief. 'Thank God,' he murmured, the tears running unashamedly down his cheeks as he stood up.

Katrina's heart went out to him; she slipped her arm through his. Side by side, they walked into intensive care to be greeted by a nurse.

'He'll be sleeping for a while yet,' the nurse said.

Katrina stood, looking down at Ross who lay as pale as the sheets which covered him. A plastic intravenous line ran from his arm to a plastic bag hanging on a stand next to the bed. The electronic gauge mesmerized her with its red digital numbers, flashing constantly like a countdown to takeoff. A heart monitor beeped regularly reminding her that Ross, a man of the earth, depended on technology to keep him alive. To Katrina it seemed so alien to the man she had come to know. Her throat tightened.

Her hand reached out for Ross's, pressing lightly, hoping somehow that he'd sense they were there. That it would be some comfort to him.

Life was like that, she thought suddenly. It could change in a heartbeat. Her thoughts settled on Sean.

If only he were here.

★　★　★

Katrina was walking along the hospital corridor the next day when she saw him moving towards her. 'Sean,' she cried out in disbelief.

He took her in his arms, pressing her close

220

to him. 'Thank God, you're safe.'

'I'm OK. Just a bit shaken up. I've been so worried about you,' she said.

Sean smiled. 'There's no need. How's Ross?'

'He's still in intensive care. The doctors said he'll pull through. He came around this morning briefly. He's been able to give the police a description of the men who shot him.'

Sean nodded. 'At least that's something.' He paused slightly. 'I can't stay, Katrina. I'm only here for one night.'

'I don't understand.'

'It's complicated. But Ross being shot changes everything.' Sean hesitated. 'I'm going to be away for a while. Helping the police with their enquiries. I'm not sure how long.'

Katrina stared at him. 'But why?'

'Let's just say I've got a few things to sort out. Things from the past.'

'And what about us?'

Sean shook his head. 'I need you to stay here. Ross will need someone when he gets out of hospital.'

'Yes . . . but . . . '

He placed a finger on her lips. 'No buts.' He bent down to kiss her.

★ ★ ★

Katrina watched the helicopter set down near the homestead ready to pick up Sean. She wanted to hold on to their night together; those precious few hours when they had lain side by side, their arms clasping each other tightly as if neither had wanted to let go. They had talked about the cottage they would live in. They'd even argued about how many children they would have. She wanted two, he wanted more. Eventually, he'd made love to her. Thinking about *that* brought a flush to her face and a warmth to her heart.

After breakfast, she had tried to hold back the tears. She didn't want to cry, to make it difficult for him to leave. Whatever it was he had to do, seemed important to him.

'When will you be back?' she asked huskily.

'I'm not sure. Depends on lots of things.'

'I don't even know where you are going. Can't you even tell me that?'

He gave a quick smile. 'It's better you don't know.'

She pressed harder. 'To Ireland?'

'I can't say.'

'To Connemara?'

'Katrina . . . ' he growled.

She put her fingers to his lips. 'I know. You can't say. But you can't blame me for trying.'

He grabbed his bag, lifted it. He put his other arm around her shoulders, drawing her in close. Together they walked towards the waiting helicopter. He whispered. 'Five.'

'Five what?' she asked, puzzled.

He didn't answer. His mouth skimmed hers, then he started to walk away.

'Sean?' she called out, still puzzled. 'Five what?'

He threw over his shoulder, grinning. 'Five children.'

She couldn't help but smile. The helicopter lifted. She waved, then waited until the helicopter was out of sight before she turned away. Her throat tightened unbearably. She tried to hold on to Sean's image. Don't cry, she told herself. It won't help. But by the time she reached her room she couldn't stifle the sob that had lodged earlier on in her chest. She sank onto the bed. Sean's towel lay beside her in a crumpled heap. She reached out for it, pressed it against her face and cried.

★　★　★

Danny Maguire picked up the *Irish Times* and settled down to read it for a few minutes. He heard Carrie's mobile phone ring. She answered it. He could see by the look on her face something was wrong.

'They what?' said Carrie furiously. She put

223

her hand over the mouthpiece of the phone and whispered to Maguire, 'The idiots. They shot the wrong man.'

Maguire lowered the newspaper and waited until she finished speaking to the caller before he asked her any more details. 'Well? What happened?'

'The two men we hired in New Zealand have been arrested.'

'And Sean?'

'He's still alive.'

'Damn it,' shot out Maguire. He threw the newspaper down. 'That could cause problems. Sean's going to want to know who tried to kill him.'

Maguire got up and made for the drinks cabinet. He poured two large whiskeys and handed one to his wife. 'We'll get Jessie to ring Katrina. Find out what's going on.' His gaze settled on Jessie sitting opposite him reading a magazine. 'Are you game, Sis?'

Jessie nodded.

Within minutes, Maguire had the information he wanted. 'Are you sure?' he asked Jessie.

'I'm sure. Sean's still at the station. So is Katrina. It was Sean's cousin Ross who was shot.'

'Right,' said Maguire. Still, he felt uneasy.

'You said no one else would get hurt,'

accused Jessie. She directed her words at Carrie sitting there with a sour look on her face.

'It wasn't our fault,' retaliated Carrie, glaring at her. 'Someone mucked up.'

Jessie looked worried. 'All the same . . . '

'Look, sometimes these things happen,' added Carrie impatiently.

'You mean like the explosion three years ago,' Jessie threw at her. 'You never told me you were planting a bomb. You could have killed me as well.'

Carrie's mouth tightened. 'We've already been over this. We didn't tell you because we didn't want to worry you. Besides we knew you had the day off from the bookshop, so you were safe.'

'Carrie's right,' her brother said eventually. 'You can't blame Carrie for what happened. Either then or now.'

Why did her brother have to stick up for her, thought Jessie resentfully? 'I never get a say in anything.'

Her brother put his arm around her, gave her a squeeze. ''Course you do. But everything we do has to go through the Army Council. It's top secret.'

'I think you should leave Sean alone,' said Jessie. 'What's done is done.'

'You're just trying to protect your friend

Katrina,' sneered Carrie.

Jessie narrowed her eyes. Sometimes she hated Carrie so much she could almost strangle her. 'So what if I am? She's never done anything to you.' Jessie remembered the time when her brother and Carrie had paid Katrina a visit at her London flat. It had been Carrie's idea. They'd found out about Sean and thought Katrina might have known where he'd gone. Not that they found anything out anyway with their heavy handed methods. Katrina hadn't known anything. If they had only asked her, she could easily have got the same information from Katrina without any fuss.

'So what will you do about Sean now?' added Jessie.

Maguire gave a grunt, but it was Carrie who answered. 'I don't know. We'll have to think about it.'

Christ, I didn't ask her, thought Jessie. 'Danny?'

Maguire poured another whiskey. 'We've got more pressing things to worry about.'

'That's right,' added Carrie sharply. 'And it would help if you didn't hassle us.'

For goodness' sake, thought Jessie, furiously. She was just trying to be helpful. She got up and walked out, slamming the door behind her.

Maguire was about to go after her when Carrie caught his arm. 'Let her cool off for a while. She's too highly strung.'

'I wish you'd try to get onside with her,' he said. 'I'm always the one who has to smooth things over.'

Carrie gave a sigh. 'I do try, but she never listens to me.'

Maguire took a mouthful of whiskey. God, women. He could never understand them. He'd rather work with men anytime. He turned his thoughts to the shipment of electronics that had just arrived, sitting outside in a white van. Khalis had picked them up from the beach. A fishing boat had brought them in during the night and delivered them to a prearranged spot.

It would take them a few weeks to sort out the equipment in the dungeons. Meanwhile, Carrie had seen to the guest-house side of things, taking in some customers, so as to allay any suspicions locally. He had to give it to her, she could turn her hand to anything. In another life, he reckoned she had probably been an actress.

* * *

Katrina's mind was on the phone call she'd received earlier from Jessie. Rushing inside to answer it, in case it was to do with Ross, she had been surprised to hear Jessie's voice.

'Is it a good time to talk, Katrina?' Jessie had asked.

'Couldn't be better. I'm here on my own,' replied Katrina, pleased to hear from her friend. She had told Jessie everything. How Ross had been shot and that Sean had really been an undercover police officer all along.

'Sean's asked me to stay. We're going to make our home here,' she said. Katrina was also about to tell her that Sean had left the station, but Sean had warned her against saying anything to anyone about his whereabouts. Katrina decided to turn the conversation back to her friend to avoid lying. 'And what about you, Jessie? Is everything going OK?'

'I'm fine. I'm in Ireland for a while. Just outside of Clifden. Some old dear wanted to sell her father's collection of books, so I'm checking them out. It's nice to be in Ireland again. I miss the place.'

There was a strained note in Jessie's voice, thought Katrina. She couldn't help feeling a sense of unease.

'Are you sure everything's OK?' asked Katrina.

Jessie gave a short laugh. 'I'm fine. Honest I am. Just tired, that's all.'

After Jessie had rung off it occurred to

Katrina that Jessie had said she was in Connemara, the same region she suspected Sean was going to. Pure coincidence, thought Katrina, shrugging off her concerns.

★ ★ ★

'I want out of this hospital. It's already been a month. If they don't discharge me, I'll do it myself,' Ross ranted.

Katrina could see Ross was in a foul temper by the scowl on his face. He paced up and down the room.

'The doctor wants to keep you in longer. He doesn't think you're ready to go home,' she said, trying to pacify him.

The nurse also tried to remonstrate with Ross, but he proved impossible. Finally, she fetched the registrar, Dr Moore.

'What's all this about?' he asked.

Ross explained. 'I just want to get home. It's not that I don't appreciate everything you've done: I do. The medical staff have been great, but I need to recuperate at home now.'

'Fine,' replied the registrar. 'We can let you go if you sign a consent form for discharge.'

'No problem,' said Ross, breaking into a smile. He signed the document which the nurse provided and handed it back to the registrar. On the way out, Ross shook hands with the nursing staff, thanking them again.

Once he arrived home, he wouldn't sit still, but insisted on doing light jobs around the farm. At least his temper had improved, noted Katrina.

Anna turned up the next day clutching an armful of books and a tin of cookies.

'I thought Ross might like these,' she said. When Ross had been in hospital she had been frantic with worry and couldn't do enough to help, often sitting at his bedside.

'Ross is in the living-room. Go right on through,' Katrina told her.

After a few minutes, Katrina found them both deep in conversation. 'Anyone for coffee?' she asked.

'No thanks,' answered Anna, rising to her feet. 'I have to be on my way. But I'll stop off again tomorrow.'

After seeing Anna to the door, Katrina took Ross a hot drink. 'I see you're making the most of it,' mused Katrina, setting the cup beside him.

Ross gave a grin. 'Too right. I didn't think it would take something like this to bring Anna running though.'

Katrina laughed. 'You're a rogue, Ross.'

He grinned. 'Maybe, but you can't blame me. Now all I have to do is convince her to marry me.'

Katrina raised her brows. 'That's fast work. You think she'll take you on?'

'I don't know. But I'm going to try my damned best.'

Somehow, Katrina didn't doubt him.

★ ★ ★

Anna arrived early the next day to find Ross chopping kindling. She put her hands on her hips. 'I thought I'd find you here. Don't you think you ought to be taking it easy?'

Ross threw her a quick glance. 'Nope.' Thump. The axe hit the lump of wood with force, splitting it in two. He bent down and put one piece back on the block.

Her eyes narrowed. 'Well, I do.'

Ross lowered the axe, then turned to face her. 'Any particular reason why?'

She moved closer. 'Your shoulder isn't quite healed. Katrina said you were in pain last night. She had to up your dose of painkillers.'

'Katrina had no right to tell you that. The last thing I want is for my shoulder to seize up. Exercise won't do me any harm. I need to keep working.' He lifted the next log and placed it in front of him. Anna moved into his way, grabbing his arm.

'Ross, will you quit it right now? I don't know what you're trying to prove.'

He lowered the axe, then dropped it on the ground. He wasn't trying to prove anything. He was working out his frustration. A man oughtn't to think about a woman twenty-four hours a day, but since Anna had been calling in every day for the past three weeks, he couldn't do anything else. He caught her around the waist as she tried to step back. 'Hold on there. For a woman who's leading me a merry dance, you're showing a lot of concern over my welfare. I don't get it.'

She looked indignant. 'I'm worried about you. And why shouldn't I? We've always been friends.' She tried to twist out of his grasp but he held on tight.

'Friends?' He rose a brow. 'Maybe we could be more than that if you'd let it.'

'Let me go, Ross. Brute strength doesn't impress me.'

Gentling his grip, but with his arm still around her waist holding her firm, he replied lightly. 'Hold on now. You don't mean that. I've done nothing but look after you. What about the time I saved you when you were ten years old? After a dare, you swam out to the middle of the river to sit on that boulder. Only you were too scared to swim back. If it hadn't been for me going out to rescue you, you'd have been there for hours, crying your heart out.'

232

Defiance flashed in her eyes. 'I would have swum back eventually. You just happened to be there at the time.'

'Yeah, sure. Or what about when you were late home after the school dance. I covered for you. Said you were at our place, that I'd invited you home for coffee. Saved you a grounding for a month.'

'That was a long time ago, when we were teenagers. We're a lot older now. I can take care of myself.'

'Is that so? So how come you asked me to fix your car yesterday?'

'You didn't have to do it.'

'No, that's true, I didn't. But doesn't that tell you something?'

Her eyes flickered. 'Maybe.'

His voice deepened. 'So what's really going on here, Anna?'

She shifted uncomfortably. 'OK. You want the truth? I . . . I don't want things to get serious between us and find out it all falls through. I just couldn't bear it.'

'Maybe you ought to trust me for once? I'm not the kind of man to dump you like the last boyfriend you had.'

She looked taken aback. 'You know about that? Who told you?'

'Who do you think? Your brother, Phil. He was worried about you.'

Her mouth set tight. 'I'll kill him.'

Ross shook his head. 'No, you won't. He did you a favour. Now I know why you've been backing off every time I come near you. You've been hurt once and now you're scared.'

She cocked her head. 'I'm not.'

'Fibber.' He gave an exasperated sigh. 'You don't need to be afraid. Not with me.' He leaned closer. 'Let me show you, Anna. Maybe then you'll change your mind.'

Her eyes widened, though he noticed she didn't move away. He continued. 'Last time I kissed you, you slapped my face,' he reminded her. 'Only trouble was, you left marks. When Sean saw them, he wouldn't let it rest. Neither would the other fellas. They baited me until I felt ready to punch their lights out.'

Anna looked shamefaced. 'I'm sorry. I really am.'

Ross leaned forward until his mouth was very near hers. He saw a glimmer of a smile. His heart leaped. Perhaps, he was getting somewhere at last. His mouth brushed hers, then moved to her jaw.

'Anna, you drive me crazy,' he murmured. 'But a nice kind of crazy. Give me a chance, huh?'

She shook her head. 'It wouldn't work;

we're both too stubborn. Besides, you've always been more like a brother to me than . . . ' She floundered searching for the right word.

'A lover?' he finished for her.

She nodded.

Ouch, he thought. That hurt. 'If you're looking for flowers and chocolates, that isn't me, so don't go expecting them. But I can find you the prettiest gemstone in the river, or even bring you a baby lamb as a pet. And I'll never let you down. Promise.'

He could see she was melting. He pushed further. 'It's up to you: this is the last time I'm going to ask you out. Take it or leave it.'

She bit her lip. 'OK,' she answered slowly. 'What time did you say that movie was playing in town?'

Ross's smile broadened, then he hugged her close and whispered in her ear. 'That's my girl. I'll pick you up at six.'

★ ★ ★

'Something isn't right,' said Katrina to Ross. 'Sean isn't returning any of my calls.'

Ross shrugged. 'Stop worrying. He'll be back as soon as he can. You know he's helping the government on an official matter. He told you that.'

'Really? So what is this official matter?'

'It's something to do with those men who shot me.'

'I think it's more than that.' Katrina gave him a thoughtful look. 'Seems to me no one is saying anything. That's the trouble. Makes me wonder why he *had* to leave. Hasn't that crossed your mind?'

Ross shrugged. 'Sean can take care of himself.'

'That's not the point.' Katrina gave an exasperated sigh. 'Waiting like this is getting me down. I've been thinking, now that you're a lot better, and can manage on your own, I'm going to Wellington to see Sean.'

'You are?'

Katrina nodded. 'Any objections?'

'Plenty. It doesn't make sense you going all that way when Sean could return any day. Besides, he may not even be there.'

'You don't know that,' she reminded him.

Ross hoped he could convince Katrina to leave well alone. He knew perfectly well why Sean hadn't returned, but he'd given his word to Sean he wouldn't tell Katrina. Sean hadn't given him all the details but he knew it was something to do with that last assignment he'd been on in London. Somehow he had to talk Katrina out of going.

Her voice broke miserably. 'You don't understand: I have to see him. There's something I need to talk to him about. Something urgent. Will you drive me to the airport?'

'No.'

'If you don't take me, I'll get someone else. Anna has already offered.'

'She has?'

Katrina nodded. 'Please.'

'I don't think it's a good idea,' reiterated Ross.

'You don't understand.' Katrina took a deep breath. 'I'm pregnant,' she confessed. 'That's why I need to see Sean.'

★　★　★

In the end, Katrina arranged with Anna to pick her up two days later when Ross was away all day checking on the stock. She knew he wouldn't be pleased to find her gone but as far as she was concerned it was something she just had to do.

The Security Intelligence Services was situated in a large building on Aitken Street in Wellington. Katrina had consulted a map that Anna had given her and after catching a taxi from the airport, she'd been dropped off a few yards away from the entrance. Apprehension coursed through her as she approached.

Earlier on, she'd phoned, hoping to talk to

Sean again but had been put through to Stephen Powell. He'd refused her request to talk to Sean, instead asking her to come in to see him just before midday.

Once inside the foyer, two security guards stood on either side of the door. She had to go through a security check. After clearance, which only took a few minutes, she found the lift that took her up to the seventh floor. Katrina glanced at her watch, noting that she was a little early. Better to be early and prepared, she thought, her heart starting to thud as the lift doors opened.

At reception she gave her name and was asked to take a seat. Soon afterwards, another woman appeared and sat next to her, and smiled briefly. Katrina returned her smile, then flicked through a glossy magazine lying on the coffee table, hoping to calm her nerves. She tried to concentrate but found she couldn't. The same question kept going around in her mind. What would Sean say when she told him she was pregnant? They both wanted children, but he'd said it would be better to wait until the cottage was fixed up. It would take a few months to renovate. While they could live there amidst the mess of renovating, having children straight away would make things more difficult. Still, she just needed some reassurance from him.

A voice called out, 'Katrina Jones.'

Katrina started. She stood up, and quickly moved forward to the man standing near reception.

'I'm Katrina Jones,' she said calmly, holding the man's gaze.

Powell introduced himself, shaking her hand. 'This way, please,' he said politely, holding the door open in front of her. Once they reached his office, he offered her a seat.

'Thank you.' She sat opposite him on the leather chair.

'I'm sorry we weren't able to talk to you on the phone,' apologized Powell, 'but everything to do with Sean is classified.'

Katrina tensed. There was a few seconds of silence. 'So where is Sean?'

'I'm sorry I can't tell you exactly. Suffice to say, he's returned to Ireland.'

'He's gone to Connemara, hasn't he?'

Powell angled his head. 'I can't comment on that. However, as you've probably realized, Sean had to attend to a matter of some urgency.'

Katrina mulled over his words, her voice quiet when she spoke. 'Are you saying that Sean *had* to leave the country?'

Powell hesitated. 'It was in his best interests to do so.'

Katrina leaned forward, her eyes glinting.

'That's what I thought all along. If you don't tell me exactly what's going on, I'll contact the media straight away. I'm sure they would be very interested in this story.'

Her threat didn't sit well. Powell's reply was swift and cutting. 'You do that and we'll have no choice but to detain you in prison.' He added, less harshly, 'Besides, I'm sure you wouldn't want to cause Sean any harm. Letting people know where he's gone could place him in a lot of danger. It could even cause his death.'

Katrina gasped. 'That's blackmail.'

'Call it what you like. But those are the facts.'

Katrina's mind reeled. She had to find out more. 'Is all this connected to Ross being shot?'

Powell nodded. 'It is. I've just read the full police report. You do realize it was Sean they were after?'

'No one has actually told us that, but we suspected as much. Have you any idea why?'

'The truth is we don't know.' Powell hesitated again. 'That's part of the reason Sean decided to return to Ireland. Unfinished business as they say.'

'Ireland? Connemara? Is it something to do with the assignment he was on three years ago?'

'Again, I'm sorry. I'm not able to answer that.'

Frustration shot through her. 'You mean, you won't answer.' When she saw there was no further response from Powell, she added smoothly, 'OK then. I suppose I have no alternative but to return to Glenroy. But if Sean makes contact, will you let me know how he is? Please?'

Powell smiled. 'I promise I'll do my best. I'll pass on any messages he sends you. We're expecting him to be in touch in a few days.'

Katrina's resolve deepened. If Powell thought she was satisfied with what he had told her, he was mistaken. She had to find Sean. She hadn't come all this way to lose him again.

And there was only one way she could do that.

Powell escorted her out of his office and bid her goodbye. Then, while waiting for the lift, she watched him go into another office and shut the door behind him. The lift doors opened. Katrina made no effort to step inside the lift. Instead, she whirled around and made for the receptionist sitting at the front desk.

'I'm sorry, I accidentally left my handbag in Mr Powell's office.'

The receptionist lifted the phone. 'I'll just page him.'

Katrina gave her a reassuring smile. 'Please, don't bother him. I'm sure he's got enough to do. I'll just nip through and collect it. It will only take me a moment.'

Without another word, Katrina made for his office, hoping the receptionist wouldn't follow her. Once inside, she leaned against the door breathing heavily. Her heart pounded in her chest. Thank goodness, her handbag was still there, where she'd pushed it under Powell's desk with her feet. She didn't bother to retrieve it. Instead, with quick strides, she made for his desk and flicked through the papers stacked in a pile. She didn't know exactly what she was looking for. But if she could only find something, anything, that might give her an indication as to where Sean might have gone . . . and why. She gave an exasperated sigh. Nothing. She saw the grey filing cabinet against the wall. The key was still in it. She turned it, and pulled open the drawer. Buff-coloured files and loose papers overflowed in the green filing pockets. Everything was labelled neatly and methodically. He obviously had an efficient secretary, she noted. Katrina ran her fingers over the labels. Finally she came to the one she was looking for: Sean McKinlay. She pulled out the file and laid it on the desk. A quick glance at the clock on the wall said she'd been in the office for five minutes. Powell would probably be back any time.

She had to find where Sean had gone to in

Ireland. She started to read the first page in the file when she heard the door handle turn.

* * *

Sean had several hours' sleep before the alarm woke him at seven o'clock. He lay in bed for a few minutes thinking things over. When he'd stepped off the plane at Dublin Airport the night before, he'd been unprepared for the rush of feelings that hit him. He was walking on Irish soil for the first time in years. A prearranged contact from the Garda had picked him up outside the airport building. Knowing Sean had come from New Zealand, the man had asked him about the country and Sean had obliged, answering all his questions patiently. At Sean's suggestion, they had stopped off for a meal and Sean had his first pint of Guinness in a long time. Smooth, black and cold. The sound of a fiddle in the background, amongst the murmur of voices discussing the troubles in the North, had made him realize that some things hadn't changed no matter how long he'd been away. He decided afterwards it was the simple things he'd missed. The oldness of the buildings, the Irish accent and simply walking along the deserted white beaches at dusk watching the waves beat the shoreline as they had done throughout time.

By the time he reached the hotel it had been almost midnight.

Sean glanced at his watch again reluctant to leave the warmth of his bed. But if he didn't get a move on he'd be late.

After a quick shower and breakfast he'd made his way to a briefing at Garda Headquarters in Phoenix Park, Dublin, arranged by Special Branch C3 section. The briefing took all morning. Photographs were pinned up on the wall.

'Any questions, Sean?' asked Detective Inspector Harvey.

'One or two. Are the local Garda in on this?'

Harvey shook his head. 'No, it's too risky. Word could leak out. We'll have a special team standing by to give you backup, if need be. We'll expect a daily report from you. If we don't hear at the pre-arranged time, we'll send one of our men in to investigate. But remember,' Harvey emphasized, 'it's only an intelligence op. We only want confirmation that al-Qaeda are involved and evidence that the castle is being used as a bomb factory. Once you've achieved your objective, you can pull out and we'll send in a team to make arrests.'

Sean nodded.

Harvey's forehead creased in concern. 'I

still think we ought to wire you up.'

'No,' said Sean adamantly. 'If I get caught, they'll know we're on to them.'

'It's up to you. But let us know if you change your mind.' Harvey pointed to the map pinned to the wall. 'Have you studied the layout of the place?'

Sean didn't need a map. He knew the place well. He'd spent his teenage years roaming the corridors and the dungeons, since his adoptive father had worked there part-time as a handyman. Sean nodded. 'As well as I can.'

'Any thought on how you're going to get into the castle?'

That he wasn't about to tell them: the less they knew, the better. 'I'll think of something.'

'One more thing,' added Harvey. 'You'll have one of our new cars. A Subaru Forester 2.5XT. Usually reserved for our undercover officers. So pick up the keys before you go.'

The rest of the afternoon Sean put in some firearms practice. On previous assignments, he'd been issued with a pistol but had never used it, relying more on his wits for survival. This time it might be different, he thought, slipping the .226 SIG Sauer pistol into his holster.

★　★　★

Stephen Powell strode into his office looking furious. 'Ms Jones, what the hell are you doing?'

Katrina stepped forward, away from the desk. 'I'm sorry . . . I left my handbag here. I just came back to collect it.'

Powell looked at the desk, his gaze settling on the file Katrina had removed from the filing cabinet. His eyes narrowed. 'You've been searching my office.'

Katrina said nothing. What could she say? She'd been caught red handed. There was no way she could talk herself out of this.

Her chin lifted defiantly. 'Are you going to arrest me?'

'I'm tempted. But I'll give you a warning instead. Go back to Glenroy, or we'll pull you in for questioning.' He lifted up the file she had been looking at and deposited it back in the filing cabinet and slammed the drawer shut. Then he swung around to face her. 'How much of that file did you read?'

She decided the truth was the best. 'Not much, only the first page. I just want to find out where Sean is. And why he's gone? That's all.'

'Don't think of leaving the country, Ms Jones, or we'll have you arrested. Now please leave, before I change my mind,' he said sharply.

Katrina's thoughts reeled as she walked out the SIS building. Thank God, she'd had time to find out where Sean had gone though not his exact address. She was no wiser as to why though. Obviously, it all had something to do with Cardell Castle in Connemara. But it was what she had read at the bottom of the page that had really stunned her.

Jessie had connections to the IRA. But how. Why?

8

When Katrina arrived back at the station she told Ross what had happened. 'Do you know what that means?'

Ross looked thoughtful. 'Jessie could have passed on information about Sean.'

'Exactly. I gave her a copy of the private investigator's report in Boston. I even told her Sean was in New Zealand. She knew his whereabouts. There has to be a link.' Katrina thought quickly. 'If I hadn't given her that information, you might not have got shot.'

'It wasn't your fault,' said Ross.

'But I still feel to blame. And now Jessie is in Connemara. At least that's what she said to me on the phone. I never thought anything of it at the time but now I'm not so sure. It's just too much of a coincidence.' She shook her head. 'I'm not staying here and doing nothing, especially after what happened before.'

Ross looked wary. 'What do you mean?'

'I'm scared I'll lose Sean. That something will keep us apart.' She paused slightly. 'He could even be in danger.'

Ross said worriedly, 'Sean's no fool. I'm

sure that wherever he is, whatever he's doing, he'll have some sort of backup.'

'But we don't know that. Powell wouldn't tell me a thing. If Sean is on a special op, things can go wrong. Just like they did before.' She faced him squarely. 'I'm going to Ireland to find him. And if Jessie has connections to the IRA, I can find out about that too. I'm leaving on the next available flight.'

Ross exhaled. 'That's not a good idea: I'll report you to Stephen Powell.'

'No, you won't, because you're coming with me.'

'Me?' He paused slightly, taken aback. 'I don't have the money, Katrina. You know we're in dire financial straits with the farm. I daren't borrow any more. Besides, Dad needs me here. We're already short on farm staff with Sean being away.'

'Don't worry about that. I've got plenty of money to cover our expenses. You can even hire an extra hand on the station while you're away, if need be. I'll pay for that too.'

Ross could only look at her in amazement. Then he laughed out loud. 'I don't believe it.'

She frowned. 'What's so funny?'

'We've been employing a rich woman to be our housekeeper.'

She couldn't resist a smile. 'Not exactly

rich, but I've got enough to help us out for a few weeks anyway. So what do you say?'

He hesitated. 'Tempting, but the answer is still no. It's too risky.'

Katrina had a feeling he was weakening. Maybe she'd push a little further.

'Too late. I've already booked the air tickets,' she added.

He sighed, took two steps closer. 'You know something. I had a feeling you would. But we're not using them.'

'Why not?' she asked, puzzled.

'Because the airports will have been warned to look out for us. We'd never even make it past passport control.' He looked thoughtful. 'One of my old university friends has a private pilot's licence. He'll take us to Australia. Then we'll catch an international flight to Ireland.'

Katrina smiled again. 'Even better. I knew you'd think of something.'

★ ★ ★

A few hours later, Ross stood in the doorway of the greenhouse, his gaze travelling along the rows of herbs neatly potted in terracotta containers and displayed on a wooden table. Anna stood there, snipping off herbs destined for the local market. A couple of years ago, she'd set up a small business growing herbs and selling them in supermarkets and gardening shops in town.

Her cheeks were flushed in the heat, her mane of auburn hair tumbling wildly about her shoulders. She wore a tight, sleeveless cotton top, low cut, along with blue faded frayed shorts that looked almost indecent.

'Thought I'd find you here,' he said, leaning up against the door frame.

Startled, she jerked back, realized who it was and smiled. 'This is a surprise. You must be feeling a lot better.'

'I am. Lots.' He stepped forward, flexing his arm. 'See? It's working just fine. I told you chopping wood would do me good.'

'In that case, you're just the person I need right now. I need a bit of muscle.'

He arched a brow. 'You do?' he mused.

'Uh-huh.' She laid the scissors down on the bench, and pointed to a high shelf. 'Can you reach up for that large container of fertilizer? Please . . . '

'Sure I can.' He squeezed past her getting a whiff of perfume. It made his head swim.

With no effort at all he lifted the large box and set it down on the ground, beside her. 'There you are. Anything else I can do?'

'Nope, but thanks anyway.' She made no effort to open it. 'I was going to ring you. See

251

if you wanted to come over for lunch today. Baked an apple pie. Your favourite.'

'That's thoughtful of you.' Damn. And double damn. Just when things were going his way. 'I would have loved to stay, but I can't. Got too much to do.'

She gave a disappointed sigh. 'Oh, that's a pity.'

His gut clenched tight. 'I've got something to tell you, Anna.'

Her gaze held his, questioning. 'That sounds serious. What is it?'

'I'm leaving for Ireland tomorrow. Katrina is going as well.'

'Ireland,' she repeated in disbelief. 'You've got to be joking. But . . . but what on earth for?'

'It's to do with Sean.'

She stared at him for a moment. 'Is he in some kind of trouble?'

The less Anna knew, the better, he decided. 'He could be. We just want to find him. Bring him back home.'

'I thought there might have been something wrong. It didn't seem like Sean to go off so suddenly like that. Whenever I asked Katrina about it, she clammed up tight. Then she finally confessed when she asked me to take her to the airport.' Anna held his gaze. 'You'll miss my birthday party then.'

Ross groaned. 'I know. I'm sorry. I really am.' He felt bad letting her down. But that's just the way things were. 'I'll be back as soon as I can. I promise. We'll celebrate together, just the two of us. I'll take you out for dinner. Do you fancy that?'

'Dinner?' she said surprised. Then she gave a laugh. 'You mean the local hamburger place in town?'

Ross shook his head. 'No. I mean a proper dinner. In a fancy restaurant. I'll even wear a bow tie. We'll have champagne and all the trimmings. Sound good?'

She laughed again. 'It sounds wonderful. But hang on a minute, you don't have a bow tie. At least, not one I've ever seen.'

Surely she could see he was serious. 'Dad's got one. He inherited it from my grandfather. I'll borrow it.'

Gently he took her fingers in his, then drew her into his arms. Touching her sent his blood pumping. All the same, he had to go slow, woo her in stages, just like breaking in a high-spirited horse. His voice lowered.

'Wait for me, Anna. At least promise me that.'

She nodded. 'I'll wait.'

★ ★ ★

Sean stopped off at the graveyard. He had been in two minds whether to visit his parents' graves. For one reason, it would distract him, make him moody, reliving memories he preferred to forget. He needed to focus on what he had to do. Yet another reason, perhaps, the most important of all, strengthened his belief that what he was doing, returning to Ireland like this, was the *right thing* to do. Sure his hand had been forced. But maybe all along things needed to be finished once and for all, so he and Katrina would be free. The more he thought about it, the more he realized the past three years had been a waiting time. Waiting until all the important pieces were ready to be played out again. In other words, fate.

With quick strides, he walked up the hill, past the graves of those who'd lived centuries ago. Some had died during the two world wars. Others during the Easter Rising. It seemed ironic that his parents were buried among them. Innocent casualties of a war where there were never any winners.

Finally, he came to their graves, lying side by side, sharing a granite headstone. In his hand he held a bunch of red roses. He found a white plastic vase, lying nearby, and filling it up at a tap near the church wall, he arranged the flowers, then carried the vase back and laid it gently below the headstone. His mother had always loved roses, he remembered.

It wasn't the first time he'd been back to visit the graves since they had died, but somehow it seemed different. The sadness lodged inside his chest was still there, but this time he felt more hope for the future. Katrina's image rushed into his mind unexpectedly. Her laughter, the way she spoke. She was what had made the difference, he realized. He wondered if his parents knew about her. Somehow they would, he thought, with a smile. He hoped so anyway.

He was just about to go when he heard footsteps. It was the priest from the church.

'Relatives of yours?' he asked quietly.

Sean told him.

'Ah, yes. I remember them well. It was a terrible thing,' he said sympathetically. 'You're welcome to come into the church for a while. Perhaps, it will bring you some solace.'

Solace? Sean shook his head. 'Another time maybe. But thanks.'

The priest smiled his understanding, and gave him a blessing. Sean started to walk away, feeling glad he had stopped by. Someday he'd come back with Katrina.

★ ★ ★

A few days later Sean arrived at Connemara. He'd thought about staying in a hotel at Clifden, but decided that it would be better to stay with his adoptive father, Finney McLoughlin, who lived on the edge of the castle estate. That way he could blend in easily. No one would think it odd a son returning home for a few days' holiday. It would give him the cover he needed.

Of all the places in Ireland, the terrorism camp was in his backyard, Sean thought ironically. It seemed a bit bizarre, yet why not? Cardell Castle was just one of the many castles sold off to foreign investors and it was situated in an isolated area. Ideal for their purpose.

Sean pulled up outside the whitewashed cottage just after seven in the morning, noting the curtains were still closed. Black smoke puffed from the chimney. Sean rapped on the door, then walked in. He called out from the hallway. No answer.

In the living-room, Finney had fallen asleep in the chair, his chin resting on his chest. A fire blazed in the hearth beside him. Sean shook him gently on the shoulder. The man opened his eyes hazily, then blinked. His crinkled face broke into a grin. 'Sean, me lad. Tell me I'm not dreaming or somethin'.'

Sean laughed, grasped Finney's hand in his

and shook it warmly. 'If you were dreaming, I'd be an angel with wings delivering you a bottle of whiskey and a fat cigar.'

'I see you've not lost your sense of humour.' Finney struggled to his feet. 'What a surprise, me lad. So what brings you back to these parts then? Something important, I'm thinking.'

Sean nodded. 'You could say that.'

Finney grunted. 'In that case, I'll make us a cup of tea. Then you can sit yourself down and tell me about it.' He gave Sean a scrutinizing look. 'You're looking in good shape.'

Sean grinned. 'You know me. Plenty of hard graft, working outdoors.'

'Aye, well I can see you've come from warmer climes with a tan like that.'

'You don't miss much. But you're right. I've been in New Zealand. Got a job on a high country station. Some relatives of my mother's own it.'

'Eh? New Zealand. Well, fancy that. I've always had a hankering to go there. Might have too, if I'd had my way. I was doing a course on tractors, way back in the 1960s, when I met a New Zealander. Canny chap he was. He offered me a job on his farm. But Mary didn't want to go. She didn't want to leave her mother who was ailing.' Finney shook his head. 'I suppose I can't blame her.'

'I'm sorry about Mary,' said Sean regretfully. 'If I could have got back for the funeral I would have. But by the time I got the message, it was all over. I was on a special op in London at the time.' Sean paused briefly. 'Did you get the flowers I sent?'

'Aye I did, lad, thanks. A big bunch it was, too. I even saved one flower and put it in the back of our Prayer Book.' The old man gave a sigh. 'Mary's been gone these three years past. But don't fret yourself over it, me boy . . . you've been away in foreign parts. I don't blame you for grabbing these opportunities as they come. I would have done the same if I had my time again.'

If only he could have been there to carry the coffin, thought Sean. He'd always be grateful to Finney and Mary for taking him in after his parents had been murdered. They had been kind souls.

'So you left the police force then?' asked Finney. 'Never thought I'd see the day.'

Sean nodded. 'I left for a while. But I've been persuaded to come back. Something's come up.'

'Ah, now would that be to do with the castle?'

'What makes you ask that?'

'Something my cousin told me. There's an

Arab who turned up a couple of weeks ago. She thought he seemed a bit odd. Margaret goes in to cook for them when they've got guests. You'll have heard they turned the place into a guest house. Bed and breakfast. But there you go.'

'Can I talk to Margaret?' asked Sean, interested.

'You can when she gets back. She's off on one of those package holidays to Spain. Not due back for another week.'

Damn. She might have been able to identify the Arab. It could well have been Hannad Khalis.

'Do you know where in Spain she might have gone?'

Finney rubbed his chin. 'Not offhand. But I can find out for you.'

Sean reached for his briefcase and took out three photos. 'Take a look at these. Have you seen any of these people? Maybe in the village or walking around the place?'

Finney reached for his glasses on the mantelpiece, slipping them on over his nose. He peered at the photos, one by one, then jabbed at the third one. 'He looks familiar. I think I've seen him walking around the estate.'

The photo was of Danny Maguire. 'You sure?'

'Aye, I'm sure.' After a few seconds Finney added. 'Is he a criminal?'

'They all are.'

'So that's why you're here.'

Sean smiled. 'Partly. And to see you as well.'

'Good. That means you'll be staying.' Finney laughed. 'I'd best make that cup of tea then.' He moved out of sight into the kitchen. There was a slight pause and a rattle of cutlery as a drawer was pulled open.

While waiting, Sean took in the cramped, untidy cottage. He couldn't remember exactly how long it had been since he'd been here. Several years perhaps. He used to keep in regular contact by phone, but since he'd been working undercover it had been difficult. On that last assignment in London, he'd only sent the odd letter or made an occasional phone call.

His gaze settled on the mantelpiece. He moved forward to look at the photos. The large black and white one in a frame was of Finney's family: a daughter and son. Another photo showed four other adopted children. Surprisingly, also a tattered photo of himself taken on his own when he was about fourteen years old.

Finney popped his head through the doorway, his large hand curving round the doorframe.

260

'I knew you'd come back some day since this is where your roots are, me lad.'

Finney was right, Sean decided. Now that he was back, he couldn't ignore where he had come from. Nor did he want to.

★　★　★

Sean picked up the binoculars and adjusted the lens as he looked through the salt-stained window of the thatched cottage. He zoomed in close. 'There's two cars parked outside. One a white Renault and the other a dark green Ford Capri,' he said to Finney standing next to him. 'There's no one up yet, by the looks of it.'

'I've just been speaking to the gardener who lives next door,' Finney said as he took off his warm jacket, revealing shabby dark overalls underneath. 'A white van has been coming and going these past few weeks. Rumour has it there's some electrical work being done at the castle but he's not so sure. If you ask me, Sean me lad, something odd is definitely going on up there.'

Sean lowered the binoculars slightly. 'That's why I'm here, checking things out.'

He swung the binoculars towards the sea. Seagulls wheeled high above the cliffs as they searched for leftover bits of fish. Dawn had come only minutes before revealing a faint mist hovering over the surrounding country-side. He swung the binoculars to the left, skimming across the jagged cliffs. A crescent of a white sandy beach came into view. For a few seconds, he watched fishermen pushing their currachs into the water. Nothing much had changed, thought Sean. The locals still relied on fishing to provide an income.

His gaze roved over the castle perched on the cliff, absorbing every detail. Dark, bleak and unforgiving, the castle had stood for centuries upon that cliff top defying battles and the rogue elements of weather.

When he'd first arrived here as a teenager, the castle had fascinated him. He'd spend many an hour roaming through the place when Finney worked there as a handyman. It had previously belonged to generations of the Gallagher family but the last owner hadn't any descendants apart from a distant cousin somewhere in South Africa, who hadn't wanted to keep it, so it had been sold.

Sean grimaced. Now, terrorism lay inside the walls. Somehow after three years of living in New Zealand, he had thought the fight had been over for him. But now that he was back, the adrenaline flowing, the challenge of a mission had him living on the edge again. Perhaps, he had missed that type of life more than he realized. Yet he had been grateful for those peaceful years in the high country — a steady, rhythmic life dictated by the seasons, where he didn't have to keep looking over his shoulder all the time to see if anyone was following him. But now his past had brought trouble to Glenroy and he had to protect those he loved.

Finney handed Sean a chipped mug of steaming tea and a bacon sandwich. 'Here you are, me lad. Get this down you.'

Sean took a gulp of the hot liquid and choked. 'Jaysus, Mary and Joseph . . . what the hell did you put in?'

Finney grinned as he slapped Sean on the back. 'Thought you'd need a bit of warming up so I put in a good dollop of whiskey, Sean. What's wrong with you, lad? Have you gone soft or something during those years you've been a gallivanting around the globe?' He chuckled.

Finney left Sean to eat his breakfast, then switched on the old valve radio to listen to the morning programme on Raidió na Gaeltachta. A deep voice boomed from the corner. Finney turned the volume down until it was a comforting chatter in the background, then went over to the fire. He lifted the brass poker, black with soot, and poked the embers. Flames shot up the chimney. He bent down and lifted out a slab of peat from the tin bucket, placed it on top of the fire, then hung the poker back on the stand. His bony frame seemed too frail for even the most menial jobs but there was a hidden strength cultivated from years of working outdoors. He stood up, with his back to the heat, rubbing his knuckles and trying to ease the arthritis which always played up first thing in the mornings.

'And what about this girl you've met? Katrina's her name, isn't it? Are you going to get wed then?'

'If she'll have me.'

Finney drained the dregs of his mug. 'Well, 'tis true women can be a bitty temperamental at times, but I know that when Mary went, all I could think of was the good times we had. Aye, we never had much but we were happy. And that's what's important, lad.' He shook his head wisely. 'The years go too fast and before you know it, you'll be old like me and wishing you had all your life afore you again.'

'So I guess I'd better make the most of it then.'

'Aye, that you had.'

Sean thought of the last time he had seen Katrina. Time had been short. After visiting Ross in hospital, they'd gone back to the homestead where they'd spent the night together. There had been unshed tears in her eyes as she had stood outside the homestead and said goodbye. He wanted to reassure her, to tell her that everything would be all right but he knew he couldn't. He didn't know what to expect. He didn't even know if he'd be able to come back to Glenroy.

Five children, he'd said to her. It was the last thing he *had* said. The thought of a family of his own, and the cottage they would renovate together, left him hope there would be a future for them both. He had to hang on to that.

And when the chopper arrived to pick him up, he watched her, never once taking his gaze off her slender figure with her arms outstretched as she waved, her blonde hair blowing softly in the afternoon breeze.

Something had shifted inside of him, intangible, gripping him by the throat until he felt like opening the door and jumping out so he could hold her just one more time. But of course, that was impossible.

Finney gave a frown. 'And does this girl of yours know you've left New Zealand?'

Sean's voice was steady as he met Finney's gaze. 'No. She might have wanted to come with me and it's too dangerous.' He didn't tell Finney, he was still coming to terms with the fact, she meant more to him than anything else in life.

Would she even understand, he wondered, that he'd had no choice but to leave her?

History was repeating itself, he told himself, and there wasn't a damned thing he could do about it right now. Fate had a habit of throwing up obstacles to prevent them being together. Why, he wondered?

Sensing the old man's wish to talk, Sean said plainly, 'What do you think's going on up at the castle?'

The old man pondered for a moment. 'Something shady obviously. You can tell me, lad, I give you my word I won't say a thing to anyone.'

Sean knew he could trust him. 'It's thought a bomb factory is being set up at the castle.' He also told him about the two assassins who had come to New Zealand to kill him.

'Aye, well, the assassins I am surprised at. But I'm not surprised about the bomb factory. I thought it might have been something along those lines.' Finney paused slightly. 'I'm not against dying for the cause, don't get me wrong. Hadn't my own father been struck down during the rising in Dublin in 1916? But there's no sense in innocent people being killed . . . women and children . . . no sense in that at all.' Finney leaned back in the chair for a moment. 'I'm against these bombs too, I am.' He paused

266

watchfully. 'You said an assassin had been sent to New Zealand to kill you. Do you know who wants you dead?'

'I have my suspicions.'

Finney rubbed his hands together. A glint of excitement entered his eyes. 'Right then, so what's the plan, Sean me lad?'

Sean smiled at his enthusiasm. 'Somehow I've got to get into the castle, find the bomb workshop and take some photos.' His brows rose. 'Pretty easy really,' he said wryly. 'Just like every assignment I've ever undertaken.'

'You know the castle like the back of your hand. If anyone can find this workshop, you can,' Finney said determinedly. He rubbed his whiskered chin again. 'They've got a guard dog which is loose at night, so you want to be careful about that. It's a vicious blighter. Nipped me on the leg when I was out poaching one night.'

Sean stood up. 'It's best if I go tonight. Get the layout of the place, check who's about.'

'I'll come with you,' Finney offered.

Sean shook his head. 'I know you mean well, but it's better I go alone.' He picked up his breakfast dishes and took them into the kitchen to wash up. The kitchen, tiny and dark, needed a good paint to freshen it up. God knows how Mary had managed to produce meals for them all in such a confined space. He remembered there had always been wholesome stews and fresh baking in the tins. If he could picture Mary now, it would be to see her with a rolling pin in her hands, her arms covered in flour.

Sean had just turned on the tap when there was a shout from Finney. He rushed through to the living room to see what was wrong.

'There's some people arrived at the castle,' Finney said excitedly, pointing out the window. 'See them — over there.' Finney held out the binoculars and Sean grabbed them, holding them up to the window. He zoomed in quickly. Condensation ran down the cracked window pooling on the windowsill.

'You're right,' murmured Sean. 'Two people.' Sean concentrated on the man who had his arm around the woman's waist. 'They look like tourists. Probably after bed and breakfast.' Sean studied the man. He was tall, wide-shouldered, dressed in smart denim jeans and a warm blue jacket. His blond hair was cut short; a number one haircut as they called it in New Zealand.

Sean's gaze shifted to the woman. Dressed casually in dark jeans with tan leather boots, she wore a thick burgundy woollen coat. He adjusted the lens to get a better view. Sean frowned. The two people looked familiar. The way they moved. The way the woman's hand lifted and brushed her hair back from her face. The woman turned around suddenly.

'What the hell . . . ?' Sean uttered in disbelief. It was Katrina and Ross all this way from New Zealand, knocking on the door of Cardell Castle.

9

Sean made himself take a calming breath. An aching hollow in his stomach started, souring the whiskey he had swallowed earlier on.

He watched Ross turn slightly and point down the driveway. As he moved out the way, Sean got a better look at the man who opened the door. He had dark brown hair, was of average height and dressed in dark clothing. Sean was sure it was Danny Maguire, recognized him from the photo Harvey had given him.

The door opened wider. Maguire was inviting Ross and Katrina inside. Sean watched, willing them to turn around and head right back down the gravel driveway, but it was not to be. Katrina went in first, followed by Ross. Then the door slammed shut behind them.

Sean lowered the binoculars slowly and turned to Finney to tell him exactly who the visitors were.

'I'll go up to the castle on some pretence, Sean. I'll find out what they're doing there for you,' Finney offered.

Sean shook his head. 'No, it's too

dangerous. If you turn up at the castle door, they're going to suspect something. Better to wait for a while and see what happens.' He handed Finney the binoculars and grabbed his black woollen jacket from the peg at the back door. 'Keep an eye on them for me. I'm going down to the village phone box. It's safer if I don't use my mobile phone. They might have a tracking system at the castle.'

As he stepped outside, cold, salty air hit him, filling his lungs rapidly. He climbed over the crumbling stone dyke and hopped down onto the narrow tarmac road. His black woollen hat was pulled low over his forehead. His tousled hair had grown even longer, curling slightly at the ends. Unshaven, he blended in well, looking just like any other villager in these parts who eked a living either from the sea or the land. Some of the clothes he wore weren't his though; the lightweight jacket belonged to Finney's son, Jake, who had left it behind when he'd gone off to Dublin to work as a builder. But as they were of the same build, it fitted perfectly. The black leather boots were slightly too big, but two pairs of thick woollen socks made them comfortable. The rest of his gear consisted of his own denim jeans and a black sweater.

Sean followed the road passing by a shrine on a corner; a petite white statue of the Virgin

271

Mary sitting on a stack of flat rocks. Sean walked briskly, his hands shoved in his jacket pockets until he came to the outskirts of the village.

On the left, perched high on the hill, a small church with its tall spire reached up to the heavens. In front of the church on the sloping and uneven lawn, Celtic stone crosses rose up at all angles in the graveyard.

Sean continued walking. Just around the corner, the bright red phone box stood out distinctly outside a row of stone cottages, their curtains tightly drawn. Everything looked so peaceful, thought Sean. He glanced up. Wisps of smoke spiralled out of the chimneys like tails of blue, every so often blowing in his direction by a vibrant sea breeze.

He had almost reached the phone box when a young woman came out of the door of a cottage and unexpectedly stepped right in front of him. It was obvious she was heading for the same place as he was. Sean cursed silently, realising he would have to let her use the pay phone first.

She smiled warmly. 'Dia dhuit.' *Good morning.*

Sean nodded, then gave her a wide grin. He held the phone box door open for her and stepped out of the way to let her enter. The girl's red hair caught the sunlight turning it to burnished copper. When she smiled again, her smattering of freckles emphasized the creaminess of her skin. 'Go raibh maith agat.' *Thank you.*

He hoped like hell she would get a move on. He needed to make that phone call to Powell quickly — every second counted.

To kill time, Sean wandered along the street a little way, noticing the local shop wasn't open yet and probably wouldn't be until at least nine o'clock. The window was full of the usual paraphernalia in a small village shop. Writing paper, groceries, cosmetics. A shabby tin sign advertising a brand of cigarettes jutted out from the wall above the shop window, squeaking noisily as the wind gusted down the main street. Cigarette advertising was banned, so no doubt a rebellious stand against the powers-that-be.

A white van came careering down the road and Sean turned his face into the shop doorway, his collar pulled upward. It was the white van which Finney had mentioned earlier on. The tyres screeched as the van braked on a sharp bend. They were in a hurry whoever they were. Sean watched the van curiously as it continued up the hill and around another corner until it was out of view. No doubt on its way to the castle.

The door of the phone box opened and Sean hurried towards it. He scrambled into the booth, then slipped in the card, and punched in the number. Detective Inspector Harvey answered within seconds. 'DI Harvey.'

'It's Sean here. Katrina and Ross have turned up at the castle.'

Harvey cursed softly. 'Are you sure?'

'It's definitely them. So what the hell are they doing there?'

'I don't know,' Harvey said uneasily, 'but I suspect they're looking for you.'

'Great. Stating the obvious,' murmured Sean. Sean's fingers tightened around the receiver. 'Powell should have stopped them: that's what we agreed.'

There was a pause as the line crackled, then Harvey said, 'He probably doesn't even know. I talked to him a few days ago. Katrina went to see him. The meeting didn't go well. She told him she was going back to Glenroy. He had no cause to disbelieve her. He also threatened her with imprisonment if she didn't do as she was told.' There was another pause as if he was pondering the situation. 'How the hell did they get past airport security? That's what I'd like to know.'

'Ross has contacts. I suspect he found someone to fly them out of New Zealand.'

Sean glanced upwards. He saw some

movement from one of the cottages. Curtains were drawn back in one sweep and he knew he had better hurry along before people emerged for the day. 'Katrina and Ross being here changes everything. I'm going in to the castle tonight.'

'We'll be ready,' Harvey promised. He didn't tell Sean, there was going to be hell to pay for the slip up.

★ ★ ★

'It's very good of you to offer to phone the garage, Mr Maguire. The last thing we expected was the car breaking down,' said Katrina with a smile.

'That's no problem. Why don't you take a seat in the drawing-room while I ring? I won't be long,' Maguire said politely, showing them the way.

Katrina and Ross followed. The drawing-room could only be described as stately with its high ornate ceiling and large glass chandelier. Maroon velvet curtains hung elegantly from tall leaded windows casting a rich flavour to a room already heavily furnished with antiques. Katrina eyed the silver tea-set standing on the Victorian sideboard, gleaming as it caught the firelight. The huge fireplace completed the picture, throwing out a ferocious heat which a slinky black cat appreciated as it uncurled its body upon the red carpet at the hearth.

She looked up at Ross. He gave her a silent look as if to say, 'We're here, so what do we do now?'

Katrina racked her brains. If the mechanic from the garage came immediately, they would have no choice but to leave since there was no outstanding reason for them to stay any longer. Maybe they should have pretended to break down in the evening, then they would have had a better chance of staying the night.

'I'm thinking,' Katrina whispered.

'Well, you'd better be quick. He'll be back any minute.'

Maguire appeared. 'I just spoke to the local garage. Unfortunately, the mechanic is away just now because some relative has died and he's attending the funeral. They're expecting him back in a day or two . . . if you want to wait until then? Otherwise, we could call the breakdown service in Galway. But then you might as well get a replacement rental car.' Danny looked at them for confirmation. 'That's the best I can do.'

'Well, I guess we're not in any hurry,' said Ross casually. 'The only problem is the bed and breakfast place we stayed in at the village last night is booked up for a few days.' Ross looked at Maguire. 'We saw your sign down the road. I know it said no vacancies but are you sure you can't fit us in anywhere?'

Maguire looked apologetic. 'I'm sorry, but we're really closed at the moment. The electricians are doing some work, renewing the wiring, that sort of thing.'

'That's a pity. Could you suggest somewhere else nearby? We don't want to travel too far.'

Maguire's voice had a slight impatient tone to it. 'Well, I can't really think of anywhere. Your best bet would be to go back to the village and ask there. I'll run you down if you like?'

A woman appeared at the doorway interrupting them. 'Just a minute, Danny.'

Katrina looked up to see a woman with short black hair and dressed in fashionable beige slacks, cross the room towards them. Her white linen shirt had a touch of lace around the collar.

Danny went forward to greet her. 'You're back early, Carrie. Did you have a good trip?'

'Good enough. I managed to conclude my business sooner than I thought.' She smiled at Katrina and Ross. 'You can both stay here, of course.'

Danny looked taken aback. 'But I thought — '

Carrie waved his excuse away. 'It's no problem at all. We still have a spare room available. The beds aren't made up but that won't take long.'

'Are you sure?' replied Katrina. 'We certainly don't want to cause you any extra work.'

'We'd be glad to have you. Danny will run your husband down in the car to get your belongings,' suggested Carrie.

Maguire didn't look pleased but obviously thought better than to argue. He jangled the keys of the car in his pocket. 'Right then. If you're ready, we'll be on our way.'

When Ross and Maguire left the drawing-room, a bereft feeling swept over Katrina at Ross's departure even though she knew it was only for a short time. She and Ross had spent a lot of time together since Sean had gone and especially when Ross was recuperating at home. She appreciated his strength and sense of humour. And what was more, he understood completely how badly she needed to find Sean.

Carrie moved towards her. 'Can I offer you a cup of tea? Then I'll show you to your room, if you like?'

Katrina nodded. 'Thank you. A cup of tea is just what I need.'

Within minutes Carrie appeared with a tray and a pot of tea for two. 'Are you enjoying your stay in Ireland?'

Katrina shifted uneasily on the couch. 'We haven't really been here very long but already I love it.'

Carrie poured the tea, then said, 'There you go. I'll leave you to it then while I'll see to your rooms.'

'Thank you again,' replied Katrina gratefully.

While Katrina sipped her tea, she thought about Carrie. The woman was too friendly for her liking and it unnerved her. The other strange thing was that Katrina felt as if she'd seen her before. There was something about the woman's voice . . .

Within minutes, Ross arrived back. 'Everything OK?' he asked, sitting down beside her.

Katrina nodded. 'Seems to be. Our rooms will be ready shortly.'

'I've left our luggage in the hallway,' Ross informed her. He went over to the table to help himself to a cup of tea and sat down beside her. He'd just lifted the cup to his lips when Carrie returned unexpectedly.

'Your rooms are ready now. Danny has already carried your bags up.'

'Good, thank you,' replied Ross, getting to his feet. He slipped his arm around Katrina's shoulders and gave her a hug. 'Why don't you have a rest upstairs? I might just go for a walk and stretch these legs of mine.' He turned to

Carrie explaining, 'I'm used to being outside working on a farm from dawn to dusk. I get a bit tetchy if I'm indoors too long.'

'I understand perfectly. I must confess I prefer the open moorland to being indoors myself. There are some nice walks along the cliffs and there's a path which leads down to the beach.' She got up and pointed out the window to the direction he should take. Ross listened while he quickly took in the layout of the land.

Following Carrie up the long and winding staircase, by the time they reached the first landing Katrina was gasping for breath. Since she had fallen pregnant, she noticed she tired easily. She peered over the banister to the hallway below, feeling slightly dizzy. Ross's arm slipped around her waist reassuringly. 'Best not to look down,' he warned.

When they reached the bedroom, Katrina took it in quickly, admiring the rose patterned wallpaper and curtains to match. 'Oh, this is nice.' The four-poster bed was large, hand carved with a white canopy draped around the four sides.

'There's an *en suite*, over there,' Carrie said, pointing to a half-open panelled door. 'I'll leave you to make yourselves comfortable. Don't hesitate to ask for anything, will you?'

Carrie smiled briefly and shut the door behind her with a resounding click.

Ross raised his brows. 'She seems friendly enough.'

'I'm not so sure,' replied Katrina suspiciously. 'I don't know what it is but there's something about her eyes. It's almost as if I've seen her somewhere before, yet . . . ' Her voice tailed off as she tried to search her memory.

Ross walked over to the window and pulled the curtains back further so he could look out. 'You know something? If I hadn't known the real reason why we were both here, I could actually begin to enjoy this holiday,' he remarked ruefully.

Katrina stood by his side. The view from the window was magnificent. She could see right down the wild coastline, along the jagged cliffs towards the grey rooftops of the village in the distance. The sea heaved and rolled fiercely as fishing boats bobbed up and down.

Ross turned to her. 'If Sean is in the area, he's hardly going to walk up to the front door and announce his arrival.'

'So what do you suggest?' asked Katrina.

'I'm not sure. I'll take a walk first. See what I come up with.'

'I just hope we did the right thing in

coming here,' she said suddenly.

'Second thoughts?'

'No, but I guess I'm just worried about Sean. We're only going to be able to stay here for so long and there's no guarantee we'll find anything out.'

'Sean will be around here somewhere. If I know him, he's probably already seen us and wondering what we're doing here.' Ross frowned. 'He's not going to be pleased. Still, I'll cross that when I see him.' He unfolded the map and stretched it out on the bed.

'Sean could be down in the village,' suggested Katrina.

Ross looked thoughtful. 'Possibly. I'd say he's probably staying with someone he trusts. I'm pretty sure his adoptive father lives around here somewhere. A pity we don't know who he is.'

'I didn't get to read the whole file while I was in Powell's office, otherwise I might have come up with something. Do you think Sean could be roughing it somewhere? What about any derelict cottages nearby?'

'That's possible too. I'll have a good scout around.'

'I'm tempted to come with you, but I know you'd probably be able to cover more ground without me.'

'True.' He took her hand and lifted it. 'I

just hope Sean realizes this ring is fake or he'll be after me.'

Katrina gave a worried sigh. 'I wonder what he'll say about the baby . . . '

Ross threw her a sympathetic glance. 'Once he gets over the shock of being a father, he'll be fine.' He moved forward to pick up the guide book and turned to the pages on Connemara, flicking through them.

'Ireland certainly is a pretty country,' he murmured. 'Full of legends, crafts and Celtic music. I can understand Sean a bit better seeing where he comes from. Imagine growing up here. Nothing could have been more different than my own upbringing. That's for certain.' After a few minutes, he closed the guide book and placed it on the table. 'It certainly explains a lot about Sean. I've always had a niggling feeling Ireland was still in his blood, only I reckoned he wouldn't ever admit to it.'

Katrina winced suddenly as a cramping pain shot through her stomach. 'Oh . . . ' she gasped.

'Are you all right?'

'I think so.' She shifted slightly trying to get a more comfortable position. 'Probably just something I ate.'

'Are you sure? Do you want me to get a doctor?'

Katrina tried to smile. 'Now who's the one doing the worrying? I'll be fine. I've probably overdone it.' After a few moments, the cramping pain eased off and she got up intending to unpack some things. 'So what are we going to do about the sleeping arrangements?'

'No problem. I'll sleep on the floor,' he offered, 'or the bathroom. It's certainly big enough.'

Feeling better, Katrina punched his arm and laughed. 'In that case, you can have the duvet,' she said generously, 'and the feather pillows.'

Ross moved back towards the window. 'Are you sure you will be OK for a while if I go out? I promised Sean I'd take good care of you.'

'I'll be fine, honestly. I'm going to have a warm relaxing bath.'

'I won't be too long,' he promised. 'Best stay in the room until I get back.'

She gently pushed him out the door. 'If you see Sean, tell him . . . ' Her voice trailed off. 'That I miss him.' Tears pricked at her eyes.

'Hormones,' Ross replied in his usual pragmatic fashion. 'Looks like we're going to have to treat you very gently.' He gave her a lopsided grin and a quick hug.

Katrina sighed. She didn't tell him it could also be fear.

10

When Ross stepped outside, he wondered which way he should go. It was tempting to find the track down to the beach but the small whitewashed cottage in the distance looked interesting, so perhaps he would head that way first.

While he walked along the track, his thoughts were of Sean. He didn't blame him for what had happened in New Zealand. It wasn't Sean's fault that a gunman had shot him instead. At least the police had caught the two men responsible and now they faced a trial for attempted murder. Once arrested, they had confessed someone had hired them from overseas but they hadn't given any names.

Ross grimaced. Danger had penetrated their life in the high country in the most unexpected way. And somehow it had brought it home to him that no matter where you lived in the world there were unscrupulous people around. The thing was, why did they want Sean dead? Was it something to do with Sean's past life? No doubt he would have made a few enemies along the way. The big question was who?

Ross neared the cottage. He thought he saw a figure move at the window, then it was gone. He hopped over a stone wall, his feet sinking into the soft grass on the other side. The garden around the cottage was rambling and attractive in a wild sort of way. Early spring bulbs were shooting through the green grass haphazardly like coloured lollipops on green stalks. Snowdrops, sitting prettily in long rows, swung their delicate bell like heads back and forward to the whisper of a sea breeze.

Ross noticed the old sheepdog tied up in the corner. When it saw him, it leaped to its feet and barked its head off. Ross, always at ease with sheep dogs, took no notice and offered his hand for the dog to smell. The dog's ears smoothed back all of a sudden and it wagged its tail furiously. It lay on the ground, its paws in the air, while Ross rubbed its tummy, speaking to it in soft soothing tones. A creak from the front door of the cottage made Ross turn quickly to see who it was.

'Gidday,' said Ross, standing up.

'Aye, it's a grand day,' Finney said cautiously, his bonnet perched on his head at an angle. 'Are you looking for someone?'

Ross smiled politely. 'Not really. Just out

for a walk. I'm staying at Cardell Castle.' He stood for a moment sizing up the old man who he reckoned to be in his seventies. 'Is it far to the village?'

Finney's weather-beaten face creased in a semblance of a smile. 'About ten minutes' walk. Just keep on following the track. You can't miss it. I'm sure you'll see some interesting things on your way.'

Something about the way he said it, made Ross's ears prick up. He was just going to ask the old man to explain when he raised his bonnet on his head politely before going back inside. He closed the door and Ross heard the bolt slide forward.

He hadn't planned on going to the village but now that he was out and about it wouldn't take long to walk there and he could certainly do with the exercise. Being cooped up on the plane and in the rental car for hours on end had made him feel out of sorts.

He had only gone a few yards when someone leaped out from over the wall, right in front of him. He wore a balaclava, his dark eyes glowing like black coals.

Ross gasped. 'What the — ' His fists clenched as he braced himself for an assault.

The man whipped off his balaclava. 'Ross, it's me. What the hell are you and Katrina doing here?'

Ross broke into a wide smile. 'Sean, mate, am I glad to see you!'

Sean grabbed him by the shoulders. 'Jaysus, Ross, I can't believe you'd come all this way to find me.'

'Then think again.' He hesitated. 'I tried to talk Katrina out of it, but she was set on finding you. I wasn't about to let her come on her own.'

Sean exhaled sharply. 'It's too dangerous. You have to go back to the castle and get Katrina out of there right now. There's no time to waste.'

Ross rocked back on his heels, a stubborn look crossing his face. 'No way. We've just managed to wangle the night at the castle. We can't leave now. It will look really odd.'

A muscle tightened in Sean's jaw. 'Forget what it looks like; just get the hell out. I'm trained for this sort of work and you're not. You'll only get in the way. The last thing I need is two civilians getting hurt.'

'You're wrong. It won't come to that.'

'You've never been involved in undercover warfare. Nothing is as it seems,' Sean told him.

'Katrina and I know what we're doing. There's no way you'll talk us out of it. So you can forget it.' His mouth firmed, ready for an argument.

At the sound of a car Sean leapt over the

wall to the other side. Ross followed suit and they both crouched down low until it passed.

Sean kept his voice low. 'I know you mean well, but it's better if I don't have to worry about you both.'

Ross had to make Sean understand. 'It wasn't you who got shot up there on the mountain. And it wasn't you who lay there in the pouring rain wondering if you were going to make it or not. I want to nail the bastard who brought violence to our home. The men who shot me have been apprehended but they've confessed someone hired them from overseas . . . someone from Ireland. They say they don't know who; it was all done through a third party.'

Sean's eyes narrowed. 'Sure. It could be one of a hundred people who are after my blood.'

'Whoever it is, they won't stop, unless we get them first. If you come back to New Zealand, we'll all be wondering when the next gunman is going to turn up again. How are we going to live like that?'

Sean grimaced. 'You don't have to tell me this — I know. That's part of the reason I'm here.' He shifted position as he leant against the stone wall, the sharp stone cutting into his back.

Ross asked curiously. 'So the gunman isn't the only reason?'

'No.' Sean hesitated. 'There could be a bomb factory at the castle. Al-Qaeda may be involved.'

'A bomb factory?' Ross repeated, his mouth dropping open.

Sean nodded. 'Now you know why I want you out of there. Right now.'

Ross whistled. 'I hadn't realized. Wait until I tell Katrina.'

Sean's forehead creased with worry. 'Is she all right?'

Ross hesitated but only a fraction. 'Katrina is fine. But she needs to see you.'

'I know. When I'm finished here, we'll sort things out. Just make sure you get her back to Glenroy safely.'

The unspoken bond of kinship tightened between them. 'I'll make sure no harm comes to her at the castle. I swear it, Sean. You know you can depend on me.'

Sean smiled. 'I know.'

'Why don't I help you? I could get you into the castle tonight.'

It was tempting, thought Sean. The sooner he could complete his mission, the better. 'What exactly have you in mind?'

Ross smiled as he leaned closer. 'I knew you'd see it my way. Here's what we'll do then.'

$\star$ $\star$ $\star$

Katrina turned on the brass taps overhanging the deep bath. She needed to relax and a long soak in hot water would do her good. A peculiar grunting noise vibrated around her as the water gushed out of the ancient plumbing.

A glass shelf near the green marble washstand held a variety of coloured bottles. She studied the labels. Soap, shampoo, moisturiser. She might as well use them. Their charges were reasonable, she noticed, after studying the tariff card on the table. Katrina stood at the mirror and looked at herself critically. There were dark shadows under her eyes, probably due to the jet lag. The bump on her stomach wasn't noticeable yet and although she'd had some queasiness first thing in the morning, she didn't feel too bad. Before she'd left Glenroy, she'd paid a visit to the local doctor for a check up and everything seemed fine. It still worried her though that she hadn't been able to tell Sean. How would he react, she wondered?

The tension eased from her shoulders once she slid into the warm perfumed water. She knew what they were doing was dangerous. The castle was connected to Sean somehow though she wasn't sure in what way. She had discussed everything fully with Ross beforehand, knowing they would be taking risks.

291

John had tried to dissuade them, putting forward a hundred arguments why it wouldn't work but her mind had been made up. She was going to find Sean.

Looking back, even if Ross hadn't come, she still would have, she realized. There was no way she was going to let Sean go out of her life now. Admittedly, he hadn't told her everything while he was being held by the New Zealand authorities, she reminded herself, but as Ross pointed out, that didn't mean he didn't care. And maybe he was trying to protect her by not telling her anything, she reasoned.

And what about Jessie? She'd left several messages on her mobile phone and at the bookshop in London, but Jessie hadn't returned any of them. Something wasn't right.

Closing her eyes, she let herself drift away. Then she heard it. A noise coming from the bedroom. It sounded like a floorboard creaking as if someone was moving stealthily across the room. Katrina stiffened. Surely it couldn't be Ross back already? If it was, he would have yelled out by now, she was sure of it. With deft movements, she reached out for her towelling robe and climbed out, wrapping it around herself tightly. She put her ear to the door and listened. Someone was definitely in the bedroom walking about.

Taking in a deep breath, Katrina swung the bathroom door open wide. A woman dressed in a black track suit was standing beside the bed, looking through Katrina's suitcase. She had Katrina's passport clutched in one hand.

Katrina's mouth fell open. 'Jessie,' she said in disbelief. 'What the . . . ?'

'Yes . . . yes, it's me.' She laid the passport on the table.

'What are you doing here?'

Jessie didn't answer straight away, just stood there looking at her. 'It's too complicated to explain right now. But you must leave here. Get away while you can.'

'But I'm looking for Sean. He's in Ireland. I don't know where exactly. I'd thought that he might have been here.'

'He's not. I've not even seen him.'

Katrina inhaled sharply. 'Are you involved with *them*?'

Jessie's brows rose. 'Them?'

'The Real IRA.'

Jessie bit her lip. 'It's not as simple as that.'

'Why don't you tell me what's going on?' urged Katrina.

Jessie took a deep breath. 'I didn't want it to come to this. I really didn't.' She shook her head. 'Danny Maguire is my brother. He's wanted by the authorities for his involvement with the Real IRA. They were formed after the Provisional IRA were disbanded.'

'I've heard of them. And you're involved with them too?'

'Sometimes. Only because of my brother. I wanted to tell you when I saw you in Boston, but I had to protect Danny.' Jessie hesitated. 'Sean is a threat to him.'

Katrina's heart started to pound. 'A threat? How?'

'Sean can identify Danny and his wife, Carrie. She hates Sean for betraying them. Carrie was livid when she found out Sean had been an undercover police officer all along. She wants Sean dead. She tried to kill him only he survived the explosion. Afterwards she wrote a letter to him pretending to be you, to draw him out of hiding. When I went out to post the letter, I destroyed it and replaced it with another letter, telling Sean you never wanted to see him again. I thought if I kept you apart, you'd both be safe.'

Katrina was aghast. 'My God, Jessie. So you were the one. I thought Sean didn't care about me. But he did. He really did write those letters. And you intercepted them.'

'It's Carrie's fault. Not mine. I only did what I thought was best. I tried to protect you. As long as Sean stays in New Zealand there won't be any trouble. But now he's here, in Ireland, isn't he? Everything's changed.'

Katrina couldn't believe she was so open in her admission of guilt. 'You lied to me all along.'

'I had to. My brother comes first, Katrina. I'm sorry.'

'Does Carrie know who I am?' asked Katrina.

Jessie nodded.

'But she's let us stay here. It doesn't make sense.'

'It does if she wants to kill Sean. She knows he'll come looking for you.'

Katrina caught her breath. 'Oh my God. They're setting a trap for him.'

'Not if you leave tonight. For God's sake, go while you can.'

Katrina took a step forward. 'Oh, Jessie, I can't believe you're caught up in the middle of all of this.'

'I didn't mean to hurt you. Honest I didn't. But you must see, I had to do it. It really was the only way.' She walked over to the door, then turned to face Katrina. 'Carrie is unpredictable. Be careful.' She shut the door quickly behind her.

Katrina snibbed the lock and leaned on the door thinking frantically. If Carrie and Danny were with the Real IRA, and Jessie had told them that Sean was in New Zealand, it must have been they who'd arranged the hit on Sean. Only it was Ross who had been hurt. Now, all the pieces were fitting together, one by one.

Katrina heard the bedroom door handle turn. 'Who is it?' she called out.

'It's Ross. Open up.'

She let him in quickly. 'Am I glad to see you,' she said, shaking.

'Are you all right?' he added. 'You look like you've seen a ghost.'

Katrina explained what had transpired. 'I just can't believe it. Jessie was the last person I expected to see here. She admitted everything to me.'

'But can you really trust her?'

'I don't know. But she did come to warn me. That must count for something.'

'Or they could have put her up to it, so she would gain *your* trust.'

'But why?'

'To find out what Sean's up to.'

Katrina shook her head. 'No, you're wrong. She's trying to avoid any trouble. We have to warn Sean, otherwise he'll be walking into a trap.'

Ross looked dismayed. 'Too late. I've already arranged to let him into the castle tonight. He's searching for a bomb factory.

He says al-Qaeda could be involved. They're in league with the Real IRA.'

Stunned, Katrina could only stare at him. 'This is even bigger than I thought. What have we got mixed up in?'

'God knows.' Ross grimaced. 'One thing I know for sure. You'd best leave straight away. Now, in fact. It will be safer. I'll stay here and see things through.'

Katrina shook her head. 'No, no, no. I'm not going anywhere. If you've think I've come all this way, just to bale out now, you're wrong.'

* * *

In the dungeons, under a harsh light, two men sat opposite each other at a long wooden table. Large boxes of Semtex, stamped red with Czechoslovakian words, were lined up against the rough stone walls.

Hannad Khalis stretched his arms upwards, throwing a dark shadow over the table. 'I could do with some fresh air. Pity we can't go out during the day. Being cooped up like this is getting to me.'

Maguire answered. 'Best you go out at night. Less chance of being seen. There'll be a full moon, so be careful.' He paused briefly. 'You never know if some local is stalking about these parts and if you're spotted we don't want any rumours circling in the village. Word can spread quickly to the Garda.' He picked up the knife and carved a pattern in the wooden table. 'Huh, a pity we couldn't have got rid of that old man, Finney. He's been snooping around the grounds these past few days, poking his damned nose into where he doesn't belong.'

'Then why don't you?' Khalis suggested, as he sat down again. He shoved his long black hair back from his forehead.

'Carrie said if we turf him out of the cottage he lives in, it could cause trouble. Sure . . . and I'm inclined to believe her. The local people around here stick together and the last thing we need is the Garda turning up at the castle asking questions.'

'I thought you had them paid off, so they'd leave you alone,' Khalis replied, inspecting an electronic component and holding it under the light to get a better look.

'Sure, one of them . . . not the whole damned police force.'

Khalis reached over for another tool, his forehead creasing in concentration. Tiredness was interfering with his thinking. Prayer would help. He began to recite the words of the Koran to give him strength. *'Bismi Allahi alrrahmani alrraheemi.' In the name of God,*

Most Gracious, Most Merciful.

While Khalis said his prayers, Maguire went forward and unlocked a large cupboard stacked full of ammunition and firearms. Reaching inside, he took out a half empty bottle of Irish whiskey, then, after pouring himself a large glass, threw himself in the armchair nearby. The newspaper was spread across the floor. He picked it up and read the headlines: 'CENTURIES OF BLOODSHED AT AN END.'

Maguire grunted. 'That's what they think.' When Khalis finished his prayer, Maguire said cockily, 'Looks like the British Prime Minister is arriving in Belfast in a week's time.' Maguire grunted again. 'There'll be a nasty surprise for him — if everything goes according to plan.' He smiled, glancing at the Sinn Fein poster on the wall.

'All our men are in place,' said Khalis. 'Now it's just a matter of moving the equipment to Belfast.' He frowned. 'What's this about Sean McKinlay? Jessie told me about him. Do you think he can cause trouble for us?'

Maguire shook his head. 'We've got things under control, so don't you worry about that.'

Khalis wasn't sure whether to believe him. He'd heard of McKinlay, how he'd infiltrated the IRA, disrupting their plans big time. 'You should have killed him while you had the chance.'

'We tried. Only he got lucky. That's the bloody Irish for you.'

'So now what are you going to do?'

Maguire laughed, a harsh sound. 'We've got his girlfriend and some relative of his upstairs. Now we're going to wait for McKinlay to come here. He will: I guarantee it.'

★　★　★

Maguire slid back the bolt on the door and stepped into the dark hallway, climbing the winding steps in front of him two at a time. When he reached the next floor, he came to a third door, heavily timbered and with iron straps, set in an archway. He swung it open. The bright light of the kitchen hit him along with the smell of cooking. Carrie was at the stove stirring hot soup.

Maguire placed his hand on her shoulder. 'Mmm . . . that smells good. Nothing like a good broth.'

Carrie pushed her hair back from her face. 'I hate cooking. A pity the cook's away on holiday.'

Maguire grinned. He walked over to the fridge to look inside. Seeing a bottle of

Guinness, he lifted it out and opened it.

'What's Jessie up to?' he asked. 'I should go upstairs and see if she's OK.'

'You'd better watch Jessie,' remarked Carrie. 'She's always had a soft spot for Katrina.'

'Jessie won't say anything to compromise us. She's got a good heart, that's all. Besides, I don't tell her everything. What she doesn't know, she can't tell, right?'

'As long as you're sure.'

'Jessie won't let me down. Didn't she report everything to me Katrina had told her? Jessie's with me on this. She always has been. Those visits to Boston as our courier proved that.'

'True,' agreed Carrie. 'Even so, she's not entirely happy about any violence.' She met Maguire's gaze. 'And that could be a problem.'

11

Sean, an ominous figure in black, waited outside the castle walls. He moved only when the moon slid behind the clouds. He stopped beside a high crumbling stone wall, his head cocked to the side, listening carefully. There was deathly quiet; only the sound of the wind as it whistled around the corners of the cobbled courtyard. Slowly, he pushed open the black wrought-iron gate, cursing the rusty hinges. The noise disturbed a small nocturnal animal, sending it scuttling off through the undergrowth.

Sean continued walking. The guard dog had been disposed of quickly and efficiently. Finney had done well. He had left some meat for the animal drawing it to a position close to the wall and while it was eating, Sean had shot it with the .226 SIG Sauer pistol Harvey had provided him with. The pistol had a fitted silencer.

He hated having to shoot the dog but the stakes were too high. Finney had then lifted the dog into the wheelbarrow and dropped the body over the cliffs.

Sean watched the kitchen door of the

castle. He could hear the bolt sliding back and waited until he could see who it was. Ross's blond head glinted silver in the moonlight as he peered outside. Then he disappeared, leaving the kitchen door slightly ajar.

Sean made a run for it. His feet made no noise on the cobbled stones as he skimmed stealthily around the perimeter of the courtyard. He just made it when suddenly the moon popped out glaringly bright. As the clouds slid over again, menacing shadows from the ramparts were thrown instantly onto the ground making it look like the setting of a gothic movie.

Sean switched on the small flashlight he carried. Once in the kitchen, he stood very still, his gaze travelling slowly around the bench tops. The stale smell of cooking still lingered in the air. The place hadn't changed much, he thought. Various pots and pans hung on brass hooks and chains from the ceiling giving the illusion of flying objects suspended in mid air. Sean listened carefully. A dripping tap reverberated loudly like the steady beat of a heart.

Focusing the flashlight on the arched door which he remembered led downstairs into the dungeons, he made his way forward slowly. He was only about a metre away, when to his horror he heard the door being unlocked from the other side. He desperately looked around for somewhere to hide. Remembering the walk-in pantry, he dived into it quickly and shut the door behind him. No sooner had he closed it when he heard heavy footsteps along the flagstone floor. His fingers tightened around the hard plastic grips of the pistol.

The footsteps stopped nearby. Sean kept very still, hardly daring to breathe. Was someone standing right outside the pantry door? He braced himself. He hadn't wanted any casualties but he might not have a choice.

Sean moved slightly, his elbow accidentally clinking two jam jars together. Damn it, he thought. Had they heard the noise?

The footsteps started up again but they seemed to be walking away from him. Sean leaned forward slightly at the sound of running water, to peer through the inch crack in the door. A shaft of moonlight shone through the large bay window highlighting the man's profile. Sean's eyes widened as he recognized him: it was Danny Maguire.

Maguire filled the glass from the kitchen tap and drank from it. Another man appeared, lean and hard-looking. His Middle Eastern accent gave him away: Hannad Khalis.

'First thing tomorrow we need to talk,' said Khalis. 'Our plans have been brought forward.'

'Why?' asked Maguire, turning to face him.

'One of our men has been arrested in Belfast. He was highly trained in explosives — a suicide bomber. The police will suspect something is up.'

'You think he'll talk?'

'I do not know. But we cannot take any chances.' Khalis paused. 'The prime minister arrives in Belfast in a few days.'

'You think you can kill him?'

'We will try. Nothing must stop us. We will show the British authorities they can never defeat al-Qaeda.' He inclined his head. '*Allñahu Akbar.*'

Both men went back through the wooden door, shutting it quietly behind them.

So al-Qaeda were involved, confirmed Sean.

He quickly crossed the kitchen floor, his rubber soles making no sound on the stone tiles. Switching on his torch, he examined the wooden door, running his fingers carefully over the edges.

Even if he was to lever it open, it would make too much noise. There was a smaller door in the grand hall that led into the dungeons, he remembered. Maybe he ought to try that. He moved stealthily into the passageway, stopping briefly near an alcove to get his bearings.

'Sean, is that you?' a voice whispered behind him.

Sean whirled around with his SIG, spreading his feet apart. When he saw who it was, he lowered his pistol to his side.

'Katrina?' His heart did a quick flip.

She rushed forward into his arms. 'Sean, I can't believe it's you. I've been so worried.'

Sean hugged her tightly, burying his face in her hair. God, he had missed her. He knew he was wasting time, bringing them both into danger, but all he could think of was he might not have the chance to hold her again. He backtracked into the darkened alcove, pulling her with him. 'Where's Ross?'

'In the grand hall looking out for you,' she whispered.

'Good. Listen, we haven't much time. I want you and Ross to get out now. Leave through the kitchen door. Meet me at Finney's cottage. Ross knows where that is. It will be safe there.'

She nodded.

He pulled back a little, framing her face between his hands and taking a long slow look at her. Dark-green eyes, with a thick fringe of dark eyelashes, stared back at him.

He had to tell her now while he had a chance. 'Katrina, I'll always love you,' he began, 'but if anything happens to me I want you to go back to Glenroy with Ross. He'll take good care of you.'

'What do you mean? Nothing is going to happen. Promise me you won't take any risks.'

He smiled briefly. 'I can't do that. I've always taken risks, but I will be careful.' He tensed suddenly. 'Sshh. I thought I heard something.' He reached out and pulled her against the wall, close to him. 'Keep very still,' he murmured.

Sean's mind flashed to alert. He waited for a few seconds. Whatever the sound was, it had gone. Sean followed her into the kitchen where he pointed to the door. Katrina had just reached out for the door handle when Sean heard footsteps behind him. He whirled around, the SIG in his hand. He couldn't see anyone but he could hear the murmur of voices.

'Wait,' he said softly. With one hand he grabbed Katrina's hand intending to head for the pantry. Halfway across the room, he halted — light flooded the kitchen blinding them momentarily.

'I don't think you'll be going anywhere,' a female voice said loudly.

Carrie walked in slowly holding a Kalashnikov assault rifle. Ross walked in front of her with his hands held up in the air. He swore loudly when Carrie prodded him in the back.

Damn it, thought Sean. Now he had brought them all into danger. He grimaced, wondering how they were going to get out of this.

'Throw your gun down, or I'll shoot the girl,' ordered Carrie.

Fear slithered up Sean's spine. If he didn't do as she said, she'd kill Katrina. She had killed before. He made a quick decision. He dropped the SIG on the floor.

'Search him, Danny. See if he's wearing a wire.'

Maguire moved forward quickly. After patting him down, Maguire said, 'Nothing.'

That was lucky, thought Sean. The covert electronic listening device he carried was disguised in a small golden stud in his belt around his waist. He'd changed his mind at the last minute about carrying a wire. Just as well he had.

'Let Katrina and Ross go,' urged Sean. His voice was quiet, dangerously so. 'Let's settle this between you and me. That's what you want, isn't it?'

Carrie shook her head. 'No . . . they know too much. And so do you now. It's a pity the gunman didn't get you in New Zealand. I should have sent one of our men. They would have done the job properly.'

Sean's eyes narrowed. 'So it *was* *you* who arranged the hit?'

'Of course.' Her eyes flickered slightly. 'What do you expect?' Carrie's mouth tightened. 'I have to give it to you, Sean, you completely fooled us. And here's us thinking you were on our side. All that time in London you were a bloody cop.'

'Carrie, shoot him,' urged Maguire. 'We're wasting time here.'

'Not yet.' Carrie swung the AK47 towards Katrina. 'You'd better start talking, Sean, or I'll kill her. Who else knows you are here?'

'No one,' replied Sean tightly.

Carrie gave a short laugh. 'Sure they don't. Something tells me you're lying.'

Another man entered the room and stood near the door. Sean looked up. It was Hannad Khalis. The Afghan said nothing, just stood there, staring at them all. His gaze settled on Carrie. 'Problems?'

'A hiccup, but nothing we can't sort out,' she replied coolly.

Sean spoke again. 'It's only a matter of time before you'll be arrested. You'll get thirty years in prison for this.'

'You think I'd let myself be taken? Then

you really don't know me at all.'

There was the sound of a van drawing up outside. Carrie turned her head slightly.

'What's that . . . ?' she started to say. It was just enough distraction for Sean to lash out with his foot. Carrie fell backwards, knocking into Maguire. Ross leaped forward to grab the AK47 which bounced off the cupboard and clattered onto the floor out of reach.

'Get the gun,' Carrie yelled to Maguire, as she picked herself up.

Ross and Maguire reached the assault rifle at the same time, both men struggling violently to gain control of it. Ross banged his head badly against the corner of the bench and fell back, clutching Maguire's arm and dragging the man on top of him.

Sean sprinted to reach his SIG but wasn't quick enough. Carrie had already retrieved it and fired in his direction. Bullets from Carrie's gun were chasing the pots and pans around Sean's head making them ring like little bells. He dived to the floor behind the wooden table, his heart pounding uncontrollably. That was close, he grimaced, wondering how many shots she had fired and how many were left.

Then the lights went off. A scream rang out, piercing the darkness.

'Katrina, for God's sake, keep down!' Sean

shouted over to her. Thankfully, she had already crawled underneath the bench. It was she who had hit the light switch.

Ross and Maguire were still fighting at the other end of the kitchen but it was impossible to see what was happening. Sean was just about to crawl over to where Katrina lay when he heard footsteps running out the kitchen. Carrie and Khalis were escaping. He had to go after them. He picked himself up and started to run.

'Stay put. I'll be back as soon as I can,' he called out to Katrina, and sprinted into the passageway.

There was light but Carrie was nowhere to be seen. He listened carefully, then felt a rush of cold air. Glancing around slowly, he remembered the small door underneath the staircase in the grand hall, the other entrance to the dungeon. Approaching it carefully, he only hoped she wasn't lying in wait for him.

★　★　★

Katrina looked on in horror at the two men fighting. Ross sent Maguire flying backwards, missing her by centimetres. He crashed into the Welsh dresser, making it rock back and forward precariously. Antique dishes and crystal glasses slid off and smashed on to the floor right in front of her.

Maguire grabbed a knife and lunged forward. Ross was ready for him and caught Maguire's wrist in mid air, twisting him round so they both fell sideways onto the table. Blood streamed down Ross's forehead into his eyes blinding him.

Maguire's weight gave him the advantage and he pinned Ross flat onto his back. Ross gave a gigantic heave and tried to roll his attacker over but it wasn't enough. The knife was now only centimetres from Ross's face.

If she didn't do something, Maguire would kill him, Katrina thought desperately. She rushed forward and picked up the frying pan. Lifting it upwards she brought it down hard on Maguire's head. He fell forward with a grunt, releasing the knife where it clattered onto the floor near Katrina's feet.

Ross's chest heaved. She heard him swear. Staggering forward a few steps, his knees buckled and he sank down to the floor.

Katrina rushed forward and knelt down beside him. 'Ross, are you all right?' She reached over for a tea towel draped across the bench and folded it over to stem the flow of blood streaming from his head wound. 'We'll have to get you to a doctor — '

He gasped. 'Never mind that, where's Sean? He might need some help.'

At that moment, the kitchen door flew open. Detective Inspector Harvey and a squad of men rushed forward, taking in the scenario at a glance. He motioned to the men to spread out one by one.

'Where's Sean?' Harvey demanded as he knelt down beside Ross. 'We heard what was happening through Sean's wire but when the fighting started we lost contact.'

'He's gone down to the dungeons after Carrie and Khalis,' said Katrina. Her hands were shaking as she pressed the towel firmly across the wound on Ross's head.

Ross tried to get up but Harvey put his hand on his shoulder. 'Don't move; you're in no shape to do anything. We've got the place cordoned off, so they won't get away.'

'It's not them I'm worried about, it's Sean.'

Harvey grimaced. 'We'll find him.' He turned to Katrina. 'Stay here with Ross.' He signalled to some of his men and a medic came over with his black bag and immediately began to administer first aid.

Katrina stood up, her heart pounding with fear. Don't take any chances, Sean, she prayed. She couldn't bear it if she lost him now.

★   ★   ★

Sean crawled through the narrow space brushing up against spiders' webs, the sticky threads clinging to his skin unpleasantly. If his memory served him right, the passage led to a bigger one and joined up to the main dungeon stairway.

He stopped and listened. Everything was quiet. So far, so good. But chances were high Carrie and Khalis had already reached the dungeons. They could be lying in wait for him.

He had no choice but to use the torch that was in his pocket. It made him a target but he needed to move, and quickly. When he reached the next passage he wondered which way to turn. Was it right or left? Momentarily disorientated he decided it had to be left and continued on his way, moving as swiftly as he could. He cursed under his breath when he got to the end of the passageway. It was a dead end. He had just wasted five minutes of valuable time.

He turned back quickly retracing his steps. Pressing up against the cold dank wall, he peered around the corner. No sign of anyone.

He continued downstairs, leading deeper into the dungeons. After two flights, he saw a large wooden door, partly open and knew it led to a cell. Could this be the bomb factory, he wondered? He approached carefully. His hand just reached out for the iron door handle when he heard someone behind him. Sean swung around.

Khalis stood there with a revolver in his hand. He waved Sean over to the side. Sean started to move. Khalis took a step forward and Sean lashed out with his foot, catching Khalis's hand and sending the gun spiralling through the air. Khalis dived to get it, but Sean gave him a side kick which sent him flying backwards, crashing into a small wooden table. It broke with a crack.

Khalis picked himself up quickly and lunged and threw a barrage of punches. Sean fended them off but one got through, catching him on the jaw. He staggered back, wincing painfully.

The revolver lay on the floor amidst the wreckage. Khalis sprinted to get it. Sean, realizing what he was about to do, tried to get there first. Both men collided, falling to the floor, rolling over and over until they reached the bottom of the next flight of stairs.

Sean was strong but Khalis was a professional killer. He knew exactly how to handle himself. Sean was scoring, but Khalis was getting the better of him. This was not fighting that involved any rules: it was survival. Sean escaped an eye gouging and delivered a head-butt to Khalis's face.

Something broke. Khalis gasped.

Sean had gained the advantage, but he couldn't capitalize on it. Suddenly pain exploded in his head. His vision doubled, then faded. He knew he was losing consciousness and tried frantically to hold on. He let go of Khalis, his fingers clutching the edge of the stone step and then he sank into oblivion.

Carrie stood there, with the leg of the table in her hands. 'Are you OK?'

Khalis grimaced. He picked himself up from the floor and gingerly wiped the blood from his broken nose. 'He certainly packs a punch,' he admitted, his chest heaving. 'Come on. We've got to get out of here.'

'No, I'm waiting for Danny,' she said stubbornly.

'Are you crazy? There's no time. He may not even make it.'

'I can't leave Danny. I won't.'

Khalis made an impatient sound. 'You can't jeopardize the mission. All that we've worked for will be wasted.'

Reluctantly, Carrie nodded. 'All right. I'll get the documents. Forget about the rest, we won't need it.'

Within minutes they piled everything into a small box and Khalis lifted it up.

'What about McKinlay?' Khalis said,

scowling. He kicked Sean viciously in the ribs as he passed.

Carrie lifted up the automatic and aimed it carefully at Sean. 'He's caused us enough trouble.'

All of a sudden a rumbling boom echoed along the passageway. Carrie's head jerked up. 'What's that?'

She called out Khalis's name as she stepped forward but her words were drowned out as the ground erupted in front of them with an almighty roar.

12

Crockery rattled on the shelves and a picture slipped off the wall, crashing onto the floor.

'Earthquake,' Ross said, knowing it was more than that even as he thought it. Ross's face was grim as realization sunk in. 'An explosion below.'

Katrina raised her hand to her mouth as the horror registered. Desperately, she ran out of the kitchen into the hallway. A man in uniform guarded the small door to the dungeons, his gun swung around in front of him.

'You can't go down there,' he informed her. He moved his bulky figure across the doorway warningly.

Katrina tried to shove him aside. 'I have to see if Sean's all right,' she cried. 'He's down there somewhere. Let me go in.'

The man struggled with Katrina for a few seconds until Ross appeared behind her, pulling her back. 'Katrina, what are you doing?'

'Something's wrong,' she pleaded. 'I know it. Sean could be lying there hurt. I have to go down to see.'

A police officer dressed in full protective gear of bullet proof vest and helmet, appeared at the entrance door, his clothes covered in white dust. He was coughing. When he managed to speak, he said, 'They've got the place wired. Someone must have set it off when we reached the next level.' Blood ran down his cheek from a splinter of wood. He wiped the sweat and dust from his face with his sleeve, then staggered forward to talk to Detective Inspector Harvey. 'I don't see how anyone could have survived that inferno down there. It's like a scene from hell.'

'Are you saying Sean's dead?' Katrina cried, breaking loose from Ross's arms.

No one answered her because no one knew. Had Sean been caught in the blast?

Harvey's mouth drew into a tight line. 'We won't know anything until we get down there. Please keep back and let us get on with our search.' He lifted his hand-held radio and issued some commands. Within minutes, more men had arrived to help break down the door in the kitchen. They were now working from two entrances.

Ross took Katrina's arm. 'You've been through enough for one night and there's nothing more we can do.'

'No, I'm not going anywhere,' she said adamantly, 'until I know if Sean's been found.'

Ross turned back to the detective inspector. 'Can we do anything to help?'

Harvey's face looked grey. 'No. We've got explosives experts down there. They're checking everything out thoroughly and when it's clear, we'll go down and take a look.' He hesitated. 'I'm sorry but we'll just have to wait.'

★ ★ ★

'Why are they taking so long?' Katrina asked again as she paced up and down the kitchen floor. She glanced at the clock hanging on the wall. It was now just before lunchtime, the following day after the explosion.

Ross had just made a cup of tea and poured her one. 'They're doing their best; they've been working all night.'

More men from the Emergency Response Unit had arrived with vehicles pulling up outside, the revving engines disturbing the tranquillity of the castle. Katrina had tried to keep busy throughout the morning, making hot coffee and sandwiches for the men, but it had taken all her effort to carry out the tasks.

Harvey appeared. 'We've found Carrie. She's dead, but no sign of Sean or Khalis. It's possible they may be in one of the other passageways which have fallen in. It's going to take a few days to clear everything out.'

'Sean could be lying hurt,' Katrina cried. 'We haven't got a few days.'

Ross spoke soothingly. 'The detective inspector's doing what he can, Katrina. You have to realize the safety of his men comes first.'

'I know . . . I'm sorry. It's just that it's hard not knowing.' Surely, after all they had been through, he had to be alive, she thought . . . he just had to be.

'Do you want to see Jessie before she's taken away?' asked Harvey. 'She's under arrest.'

Katrina wasn't sure. And yet, something made her nod her head. 'Perhaps, just for a few minutes.'

Jessie was under guard in the drawing-room. She gave Katrina a silent regretful look as Katrina walked in. 'Have they found Sean?' she asked.

Katrina shook her head. 'No, not yet.' Katrina felt awkward. She ought to be angry at Jessie but found she couldn't be. 'Your brother Danny's been arrested. And you'll be in prison soon too.'

'Yes,' whispered Jessie. 'For what it's worth, I'm sorry. It's just the way things worked out.'

Somehow sorry just wasn't good enough, thought Katrina. Not this time. Jessie had betrayed their friendship.

Jessie's eyes brimmed with tears, then she was led away.

★ ★ ★

'I can't believe I was so easily duped,' said Katrina. 'Jessie encouraged me to go to Boston in the first place. Naturally I accepted her advice because she'd helped me so much since the attack in London.'

Ross grimaced. 'Don't you go feeling sorry for her. She knew exactly what she was doing. She led a double life feeding you one story when all along she was actively involved with the Real IRA.' Ross came up to her and gently placed her hands in his. 'Katrina, it's been three days now since the explosion. Maybe it's time we thought about leaving here.'

'What? How can you say that? We still don't know what's happened to Sean.'

'Sometimes you have to let go,' he said gently. 'The detective inspector thinks he's probably been buried in one of the passageways. We may never find him.'

'If you want to leave, then you go right ahead. I'm staying right here until I know for sure.' Ross gathered her close. A sob rose in her throat as she buried her face in his chest.

'Two more days, Katrina, and then I'm taking you back to Glenroy where you belong,' he said firmly. He held her for a few more minutes before he added quietly. 'All this stress is not good for the baby. Surely you can see that?'

She wiped her tear-stained face with the back of her hand. 'You're right. It's just that I need to know for sure before I can leave here.'

'You don't have to explain to me.' Pain shot into his eyes, turning them a dull blue.

Katrina lifted her head, realizing how selfish she had been, thinking only of herself. 'I'm sorry. I know it must be hard for you too. I just need time . . . '

He nodded understandingly. 'Yeah . . . we all do. But I can't help thinking if we leave here, we can put this all behind us. I think Sean would have wanted that.'

'You're already speaking of him in the past tense — as if he is dead.'

'You have to face up to it. He might not be coming back.'

His words were unwelcome. Desperately, she said the first thing which came into her mind. 'Oh God, I wish I could die too, everything is so unfair. We were almost given another chance to be together and then all this happened. We shouldn't have come to

Ireland. I'm responsible: I've caused his death.'

Ross stared at her. 'No. You're wrong. We did what we thought was best at the time.'

Katrina knew Ross was right but it didn't make it easy.

'You have to carry on, for Christ's sake,' added Ross. 'How do you think I feel?' His voice was strained. 'Sean's like a brother to me. We worked together from dawn to dusk, side by side, ever since that day he turned up on our doorstep.' He took a breath. 'I didn't want to like him . . . ' He saw Katrina's surprised look but felt he had to make her understand. 'Oh, yes, I'll admit it. I didn't even want Dad to like him. I was scared, damned scared. And if I was honest with myself it was because I didn't want him getting a place on the farm. I was jealous you see. Then there was Anna. I've always had this thing about her since I was knee high, I even wanted to marry her but she turned me down. It was obvious when Sean came along who she preferred. But when I got to know him I realized how stupid and immature I had been, and as for Anna, well, there are things I still have to sort out with her.' He shook his head. 'Sean had demons which haunted him, I always knew that and understood, but there was a strength about him. You could trust him. He gained my respect — he gained everyone's respect.' He took another step forward, his hands trembling slightly. 'Sean's my best friend, can you understand that? I just can't imagine Glenroy without him.'

Those simple words reached her. She wanted to comfort him, but there wasn't much left. Her eyes blurred with tears. She reached up and kissed Ross lightly on the cheek saying gently, 'I know.'

Ross reached out for her with one arm, clamping her to him. He shut his eyes to hide the grief he didn't want her to see.

★　★　★

A couple of hours later, Katrina stood at the window looking out. Black clouds were gathering over the horizon, slowly rolling towards land. The sea was whipped into a frenzy with gigantic waves exploding onto the white, sandy beach. The wildness reached out to her. Perhaps a walk might do her good, she suddenly thought, feeling restless. She had been cooped up all day, unable to rest or think properly. She had hardly eaten, her nerves on edge all the time.

'I'm just going out for a while,' she said to Ross.

'Do you want me to come with you?'

She stood at the doorway, her hand on the door. 'No. I really want to be alone. I need to think things over.'

He nodded. 'OK. Then don't be too long, there's a storm brewing. And it will be dark soon.'

She shut the door behind her firmly, and slipped on her woollen jacket. The night before, the doctor had told her she was suffering from shock and needed to rest. But she couldn't. All she could think about was Sean and whether she would ever see him again.

Her feet sank into the wet grass, slipping slightly as she climbed uphill. The wind embraced her, whipping her hair across her face. When she reached the edge of the cliff, she stopped and looked down at the sharp drop to the ocean below. The tide was coming in. It would be so easy to jump over the cliffs and end it all, she thought dully. Just one step.

That's a coward's way out, something told her sharply. She was only thinking of herself, not the baby.

Oh Sean, will I ever see you again?

She lifted her head to face the wind, trying hard not to cry, but somehow the tears came anyway, falling hot down her cheeks. She wiped them away with the back of her hand. The rain started and she began to shiver. She had to keep moving to stay warm.

Her gaze travelled to the roughly hewn steps leading down to the beach. She hurried down the path, her feet sliding beneath her on the loose rocks. When she reached the bottom, the full force of the wind hit her with such fury she fell to her knees onto the soft sand. This time there was no stopping the tears. They blinded her, along with the full onslaught of the sea spray as each wave hit the shore. The sobs rose in her chest, one by one, until she could hardly swallow.

Why, Sean? Why?

Something drove her to her feet and she started to walk. Misty air enveloped her like a soft wedding veil. The slimy stone walls of the cliff wall soon loomed up before her. If she went any further along the shore she wouldn't be able to get back. Yet something pushed her on.

It was then she saw it. Something moved suddenly from behind the black rocks. She blinked. A figure emerged, then disappeared. The soft mist of sea spray clouded her vision again. Surely she wasn't seeing a ghost?

She stopped, waited a few more moments. The cold water rose higher, swishing around her feet and chilling her body. An oddest sense of calm descended as if she was losing sense of time. With a great effort, she turned. She had to make it back to the stone steps and up to the cliff, otherwise she'd be trapped.

Someone coughed from behind her. Katrina whirled around. All she could see was a cavern, the darkness never ending. Her eyes gradually adjusted. Surely — it couldn't be? It was an outline of a man. She had to be hallucinating. Taking a step forward, she clutched at the large rock in front of her, shaking uncontrollably.

The way the figure moved seemed familiar. 'Sean . . . ' she murmured.

A figure moved towards her. 'Katrina?' she heard him say.

It was him, she thought. She rushed forward and then she was in his arms. He held her so tight, she could hardly breathe. Pulling back, she said, 'Tell me you're real.'

He lifted her hand to his chest and pressed it flat.

'Feel my heartbeat,' he said. 'Sure . . . I'm real all right. And I'm standing right next to you. Cold, but alive.'

'B . . . But where did you come from?'

He pointed towards the cavern. 'Over there. A secret passage from the castle to the beach. There's a myriad of them in the dungeons. I used to explore them when I was a teenager.' He looked at the sea, circling around them, rising slowly. He grimaced, his hold on her tightening. 'We have to get out of here. In a few minutes the sea will cover these rocks. We'll never make it back along the shore now, the tide will beat us.' Sean looked upwards and frowned. Seagulls swooped and dived erratically straight above them. 'We're going to have to climb the cliffs. Do you think you can do it?'

Katrina nodded but her heart sank. 'I don't know. It's an awfully long way up.'

He gave her an encouraging smile and she felt his energy surge into her body. 'I'll be right with you all the way,' he said reassuringly.

He helped her up the first part but then Katrina started to feel dizzy. She couldn't move. Her left hand wouldn't go where she wanted it to. And she was cold . . . oh so cold. Her teeth started to chatter.

'Sean,' she said hoarsely, her throat unbearably tight. She clung onto the cliff face, pressing herself against the green tinged stone. A wave of nausea swept over her at the strong smell of seaweed, and then suddenly her foot slipped and she nearly fell.

'Don't look down,' he shouted frantically, reaching out for her hand. 'Just follow me

. . . nice and slowly. OK?'

Katrina took a deep breath. She had to get a grip. 'The rocks are so slippery.'

'I know. Be careful.'

They began the steady climb up until finally they reached a rocky ledge about a third of the way up the cliff. There was just enough room for them both to huddle in a sitting position. If she stretched her legs out they would dangle over the edge.

Katrina felt worse, much worse, and closed her eyes to shut out the heaving sea below. Waves of nausea were coming regularly causing her to start retching. 'I can't go any further.' She clung on to him. Sharp pains shot through her abdomen. My God, she thought, what was wrong with her?

Sean held her in his arms tightly. 'You're going to be just fine. I'm right here with you.'

She gasped. Another spasm shot through her, making her jerk. And then she knew. The baby.

'What's wrong?' asked Sean.

'Sean, there's something I have to tell you: I'm . . . I'm pregnant.'

'You're what?' He took a deep breath. 'Of all the places to tell me . . . '

'I'm in terrible pain,' she mumbled. 'Help me, please.'

He held her against him, quickly weighing

up the situation. 'It's the shock. The adrenaline has probably set off contractions. Try and breathe slowly until they pass.' He swore softly as he looked at the sheer rock face rising above them. This was as far as they could go with Katrina like this. Defeat stared him in the face, but he wasn't about to give up.

'I'll go for help.'

'No . . . no . . . please, don't leave me.' Katrina's voice cracked a little. 'Promise me you won't leave me here.'

'Katrina, if I don't go . . . ' he anguished. 'All right. Let's hope someone will be along soon. They'll miss you at the castle — we'll just have to sit tight and wait.'

Sean wasn't sure how long it was. He'd never prayed for anything more in his whole life, that someone would find them. He was still reeling from what Katrina had told him. She was carrying his child.

It was exactly an hour later as dusk descended that Sean heard Ross's voice calling from above. He was shouting Katrina's name and peering over the cliff. Sean lifted his arm and waved. 'We're here,' he yelled. 'We're right here.'

Sean looked down at Katrina. She couldn't stop shivering, although Sean had tried to shield her from the wind and the rain. Within minutes, one of the rescue squad had descended with a long rope and lifted her into a harness. By the time she reached the top she had lost consciousness.

★ ★ ★

Khalis crawled out of the narrow dark tunnel and hunkered down onto a rocky ledge gasping for breath. Sweat poured down his forehead. He glanced down at his knees and elbows, the skin shredded from moving along the rough rock. Pain sliced through his chest every time he took a breath. He probably had a few broken ribs as well. Apart from that he thanked Allah for sparing him from the explosion. If it hadn't been for Allah's guidance to him finding the old map in the castle library showing the mass of tunnels leading to the sea, he'd have died, trapped forever in the dungeons. Not that death worried him. The thought of seventy-two black-eyed virgins as promised to martyrs in the Koran were riches indeed. He didn't have a wife, nor did he regret not having one. His work had made it impossible to forge any close relationships while he had been based in England for the last few years.

Crouched on his haunches, he thought about his next move. He'd already planned his escape from Ireland just in case things had gone wrong. The mission hadn't entirely been unsuccessful. They might not have killed the British Prime Minister this time, but there would be another opportunity some day. He'd also learned more about explosives from Maguire and vice versa. The information and contacts Maguire had given him had already been passed on.

The British Government would realize that al-Qaeda could never be beaten. The bombs back in July 2005 had been the biggest attacks in London they had ever seen. He'd been a part of that.

Feeling around the rock beside him, he found the hole and the waterproof backpack tucked into it which he'd placed there some time ago. Inside the backpack were a torch and spare batteries, two small candles and a disposable lighter, a flask of water and three ration bars, a mobile phone, and an emergency blanket. Shivering, he wrapped the silver foil-looking blanket around his shoulders and drew it across his chest while he thought what to do next.

The tide was still high, the waves making a sucking noise below him. White bubbly froth coated the rocks along with green seaweed. In a few hours it would be low tide. He would have to wait until then before he could arrange a pick up. The mobile phone had no reception in the cave so he would use it further along the beach. He flicked his wrist to see the time on his watch. His mouth fell open. The watch had gone. He must have lost it somehow. Anger surged through him. It had been a gift from Maguire. Something he'd valued.

Several hours later, Khalis stood on the beach. He'd dialled his contact and given the password. Now it was a matter of waiting for the dinghy to appear that would take him to the fishing boat waiting further along the coast. Already his mind drifted to the next operation. But first he would go home to Afghanistan and be amongst his own people for a while. There he could recuperate and give thanks to Allah for saving him.

* * *

Sean sat in the tapestry chair opposite the bed, beside himself with worry. His hand reached out to touch Katrina for the thousandth time but she was still fast asleep. If only, she had gone to hospital, but she had preferred to stay with him and be attended by a local doctor. He got up to stretch his legs, wincing at the sudden movement. His headache was better due to the morphine shot he'd been given but it would be a while before his head wound healed. It was lucky Carrie hadn't killed him.

He stared out the mullioned window. The storm had lifted and in its place was a beautiful morning, the sun streaming through the thin panes of glass, basking the room in a rosy golden glow. Ireland was like that, he thought. One minute she was unleashing the elements in a screaming fury, the next she was calm and seductive. Just like a woman, he mused, his gaze shifting back to Katrina.

He had brought her nothing but trouble but he'd make it up to her. He'd swear it. When she was better, they would start afresh. They had each other, a baby to look forward to and a lifetime before them now.

He reached out for some paper and a pencil and started to sketch her picture as she lay in bed, her hair streaming gold against the white lacy pillow.

After a few moments, she stirred slightly. He put his drawing pad aside.

'Katrina,' he said softly, leaning over her. He blew softly on her face. 'Wake up, my love.'

Her head turned towards him, then her eyes slowly opened. 'Hello,' she said uncertainly. A flicker of a smile.

'Have a good sleep?'

'Mm . . . sort of. The last thing I remember was being on the cliffs.'

He smiled. 'You're safe now.' His hand slipped into hers, squeezing her fingers tight. Then he lifted her hand to his lips, where his mouth skimmed across her knuckles. 'How are you feeling?'

'Exhausted.' Panic leaped into her eyes. 'The baby? Oh . . . Sean — '

'Everything's OK. But the doctor would like you to go to hospital for a scan. As soon as you feel able to. Just to make sure.'

She nodded. 'I will.' Her hand lifted, touched the bandage on his head. 'You're hurt.'

'It's nothing. I'm fine really.' He gave a smile to show he meant what he said.

Silence fell between them. 'What now?' she asked softly.

He pursed his mouth. 'First, you have to get better. Then we'll talk. There's a few things I have to sort out with Detective Inspector Harvey, so you might as well rest up until then. There's no rush. I want to make sure you're well enough before we leave here.'

'The baby . . . are you pleased?'

'Am I what?' A smile broke out on Sean's lips. 'An unexpected surprise. I'm thrilled. I've even been thinking about names. I don't mind if it's a boy or girl. Either's fine with me.'

A knock at the door interrupted them. Ross entered carrying a breakfast tray for Katrina.

'Ah, the sleeping beauty awakes. About time too,' said Ross lightly.

Sean looked at the tray of food. 'You've got enough there to feed an army,' remarked Sean.

'Thought you might be hungry,' replied Ross. 'Besides, Katrina's eating for two. And knowing your appetite, Cousin . . . '

Sean gave a grin. He'd missed Ross's banter. 'Thanks.' Sean took the tray from him and set it down on a small table. He poured Katrina a cup of tea and helped her sit up.

Ross turned towards Sean. 'The detective inspector would like to see you. Can you spare him a few minutes?'

'Sure.' Sean glanced at Katrina. 'Is that OK?'

Katrina nodded. 'I'll be fine. I'll be too busy eating to notice you've gone,' she teased.

'Good. I'll be back as soon as I can.'

After Sean shut the door behind him, Ross sat down on the chair, next to the bed. 'Talk about being attentive. You know, I'd say Sean is head over heels in love with you.' He gave her a speculative look. 'Funny, I've never seen that side of him before.' He wagged his finger at her. 'And by the way, you gave everyone a fright disappearing like that. I ought to give you a telling off, but I'm just too glad you're OK.'

'I know. I'm sorry,' she murmured. She stared into space for a moment not sure what to say and whether Ross would even understand the desperation that had sent her to the cliffs. She had been at a very low ebb.

'It's amazing what true love makes us do,' he said.

Katrina smiled. 'Don't I know it?'

She had followed Sean from one end of the world to the other and back again. Faced danger, and loss, only to find happiness at the end of it all. It had been worth every single minute.

'I can't wait to get back to Glenroy,' Ross added. 'Back to normality. I really miss the place.'

'You're a farmer at heart,' Katrina said. 'Somehow, I can't imagine you living anywhere else but the high country.'

'Yeah, I suppose that's true. But in spite of what happened here, I've enjoyed seeing this part of the world. It's certainly broadened my outlook by a long shot. Got some news for you. I phoned Dad this morning.'

Katrina's eyes lit up. 'How is he? Is he managing OK without us?'

'Better than I thought. He'd just been at a horse sale with Anna. Wish I'd been there. Sounds like there were some beauts for sale. And he's got you a pony.'

'A pony for me? I never expected that. Your father is too kind.'

Ross smiled. 'He thinks a lot of you.' He paused briefly as if something else was on his mind. 'I also spoke to Anna as well. Seems like she's really missing me.'

Katrina smiled. 'Maybe she's realizing how much you mean to her after all.'

'I hope so. Because I sure miss her.' He gave another sigh. 'Are you and Sean coming back to New Zealand with me?'

Katrina put her cup on the saucer. 'I think so. It's not something we've discussed yet. I'm going to stay here with him until he feels ready to leave.'

Ross gave her a long look. 'I hadn't expected anything else. But let's hope it's soon. Glenroy won't be the same without you both.'

* * *

Detective Inspector Harvey was sitting in the dining-room at the long mahogany table, drinking a mug of coffee, when Sean found him. 'You wanted to see me?'

Harvey rose to his feet and gave a smile. 'This won't take long. Just a few things to tie up.'

Sean accepted the coffee that was offered to him and took a seat. He slid the blue folder across the table towards the inspector. 'The report's completed.'

Harvey raised a brow. 'Already? I am impressed.' He opened the folder and flicked through the papers. 'Have you recorded everything you saw in the dungeon? The explosives. All the equipment.'

'As much as I can remember while I was fighting with Khalis.'

'Good.' He gave a grim smile. 'You were lucky they didn't kill you.'

'Sure, the luck of the Irish,' mused Sean. 'But seriously, I still can't figure that out. They would have had time, I'm sure of it.' Did Carrie balk at pulling the trigger, he wondered? It was a question that would haunt him for the rest of his life. 'As soon as I came to, I realized what had happened,' added Sean. 'The place had blown apart. There was rubble everywhere and no sign of Carrie and Khalis. At first, I thought I was trapped but I managed to crawl out and make my way along another passageway. That place is like a rabbit warren down there.'

'We tried to reach you as soon as we could

but we had to proceed carefully,' Harvey explained. 'We suspected they would have wired the place. But Khalis was clever in setting the trap. We slipped up, I'm afraid. The place blew taking the whole factory with it.' Harvey looked worried. 'We've found Carrie dead, but not Khalis.'

Sean took out the gold watch from his pocket and slipped it onto the table. 'I found this in one of the passageways that leads to the beach. Take a look at the inscription on the back. It's a gift from Maguire to Khalis.'

Harvey turned the watch over in his hand and examined it closely. 'You think Khalis is still alive?'

'I don't know. But I'm a hundred per cent sure the watch was on his wrist when we were fighting. That means he must have lost it sometime afterwards.'

Harvey looked thoughtful. 'It's possible he's been entombed in one of the cells, but I guess we'll never know. Not unless he turns up again.'

Sean nodded. He felt uneasy. But at least there was some consolation that if Khalis had survived, chances were high he'd already have left the country. Still, that wasn't something Sean needed to worry about now.

'So what's the intelligence update?' asked Sean.

'Looks like we've wrapped everything up. Carrie and Maguire were the leaders. Khalis was al-Qaeda's front man.' His voice lowered. 'It looks like they were going to set up a bomb to kill the Prime Minister. He was due to visit Belfast next week.'

Sean raised an eyebrow. 'An ambitious plan. What about Jessie? Did she know what was going on?'

'She claims she didn't. Her brother confirmed that. We think she's telling the truth.' The detective inspector paused as he lifted his mug. 'She'll be charged with a variety of offences. And since she's completely co-operated with us in our inquiries and made our job a hell of a lot easier, it will go in her favour.' He pursed his lips. 'What about you? You'll be going back to New Zealand, I take it?'

'You guessed right.'

Harvey leaned back in his chair. 'I must admit things didn't turn out exactly the way I'd expected. I wanted a clean, smooth operation with no casualties. Your job was to locate the bomb factory, gather intelligence and get out. It was all very clear cut, Sean. I'm still trying to understand what exactly went wrong.'

Sean gave an ironic laugh. 'That's how things work out sometimes. Operating under-cover is never easy.'

Harvey smiled. 'You're right. My apologies. You know, I knew Andy Davis, your previous controller. He was a good man in spite of him turning informer. Maguire was responsible for killing him. He was the official commander of the group.'

Sean frowned. 'You never told me he killed Davis. You only said it was a possibility.'

Harvey looked embarrassed. 'We didn't want you shooting Maguire. We wanted him alive for questioning. Still, the terrorist group is now out of action. No longer a threat to the peace process in Ireland.'

'And al-Qaeda?'

'The fight goes on.'

'I'm glad I live in New Zealand,' stated Sean. 'One of the most peaceful countries in the world.'

'That might be. But one day terrorism *will* reach you.'

The same thought had occurred to Sean. He'd do anything to protect his home and those he loved. 'I hope not.' Sean rose from his seat and Harvey held out his hand, gripping Sean's firmly.

'Thank you for your help,' the police officer said quietly.

The question was in his eyes and Sean knew it was coming. But he was prepared.

'Can we call on you again?'

343

Sean smiled. 'No. My days as an undercover agent are finished. There are other priorities in my life now. Katrina and I are having a baby.'

Harvey's eyebrows shot up. 'Now that's cause for celebration.'

'My thoughts exactly,' replied Sean grinning. 'I've already ordered the champagne. I hope you'll join us tonight.'

'I'd be pleased to.' Harvey stood up, straightening his jacket. 'I might look you up sometime in New Zealand. Experience some of that Kiwi hospitality I've heard about. I'm meeting Stephen Powell later this year to discuss security in both of our countries.'

Sean nodded satisfactorily. 'There's always a bed for you at Glenroy. You'd be more than welcome.'

★ ★ ★

After lunch, Sean grabbed Katrina's hand. 'Come on, let's go for a walk. There's something I want to ask you. Something important.'

They walked together for a while along the cliffs, taking in the windswept scene around them. The salt air was strong, the sky so blue it made Katrina's heart sing. All the worries of the past few months faded into insignificance. She was in love with Sean, would always love him, and she knew he felt the same about her.

Sean turned to face her. 'I've been thinking, would you like to stay in Ireland for a while?'

He was testing her, she knew that. 'On holiday?'

'Call it a long honeymoon. Let's get married straight away. We've waited long enough.'

'Oh . . . Sean . . . '

'We can spend the summer here and then after the baby is born, the three of us can travel back for Christmas,' he added. 'If you want to, that is?'

'Yes,' she said enthusiastically. 'I'd really like that.'

He drew her closer, slipping his arm around her waist. 'Everything has turned out for the best. There really is a future for us now.'

Katrina's eyes lit up as happiness surged through her. 'A future? For you and me. That's something I've been counting on, Sean McKinlay.' She prodded him in the chest. 'Just make sure you don't go disappearing on me again. Twice is enough to last a lifetime.'

He laughed, pulling her down on the grass beside him and said, 'Sure. And that is one promise I will definitely keep.'

We do hope that you have enjoyed reading this large print book.

Did you know that all of our titles are available for purchase?

We publish a wide range of high quality large print books including:
Romances, Mysteries, Classics
General Fiction
Non Fiction and Westerns

Special interest titles available in large print are:
The Little Oxford Dictionary
Music Book
Song Book
Hymn Book
Service Book

Also available from us courtesy of Oxford University Press:
Young Readers' Dictionary
(large print edition)
Young Readers' Thesaurus
(large print edition)

For further information or a free brochure, please contact us at:
Ulverscroft Large Print Books Ltd.,
The Green, Bradgate Road, Anstey,
Leicester, LE7 7FU, England.
Tel: **(00 44) 0116 236 4325**
Fax: **(00 44) 0116 234 0205**